The Tenth Realm

MICHAEL CHATFIELD

Cover Art by Jan Becerikli Garrido
Jacket Design by Caitlin Greer
Interior Design by Caitlin Greer

eBook ISBN: 978-1-990785-02-3
Paperback ISBN: 978-1-990785-01-6

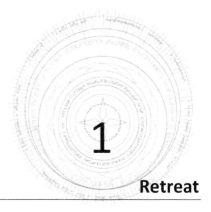

1

Retreat

Rekha Bhettan, first disciple of Xun Liang, the last head of the Imperium, wrapped her braid up in a rag, her brown eyes never leaving the storm clouds advancing in the distance. The Tenth Realm was hell and heaven, lands of plenty, untouched forests, floating islands, and underground worlds, all waiting to be discovered. It was filled with the strongest creatures and people of the Ten Realms, but also Elemental storms that could tear apart body cultivators and mana storms that would overload the strongest mana cultivator.

Those were natural occurrences; the approaching elemental clouds were anything but. Mountains framed the horizon as the storms, attracted by their masters, hung above or rumbled below.

She pulled the rag closed with a final tug, drawing upon her mana. Wisps of a spell appeared over her fingers, and she passed it over her face. Her vision *reached* across the kilometers. Ravagers, creatures of the Shattered Realms that cultivated Elements ate up the open ground, crossing the plains rapidly. They moved in packs, grouped by their elements and beast type. At their centers humanoid creatures moved upon their elements, surrounding them, responding to their command.

Devourers.

Ravagers gave them a wide berth, not daring to close with them unless summoned.

Rekha's eyes flicked from the creatures on the ground to the ones in the air. She blinked against her fatigue, and the grit that seemed to fill her eyes. "Here we go again." She sighed, wondering absently when she'd last been out of her armor.

"I can't see who their leader is," Sam, one of her closest friends and party member, muttered. His elven ears twitched in frustration as he ground his casting staff into the catwalk.

"They have to be powerful to have this many sworn." Rekha dismissed the spells from her eyes. She could see the elemental energies twisting the very fabric of the realm without their aid.

"A lot of changes in three weeks," Sam said.

His somber tone caught her off guard. She followed his gaze, watching a party leader, an Imperium veteran, checking on the latest reinforcements bolstering the ascension platform's fortress. Rekha recognized them as fellow students of Avegaaren.

Former students.

A familiar stab of grief ran through her. Three weeks ago, they had lost Avegaaren, the only place she had called home and where she had been accepted. Three weeks ago, the Imperium lost their leader, and she had lost a man she had thought of as her father.

She steeled her heart, quashing her anger and retreating into that colder, darker place—the place that had seen death and dealt its hand. She gripped the sword on her hip, her master's sword, sending a ripple through her heart. The runes across her armor brightened with the fluctuation of mana and elements flowing through her body.

She studied their defenses. The fortress lay on a rise in the vast plains. Three four-sided stars at ninety-degree angles to one another and fifty meters taller than the one before them, cut up the hill that the ascension platform stood upon. Their white and grey walls were covered in the flowing script of Star-rated formation masters, as thick as a person's fist, and filled with catalysts that glowed like gems.

In the center of the fortress stood the ascension platform, a spike of formation-layered stone and metal, untouched by nearly two millennia. It stabbed into the heavens, its peak wreathed in clouds, taller than any mountain across the Ten Realms.

Dozens of warships held position around it, facing the enemy advance. Rolling grasses shifted with the wind. Here, unlike the rest of the realm, there were no natural mana or elemental storms.

"You think it works?" Sam asked.

"The ascension platform?" she said.

"Yeah."

"The first ascendants that created the Tenth Realm made the tower to replicate how they ascended. One needed to reach the Tenth Realm with their own strength, then pass through the ten trials before they might attempt ascension."

"Yeah, and in two millennia, we haven't had a single new ascendant. Not even one person has made it out of the tower. Once you start climbing the tower, you ascend, or you die."

Cayleigh, the gnome and last member of their group, pumped her arms as she ran from the command center. Behind her, fighters started talking to one another and gathering their gear.

We're attacking them? On open ground? That's suicide.

Cayleigh made it to the stairs. The higher elements and mana made one stronger, but it was also harder to move, like wearing armor while being stuck on the seabed. Jumping fifty meters was impossible in this realm, forcing her to use the stairs. "'Scuse me! Watch out, make a hole!"

A crash followed with cursing. Cayleigh appeared at the top of the stairs a few minutes later. Her hair was cut short, and colored red, yellow, and silver, her boisterous ways in contrast with her reserved grandmother, Weebla. "Well then."

She huffed and took a deep breath, resting her hands on her twin short axes, getting her breathing under control.

"What's happening?" Rekha asked as fighters made their way down the stairs, abandoning their positions on the wall.

"We're pulling back to the Seventh." Cayleigh exhaled the words like ripping off a bandage.

"What?" Rekha yelled, pinching her brows together.

"Clive Andross has ordered us to consolidate our forces in the Seventh Realm."

Rekha gritted her teeth, her knuckles whitening on her grip. "Doesn't he realize that once we lose this position, we might never get it back? This is the bulwark against the Shattered Realms."

"Rekha," Sam's voice warned.

"What? It's true."

"And you're the last Imperium head's disciple. Right now, we need to be united. If people think you don't agree with Clive, it could cause the Imperium to break."

"It wouldn't." *Would it?*

The academy itself, untouched for millennia was attacked directly, and the head of the Imperium, who was usually only replaced when their term was up, was killed.

"The lower realms cared little about what we did and now everything is coming apart. They're looking for someone to blame," Cayleigh said.

"I'm sure he has a plan," Sam said, but Rekha knew him too well. He was anxious and unsure as well.

Fighters retreated without panic or fear. Teleportation pads flashed as the formations on the warships powered up.

Three weeks of fighting and we're falling back at the first sign of battle.

The fortress would bloody the Shattered, but she knew that they always had more to throw into the fight. This was only the start.

"The warships are tasked to hit the creatures as they approach. Activate all traps and then we get out of here," Cayleigh said.

"We're *giving* them the ascension platform." Rekha threw up her arms and stalked to the crenellations, smacking her palms into the stone.

Sam and Cayleigh waited a few moments before walking up on her left.

"Them's the orders," Cayleigh said.

Sam pressed his lips together, but there was no fight in him.

Rekha wanted to yell at the sheer frustration of it, but there had to be a reason the new head needed them in the Seventh. "I—" She let out a breath that did little to quell her anger.

"Don't worry. We'll pay these bastards back for what they did here, and for Avegaaren, and—"Sam's voice softened as he looked from the approaching elemental storms."—for Xun Liang."

Rekha gave a short nod, gathering herself before joining the rest of the retreating fighters. She felt numb, as she had for the last three weeks, like the world was covered in a cloth she couldn't reach through, or maybe she was wrapped in a cloth she couldn't escape.

They teleported to the waiting warships, floating out over the fortress. The seer screens showed the approaching enemy in their thousands, swarming from the sky and the ground. She could make out their individual formations with the naked eye now.

The warships accelerated away from the platform. Mana cannons and mages along the upper decks, together with the side batteries, lit up the sky. Explosions with titanic force tore through the aerial Ravagers as Devourers covered themselves with their elements, creating shields and advancing without pause.

As one fell, another would take their place, charging across the broken plains.

The batteries on the underside of the warships fired, spells trailing light as they hit the ground, rippling under the Ravager's and Devourer's feet.

The Shattered spread out, roaring, swiping and releasing their pent-up elemental attacks. Red, blue, silver, brown, grey, and green thundered across the open space. The air brimmed with energy. Counter-spells crashed into elements like rocks against the ocean.

Aerial Shattereds' attacks peppered the warship's interlaced barriers like rain on a skylight, with the sounds of Armageddon.

Rekha watched the strikes hit, grimacing with the blows and wishing there was something she could do to lessen them, but knowing she couldn't.

She had viewed the warships as untouchable, inviolable war machines, but had learned otherwise in the last three weeks of fighting.

The fortress' automated defenses activated. Spell formations as large as a person appeared across the walls, unleashing beams of destruction, pure mana that tore through grasses and dirt with their passing, their integrity breaking apart under elemental attacks before they hit a target to discharge their energy or lost spell integrity.

Shattered attacks splashed over the giant barrier like colored water balloons against a window.

Ramps opened around the fortress as golems, twice the size of a human, made of the same material as the walls, and covered in ancient Gnome and Elven script, marched out holding swords and shields.

Shattered rushed them, meeting the golems' weapons as they pushed out to create a semi-circle from their ramps.

Golems took down dozens of the Shattered, their progress slowing to a crawl without the support of fighters on the wall and the ramp limiting the number that could run out at a time.

The crawl turned to a halt, semi-circles of golems against a seething tide of Shattered.

"The golems are being pushed back," Cayleigh hissed.

The Shattered used the bodies of their dead, the physical weight pressing upon the golems as they jumped down on them, attacking them from several angles.

The golems marched back in lockstep. The Shattered flowed forward, several latching onto a golem. It hacked apart two Shattered, three jumped on it, cutting through its runes. Its legs collapsed, still swinging its sword until its arm was torn free. The golem was buried under the flow of Shattered that pressed on, entrapping more golems, bringing them low and finishing them off.

Other golems were lost among the press as they drew back.

Shattered dug their claws into the sections of walls left uncovered in their retreat, scaling them.

A Devourer from the front unleashed a beam of chaotic elements. The twisted kaleidoscope of colors slammed into the fortress's outer barriers.

Another added their beam to the first, strengthening it, then a third, a fifth, a tenth. The barrier colored and spasmed.

All those skirmishes, shutting down dozens of tears, weeks without sleep. Rekha gritted her teeth against her scream, the cloying fury at their retreat, watching their final redoubt in the Tenth Realm folding like a sandcastle against the tide.

Spells bombarded the Devourers from the warships. Ravagers cast their own elemental attacks, defending their masters.

Growing from several centimeters to a dozen meters, more beams lanced out at the fortress. Chaotic beams of swirling, twisted energies crashed into the outer star wall, the formation script straining under the attacks as more Devourers added their power.

"Devourers don't work together." A guard said, blinking at the truth that lay waste to his words, his prayer.

The formations stuttered. Rekha's heart leapt into her throat. The very fabric of the realm shimmered like air above a smith's forge.

A beam cut through Shattered and the Imperium golems, detonating with a thunderclap. A twenty-meter-wide crater appeared in the heart of the golem line, throwing them from their feet.

Shattered rose. Those out of the blast surged forward to kill the remaining golems. A living arrow through the heart of their golem defenses, they attacked the golems on all sides. Others rushed the walls behind them.

"They're getting over the walls!" Sam yelled.

"And there's not one fighter to meet them," Rekha hissed back.

Finding no defenders, Shattered charged into the fortress.

"Shit, look! The barrier!" Rekha followed Cayleigh's finger. Golden cracks burned up and away from the impact points of the chaotic beams, shimmering through colors, blackening its trail as they ate upward and across.

Beams drilled into the outer walls, their formations flaring to withstand the destructive might. Elemental attacks landed among the retreating Imperium forces, throwing them like chaff in the wind. Meteors of flame, cracked apart with the force to lay forests flat stained the fortress' clean lines; beams melted stone as gales with sword-sharp winds tore up stones and scarred runes.

A dozen—hundreds of beams lanced out to strike the walls.

Sections were blasted away, and cracks appeared. Walls that had stood for a thousand years crumbled and formed a ramp for the Shattered horde to use.

"The ships are retreating!" Sam pointed at the warship fleet flying away as the aerial Shattered piled attacks upon their barriers, no longer protected by the tower's.

A warship took several hits, flames blowing out another section of the ship. Its runes flashed and died as it lost power and dove toward the ground.

Runes flared to life, brimming with light stronger than the sun. The ship transitioned, debris that had been torn free, crashing into the plains, sending up plumes of dust.

"Prepare for transition to the Seventh Realm in twenty seconds," the fleet's admiral announced.

Rekha's stomach turned. They had lost the Tenth Realm before, but had never lost the ascension platform.

"Transitioning."

2
Head of the Imperium

Eli'keen, administrator of the Imperium, and a member of the elven council, studied the map table in the middle of the Imperium war room. It was the largest of the nine tables. Ten smaller tables created a nearly closed C shape, the open side facing the one main door, with a massive table in the middle. It was large enough that it would take twenty men holding hands to circle it.

Since he joined the Imperium, he had only needed to be in attendance in this room three times in the last millennia.

The main table showed a replica of the ascension platform. Shattered had smashed through gates and barriers and were spreading through the fortress' defenses.

The remaining golems fought on, taking down a few Ravagers, but they were isolated and overwhelmed and soon collapsed.

Eli'keen's heart shuddered. No one had attempted to challenge the ascension platform in the last two thousand years, but it was a hope and goal for many. The map stilled. The last of the warships transitioned to the Ninth Realm.

The door opened to the sound of marching boots, breaking the silence that had settled across the room. The administrators snapped their heads up to the man who entered—the newly appointed head of the Imperium.

Clive Andross entered with his group of advisors and guards. His armor was well used and had been repaired recently; his sword hanging from his hip was almost a part of him. His balding head had been shaved, and he had an ever-present scruff of a beard. He looked like a man who was born to frown, with deep lines across his forehead.

His severe green eyes cut through man, maps, and lies, getting to the heart of the matter. An athletic man, who had gained his size through fighting rather than body alterations.

"Change it to the Ninth."

An attendant moved the controls on the table. The tower was replaced with a floating spherical map of the Ninth Realm.

Clive paused at the edge of the table, looking at the others gathered around its edges. "It's time we cleared this fuck-up. I've ordered all remaining forces in the Tenth and Ninth back to the Seventh Realm. Associations and the mission hall are coordinating with the sects and alliances. It's about time they put in some work to defend their freedom." He rapped his fingers on the wooden table, getting a few snorts and mutterings of agreement.

Clive swiped his hand across the map, bringing up the Seventh Realm map, closing the matter.

"Eli'keen, can you get us all up to date?"

"Yes, head." Eli'Keen bowed and stepped forward. "Since the loss of Avegaaren, fighting has moved to the Seventh Realm, with sporadic fighting in the Sixth Realm. The Mission Hall and heroes are containing the tears in the Seventh for now.

"Some have gone to the Eighth Realm and are fighting the creatures there. The place is filled with dungeons and fighting constructs. They've reaped a bloody harvest.

"I've ordered the totems closed off to the Tenth Realm, and that one can move up any amount of realms, but they can only descend one realm at a time. That way, the Shattered can only travel to the Ninth, then the Eighth and then the Seventh, instead of jumping from the Tenth to the First."

"Are they cultivating?" Clive asked, leaning his chest over the table, commanding it.

"They are, and they're increasing in ability quickly. A few die from it, but they're getting stronger overall." Eli'keen noticed Weebla enter the room from a side door, staying in the back and watching. "Alvans and their allies support us in the Seventh Realm, combined with the assistance of other groups. The Seventh Realm is banding together for the first time since the Imperium was created."

"*Alvans,*" Clive muttered and shook his head. "*We* hold the Ten Realms. We have for centuries. They've barely been in existence for a decade. Thank you, Eli'Keen. All right, so we've fought the Shattered before, done so for as long as the Imperium has been standing. We've just got a few more of them to deal with this time. Once our forces have gathered in the Seventh Realm city of Cronen we'll lead an assault and retake the Ninth Realm. We'll even draft the Alvans in, give them a lesson on how to deal with Shattered."

Eli'keen hid his grimace. Clive was approaching this like an ordinary mission to close tears. Eli'keen studied the map. The Shattered were attacking everything they could. The last three weeks spoke to planning, not coincidence.

"That should let them redeem some honor for losing the Ninth Realm." Clive sneered as he stood upright and waved over his commanders.

Eli'keen closed his eyes and sighed. The loss in the Ninth Realm had been a big one and had hurt the Imperium's pride deeply. While people wanted someone to blame, there simply was no one. There were fewer and fewer that dared to go into the Shattered Realms. Their only source of information was the tears that opened in the Tenth Realm and the sneakier Shattered that were able to establish a hidden outpost in the Tenth to slip into the Ninth.

Maybe it is just our nature to need someone or something to pin the fault on.

Clive and his commanders strategized on entering the Ninth Realm and reclaiming it as Eli'keen moved beside Weebla, against the wall.

"He's a party leader, not a military commander," Eli'keen said.

"He's got the charisma, strength, and age. Too old for us to mold into a leader, young enough to be an idiot," Weebla said.

Eli'keen gave a twinge of a smile. Xun Liang's loss and the loss of so many friends and family members had hit them both hard.

A messenger walked in, scanned the room, and walked toward Eli'keen and Weebla. "Report from our people in the Tenth Realm."

Eli'keen pushed off the wall and took the scroll the messenger gave him. He reviewed it, his frown quickly turning to alarm. "Akran? Are you sure?"

"Yes, sir."

He looked at Weebla. "We thought he was dead."

"Hoped he was, devious little bastard."

"If Akran's back in the Ten Realms, that doesn't bode well. He's anything but a dumb beast. Where is he?"

"At the ascension platform."

Weebla scoffed. "Rekha wanted a strong opponent."

Eli'keen's frown deepened. "There's no one defending the platform."

"What?" Weebla hissed, stepping toward him.

"*Everyone* was pulled back from the Eighth and higher."

Weebla's eyebrows pinched together as her eyes widened. "You can't be serious?" She studied him, turning a shade whiter as she ran a hand over her forehead, holding it there. "If he destroys it, we'll never have another ascendant. Those formations were made by them. We haven't any idea how they work *still*." She hit her fist into her thigh. "Fuck."

Clive and his retinue looked over. "Weebla, you might have taught the previous head of the Imperium, so I'll forgive your outburst, but we need rational heads here. While hundreds have gone into the tower, none have made it out. We can't definitively say if it will turn someone into an Ascendant. Even the Ascendants who built it based upon their understanding of ascending, didn't use it to ascend."

Eli'keen held out a scroll and walked toward him. "You might want to read this."

"What is it?" Clive took it.

"A report on Akran. The leader of the Shattered's push. He's the strongest Devourer we have ever seen. Nearly four hundred years ago, he attacked the Ten Realms, and he was just a level three Devourer then. Scrying formations were able to get a reading on him. He's a level five now, all the elements packed into one body."

Clive let out a low grunt.

"He has to be the one coordinating this."

Clive finished reading and closed the scroll, passing it back. "He may have many sworn, I'll agree, but *leading* this… *really*? The Shattered are little more than beasts. Yes, some can take human form, but they're not like the demi-humans we have in the Ten Realms. It says here that his sworn have spread out and are creating tears from the Shattered Realms to the Ninth. Sure, he can control his sworn, but the other Shattered? Ain't no way."

"What about the ascension platform?"

Clive sighed and put his hand on Eli'keen's shoulder. "In two millennia, not one person has ascended. While I'd love to have a few ascendants on our side, it's not going to happen. If this Akran takes a liking to the place and gets comfortable, I'll thank the gods and skip down the halls. If Akran moves toward the front lines, we'll deal with him. Right now, we have to retake the Ninth." Clive patted him. "Get me the number of Elves and Gnomes that can fight in the Ninth Realm. We'll need them to assist." He turned back to the commanders. "Now, where were we?"

Eli'keen returned to Weebla.

"Pretty sure of himself." Weebla transmitted her voice through mana to his ears, so no one could overhear.

"What is Akran up to? He's been gone for so long, and now he just shows up at the ascension platform to destroy it? No, he must want something with it."

"I agree, and as for leading an offensive on the Ninth Realm, that's more about vanity than a tactical choice. You see how they're planning to regain the academy and the city. Plenty of room beyond to create tears."

"What do you mean?"

"We've lived beyond the Sky realms for years. Few of the sects or other powers in the realms have made it into the Ninth Realm—and fewer still have seen the might of the Imperium within the Tenth Realm. There's talk of securing our land and considering our options—using this as leverage against the other realms," Weebla said. "The Celestial and Divine realms are myths—fantasies to the lower realms. They have come up with tales of our strength, but they've never *seen* it."

"That's—" Eli'keen shook.

"The Imperium originates from the Associations, a group that barters with power daily. You think they'd be against using leverage to get a better deal with the rest of the realms?" Weebla reached up and patted his arm. "Don't worry, there are others that care about saving the realms first, like you. Though we'll need information to convince them."

"The Imperium has stood longer than the Ten Realms have existed. Its foundations are firm and unwavering."

"A society is built upon people. Its roots are in its past, but the living guide it. I feel that history is being made, and our actions will see us to tomorrow or cut us off thinking of glories past."

3
War Machines

ooks a little different." Erik West leaned against the office window, staring over the Thunder Mountain Range shipyard below.

The original yard had been widened using spells and formations. Several bays had been cut into the mountain range. Doors led to workshops deeper inside, building the parts to be assembled within the massive bays.

Metallurgy, dungeon core research, formations, weaponry advancements and modern aerodynamics came together to form Alva's newest warships. Hundreds of men and women taking raw materials to create these massive machines.

He caught his reflection in the glass. The years had added a few more lines to his face, some patches of silver showed in his beard, but his eyes were as bright as ever, a piercing blue.

"Last time we got here, all three of us were half dead with half-fused bones and trying to keep a group of Rocs off our asses. Damn flying assholes," Rugrat muttered.

George rolled his eyes. He stayed in his human form more often now, and was reading a book on cultivation while eating a sandwich Momma Rodriguez had made for them. Even as the mayor of Alva Dungeon, there was no way in hell she was letting her boys leave without food.

"Ubren's little bolt hole in the mountains. Now our fourth biggest shipyard." Taran, Alva military's technology development director, damn good smith, friend, and originally from Alva village, walked into the office, talking to someone just outside the door. "And make sure they check the damn mana drill formations. Stick a fricking arrow on it, pointing at where it's aiming. I don't know, just *don't* point them *into* the friggin' ship!"

There was a series of, "Yes misters."

Taran's feet shuffled as he turned, stopped as he saw the trio in his office.

"Was that meeting about the ship progress today?" he yelled.

"Yes, and you're late!" his secretary shouted back, like a mother finding her child late back for dinner. Taran winced, pulling his head in at her tone.

"The others?"

"Are *also* running late."

"Be careful now, else your secretary's gonna have you over her knee and tan your hide," Rugrat said, the corners of his mouth lifting into a smile.

"Thank you, Sarah," Taran said placatingly and closed the door.

"I thought it would be Glosil or the Silaz boys or something. What're you two doing haunting my office?"

"Glosil wanted us out of his hair and probably away from the front line for a day or two. Sent us here to learn about the ships." Erik turned, and they moved to a drafting table and chairs in the corner of the room.

"And they dragged me along for the ride." George glared at them over his book and continued eating his sandwich.

"You got mayo all up in here." Rugrat gestured around his mouth.

"Thanks." George's cheek tremored at the edge of a smile, taking out a napkin to wipe his face.

Rugrat sat on a stool, grinning at Erik.

"What are yo—"

Rugrat pushed off the floor, the wheels carrying him toward the drafting table. He tightened up as he got closer, coming to a perfect stop next to the table. He tapped on the table and clapped his hands at his win.

"Should've tried out for water polo," Rugrat said.

"It's not water polo, its ice curling. How many times do I gotta tell you?" Erik shook his head, leaning back against a table. "Water polo is when you tread water like a fucking mad man and throw a ball at a floating net. Curling is when you take a big stone and roll it down a slab of ice at a target. Like ice bowling."

"Why is it that there's polo with horses, sticks and balls, then there's water polo that's an aerobic nightmare of volleyball and floaties?"

"Can't use floaties."

"Fucking bullshit is what it is! Why can't they just call it water football or horse golf? And as for curling, that's not like a curl at all." Rugrat curled his arm. "That's a curl. How you doing, precious?" He kissed it.

"Annnd we've lost him." Erik smiled at Taran. "Rugrat, guns, ships, armor, bang explosions."

"Well, what've you got for us?" Rugrat asked.

"A straight jacket." Erik coughed.

Rugrat flipped him the bird as Taran shook his head.

"Good to know that some things don't change."

The door opened as Delfina walked in. She came from south American origins, shorter than Erik but built like someone that worked on machines constantly, complete with jumpsuit and grease on her cheek. She looked like she'd just woken. "Mornin'." She flashed them the peace symbol and dragged herself to a stool, hunched over, resting her elbows on her knees.

"Do you want to go over the ship designs?" Taran asked.

Delfina yawned. "You know as much as me."

"You speak military better." Taran sighed.

"All right." Delfina pushed over to the wall with the chalkboards on it. "How dumb do we need?"

"Marine." Erik gestured to Rugrat.

"Hey, and who out of us knows more about formations?"

"Still a marine."

"Oorah."

Delfina smiled and cleared her throat. "We've got designs for seven ships and have only built or converted four types so far. We've got twenty corvettes. Think of them like big bombers and troop transports. Frigates, nine of them, packed from nose to ass with missiles. Three destroyers, multi-role, got some cannons, some missiles, some aerial beasts, and ground forces. Last but not least, the cruisers, three in service, ship killers, larger aerial contingent, as many missiles as a frigate, four centerline accelerators, phoenix breath cannons, without exposing our oh-so-gooey centers and using railgun principles."

She moved the chalkboards on their rails, several others underneath, finding an image of the ships.

"Looks like a Russian tank screwed a stingray that looted an armory," Erik said.

"It's fucking awesome."

"We took what we learned from fighting with mana barriers and our enemies, and then Elan's Intelligence department stole information about everyone else's barriers. They're solid, with outer barriers that can inter-link with the other ships, and near armor barriers interlink across the ship, creating a second layer. That bastardized PPSH machine gun? We took it, added sensory formations, chambered in twenty-millimeter flak rounds, new defensive weapons. Armor plating is sandwiched composites, reactive armor, on the outside, Celestial Iron along the core areas, whole ship is run from the spine." She pulled out a sheet with a blueprint cross section of the ship and stuck it to the wall.

"Center of the ship, wrapped in armor, gunners, pilots, crew, everything is housed here. We lose the outer ship, our people are protected. Need to take one hell of a pounding to take her out of the fight."

"Nice," Erik said.

"Hey, you and Rugrat got us the Iron with your mission points. So, carrying on, we've got the newest version of the rail cannons. With the autoloaders, we only need one person per cannon. Can even slave them all together if you wanted. We've got bombs that'll fucking rattle your grandparent's teeth. Missiles have better seeking systems and more bang." She gave Erik a worried look.

Rugrat was about to tip his stool forward, bouncing both his legs, with throaty breathing.

"Ahem, spell formations upgraded for power. Basically, we've got jet engines. Didn't have time to develop real jet engines, but enough formations, mana, and fuel." Delfina shrugged. "Mana gathering formations we took from Alva, and remote mana gathering formations. Also, mana drills. Egbert came up with a way to locate the ley lines and the mana stones in the ground. We find a cache or line, drill into it, tap and fill. You can also use it as a ground-based weapon."

"How did you get this much done?" Erik asked.

Delfina sat back, cracking her neck. "Well, with dungeon cores, we could prototype in a few hours. No one to say what we couldn't do. Then we used the dungeon cores to print gear, bought the components we could outsource, and had the factories building everything else. When you and Rugrat were working on this stuff, there was what? Maybe ten of you in a shop?"

Erik nodded.

"Well, we've got a few thousand crafters now. Some from Earth, some from the Ten Realms, most of them experts in their own fields. Co-opted in the military's engineers and those that were engineer trained, which gave us a few hundred thousand more bodies. Crafters from Alva. The dungeon cores for the ships were fed materials and power to get started."

"And we had like half of the ships coming through the Sha," Taran said.

"Okay, okay I get it."

"Magic allows us to take a lot of shortcuts. These ships are smaller than anything in Alva in their class, but they're built to be airships first, taking all we know about modern warships, helicopters, fighters, and submarines, even some theoretical stuff on spaceships." Delfina grinned at Rugrat. "You did make a railgun."

"How have things been going with Edmond and Esther?" Erik asked.

"I thought there might be some issues with them selling their warships to Alva." Taran shrugged. "Haven't run into any issues. Well, sure, it'll take them some time to get used to everything. Little harder to retrain things that have already been trained into them. Though they have enough general knowledge that they're about as fast as our people learning it all new," Taran said.

"They're our people now too," Erik said.

"Ah, right, yeah, just..." Taran scratched his head, chagrined. "Yeah, you're right. Thanks for catching me on that."

Delfina cleared her throat. "Chonglu has been training his Crows alongside them and the crews are all Alvan, some old Sha are mixed in. They all swore oaths." She paused, mentally weighing her next words. "Overall, I think the groups have integrated well. Better than I thought they would. When the Sha started, there were many new things. It was exciting. We've found that excitement again with the new gear and warships. Its motivated them anew."

"Elephant in the room is levels," Rugrat said, drawing the other's eyes. "We have a lot of good soldiers, but not everyone has reached level seventy and passed their Eighth Realm trial. That takes time and we're running low on it."

"How many could fight in the Ninth?" Erik turned back to the presenters.

Taran rubbed the top of his head, boring a hole in the ceiling. "Couple of corvettes, a frigate or two, maybe a destroyer?"

"Ouch," Rugrat shook his head.

The door opened and Julilah and Qin walked in.

"Nice for you to show up," Taran said.

"You want to go over the flying formations?" Qin said.

Erik held up his hand. "Got it."

"The barriers?" Julilah asked.

"All good," Delfina said.

"Oh." The girls glanced at one another and took a step backward. "Do you need us for anything?"

"Thank you both for all your work. These ships sound like some nasty business," Erik said.

"Just doing our job," Taran said.

"More to be done still! Nice to see you. We've got some testing to work on!" Julilah said.

"The formations in the corvette glide system are still giving me a problem. I swear I could get ten percent more power!" Qin growled.

The two girls seemed to have forgotten about them already, speaking in formation master code as they left.

Erik smiled. They had both taken the deaths of Tan Xue and Tanya hard. Taran had helped Julilah get back on their feet and they had jumped into developing any technology that could help the military.

"You think that I could fire one of those machine guns standing?" Rugrat asked.

"If you don't want working shoulders." Taran shrugged.

"We've got healing spells for that, right?" George asked.

Erik sighed, shaking his head. "Never change, Rugrat. Never change."

4

In Defense of the Realms

hree tears, elemental energy flickering at their edges, cut a path from the Ninth Realm to the Eighth, Ravagers pouring from the grassy plains into the Eighth Realm's jungle forest. The constructs of the realm, built to test those seeking passage to the Ninth Realm, grew from the ground, pushed out from the trees and dropped from the skies, clashing with the intruders.

Storbon's team advanced between the trees, an Alvan company on either side. The air filled with tracers cutting one way as elemental attacks cut another.

A blast of water struck a tree, turning the trunk to shrapnel and pulping the rest. Storbon braced against the tree, hitting his armor, firing a burst through a charging ravager.

They had the Shattered contained now, a clear demarcation of his lines and those of the enemy.

"Grenade launchers!" Storbon yelled over the sound of two Alvan companies fighting. "Aim through the tears! Thin out their reinforcements!"

The updated grenade launchers fired, more like close range mortars now. Rounds passed through the tears, exploding on the other side in the Ninth Realm.

Attacks hit a machine gun position, throwing back two soldiers. Others moved to pull them out of the fighting line, others stretching out to cover the gap.

Damn, I wish I had arty.

The grenades laid waste to the Shattered on the other side of the tears, grenades landing among pockets of Ravagers that had found cover between tree roots or defilades in the forest.

The Shattered lines collapsed under the fire, their reinforcements cut off, any that used long range attacks getting the attention of the grenadiers too.

"Mages!"

Spells crashed into the tears, destabilizing them. They shuddered and frayed at the edges. They fought against the opposing energies, shuddered and collapsed.

Anything caught between the tear's lines was severed.

"Hold steady! Pick your targets!" Storbon yelled. They were so close he didn't need people seeking glory.

The Ravagers didn't have reinforcements, they were cut off from their Devourer leaders.

Storbon cut down a Ravager fleeing from the fire.

It was the turning of the tide. Ravagers bolted in any direction they thought was safe, away from the Alvan's firing lines.

Storbon ducked behind the mound he was using as cover, reloading. *Left holding steady, not advancing. Right is good too.* The troops held in, not moving an inch or giving into the desire to charge after their broken enemy.

Everyone knew their job and acted with cold, calculated ruthlessness.

"Launchers, target rear back position!"

Grenades fell on the pre-planned area. Detonations created a wall, turning the fleeing Ravagers. Spells and weapons fire cut down the rest.

Slowly and then suddenly, weapons ceased firing across the line.

Storbon scanned the area. Bodies covered the jungle. Dungeon monsters of the Eighth Realm regenerated, chasing the few Ravagers that had gotten away. Silence swept across the battlefield.

"Move to clear the field, rifle squads."

Rifle squads came off the line, fixing their bayonets. They moved to the right flank and made sure there weren't any Ravagers left alive.

No Devourer.

Storbon gnashed his teeth. His people had operated well. It was a textbook tear-clearing operation. They'd had plenty of practice the last month. Though without killing the Devourer's that opened them, they could recover and open more tears.

Units reported their status, checking on people and supplies. No one was injured that couldn't heal themselves, just ammunition expended.

Yao Meng jogged over as the rifle squads finished their sweep.

"Get the element harvesters up," Storbon ordered.

Formations glowing with monster cores floating in their center were set up. Streams of each element swirled through the formation and up into the core, becoming brighter with each second.

"Another day, another tear."

"Three weeks ago, it was a tear every three days," Storbon said. "The hell is the Imperium thinking?"

"I heard they're going to take back the Ninth Realm. Takes time to plan to take a realm back." Yao Meng shrugged.

Storbon sighed. The special teams had been deployed with the tear clearing teams in case a Devourer showed up. "The Devourers are getting smart, opening up tears, staying in the Ninth and sending over waves of Ravagers."

"They're going to have to come over eventually, losing all their sworn."

"Yeah, but they own the battlefield. We'll clear up the elements here, but they'll just punch through to another region. Won't be long before we're fighting Devourers every day. These are probing attacks."

"You know, for a guy who just got a girlfriend, you're a bit of a downer."

"Jackass." Storbon rolled his eyes.

Yao Meng laughed. "So purge the area, get them grouped up and head back?"

"You know the plan. Honestly, I'm a little scared we're going to get so used to this that we lose our edge. Got to make sure that everyone's head stays in the game."

"Sure thing, boss."

Rugrat's machine gun was strapped across his body, his gear tied down and checked. The lighting in the corvette's drop-hangar bathed his helmet and gear in red.

Soldiers chatted, checked their gear, or closed their eyes to get some last seconds of rest. "Five minutes, up!"

The first group stood. Rugrat was back from the front, special team members ahead and behind him. His seat snapped up against the wall as he grabbed the bar above his head. The corvette shook like a subway car switching tracks.

Rugrat accepted an incoming call. "Go," Rugrat said.

"Rugrat?"

"Kay'Renna?" He was momentarily stunned by the female voice. He laughed at the absurdity of the moment. "How's life treating you? Sorry, I might have to go at any minute, about to jump into a bunch of Shattered."

George, standing in front of Rugrat, turned around, picking up his change in emotion. Rugrat waved him back the way he was facing.

"I know," Kay'Renna drawled. "You're coming into the city I'm stationed in."

"Small realm, ain't it?"

"Something like that." Kay chuckled. "You're coming in back from the walls. I need you to reinforce the northeastern wall. We're getting pushed heavy on this side and there are a number of breaches."

Rugrat added in Lieutenant General Yui.

"Yui here."

"This is Rugrat. We're to reinforce the northeastern wall. Kay'Renna is the Mission Hall leader."

"Enemy inside the wall?" Yui asked.

"We think there might be. Reports are spotty. Leadership on the wall got messed up. Clear up to the wall, regain command and control," Kay'Renna said.

"Understood," Yui said. "Two minutes out. We're going to have our corvettes as close-in support."

Rugrat felt the corvette's machine guns through his feet.

"One minute!" the corvette captain barked.

Armored ramps unlocked and opened, the wind howling as the light of day, spells, and explosions ignited outside their hangar.

"Can confirm the enemy is inside the walls. Maps will update with our telemetry," Yui said.

"See you on the ground and, Rugrat?" Kay'Renna paused for half a breath. "Glad you're okay. Wasn't sure after Avegaaren fell. Don't get killed now."

"I aim to please." Rugrat grinned.

The corvette's engines flared as Rugrat closed the channel, dust and shit going everywhere.

"Go!" The first man jumped off the ramp. They followed one after another, not pausing for a second.

Daylight streamed in as Rugrat jumped out into a marketplace. He fell twenty meters, the corvette's formations flaring as it came down to land and edged forward, creating lines of soldiers as they cleared the warship.

The force of the corvette's wind formations scoured the dust free of the square, pulling at the Alvans' armor and clothes. Stalls, crates, and leftovers from the market broke and tumbled across the open space, crashing into surrounding walls.

"First team, up in that building. Second, up there. Third, take that corner. Fourth, get down to that entrance. Fifth, with me!" Niemm yelled, pointing at different locations.

The special team came apart, running across the open ground in their fireteams.

Rugrat was part of team three with George.

He followed his team member, jumped, and wrapped themselves in mana, flying up several stories to the roof.

They had a commanding view over the city. It stretched through mountains, turning them into compounds and homes. Several massive sect buildings rose into the sky.

Spells and cannon fire illuminated the wall line just a few blocks away.

Warships fired over it, their batteries firing into the open ground beyond. The impacts rolled so loud that the wall, the buildings added in their own notes to Rugrat's ear. A section of wall exploded inwards.

"Ah, shit." Rugrat cast spells on his eyes and raised his scope.

Ravagers charged through the opening before lightning and fire spells covered the breach, opening it wider under the bombardment. The fire lifted as mounted aerial fighters charged across the sky to hold the breach.

The wall ran across Rugrat's vision, from one hilly area to the left to another far to the right. The city ahead of him was barren. He turned. Everywhere people were in the streets, in the air, fleeing the areas closest to the wall. They lined up at teleportation hubs, running through with all their belongings they could carry.

Rugrat saw it, but his brain couldn't put together just how many people were there. It was a massive undertaking.

"I have the left flank," Rugrat said. They fanned out, controlling the roof and scanning the streets. The corvette emptied, additional units tightening their perimeter.

"I've got the right." George was a natural with a rifle. He'd seen Rugrat use it enough times and Rugrat had been happy to teach him.

The second wave of reinforcements ran through the teleportation pads inside the corvette and off the ramps, jumping clear of the ship.

They grouped together, running for the wall.

Two supporting corvettes, two frigates, and a cruiser hovered above. Another corvette in a courtyard to their east released the last of Yui's Tigers. The wind picked up as the corvette's formations and engines blasted the streets clean, rising in altitude, cannons and guns scanning the surrounding area.

A squad made it up on the roof.

"We're to relieve you."

"Welcome to it," Rugrat said. He and George covered them as the five-person squad took their places, setting up machine guns and defenses on the roof.

"Have fun." Rugrat and George left the roof and walked into thin air. Mana warped around them as they flew over to where Special Team One was mustering.

"We're reserve force, Devourer clean up. Good to go?" Niemm looked at the others as Rugrat landed next to him. Niemm barely glanced over, giving him a shadow of a nod. "Okay, let's get going, spread out, staggered down the street."

They spread out and followed the line of advance toward the wall.

Groups came under contact, killing Ravagers or holding them in place long enough for the corvettes to bring their weapons to bear.

Rugrat passed buildings that had been chewed up and holed by the heavy PDCs.

"Gotta get one of those as a gun," he said.

"The beast is nearly as long as you are tall," George said.

"Yeah, but it's semi, that's full auto."

"Move up," Niemm said as the corvette's weapons ran silent. "Just a few blocks from the wall, heavy rain incoming.

The cruiser and frigate opened fire. Missiles popped their hatches as rail cannons bellowed. The cruiser's accelerators fired in a series, a streak of light across the battlefield that hit beyond sight, the resulting explosion shaking buildings.

Railguns stitched the air as Sparrows around the cruisers and frigates engaged aerial Ravagers, tearing them apart and sweeping back to their charges.

They reached the wall, a four-story behemoth of enchanted and compressed stone. Alvan engineers had rebuilt the broken sections of the wall, teams running into the bottom level of the wall, creating firing slits to shoot into the Ravagers.

"Third floor!" Niemm yelled as they entered a tower and ran up the stairs.

The walls shook with their artillery cannons and spells. Rugrat caught glimpses of the battle through passing arrow slits. Accelerators hit, burning the ground, and creating a cone of destructive force through the enemy lines, stone, and trees beyond.

Ravagers of all varieties charged around obstacles and attacks. Spells threw the Ravagers back, the elements thick with their deaths.

Rugrat stopped at a casting balcony with a series of windows.

"This is us. Fire at targets of opportunity! Call out Devourers!" Niemm yelled.

Rugrat moved down from the casting balcony, taking a position at one of the arrow slits.

"Devourers! Shit, they're thick!" Niemm fired on several demi-humans that shed their human form, growing in size, shields of elemental energy-destroying attacks aimed at them.

"They're going for the breaches," Rugrat yelled, firing five shots as fast as he could pull the trigger. He aimed at a fire element Devourer, imbuing his shots with water to overpower its defense.

The rail cannons' rate of fire shot up, impacts dotting the Devourer's advance. Two missiles hit the ground, killing two of the creatures, and leaving an empty crater in the middle of the Shattered horde.

"Change targets. They're dead," Rugrat yelled, feeling the wash of elements from the Devourers. He reloaded his rifle, picking out Ravagers closing with the wall and ranging back further.

Three Devourers launched themselves toward one of the city's frigates. Spells tore through the sky from several directions, the Devourers broke through them and crashed into the ship, tearing into its sides. The crew and the Devourers savaged one another before the first Devourer dropped. The second was fighting inside the frigate, which shook and plummeted from the sky, crashing into buildings. Groups rushed the frigate to kill the beast.

Sworn were fleeing the city in droves as their Devourers were targeted and killed. Rugrat shot at them as they ran. Then all of the Ravagers broke.

The corvette's engines howled as it surged forward, surrounded by Sparrow wings. Their PDC's *brzzt's* and cannon's chest compressing blasts raked nearby targets. It accelerated, gaining altitude and speed, well above the Ravager's range. *Follow them back to their tears.*

A few minutes later, the wall fell silent.

"Must have killed the one in the frigate," George said.

Niemm walked up to Rugrat and tapped him on the shoulder. "Lieutenant General Yui wants to you meet him at the main command center."

Rugrat pulled out his map.

"Four and six, you're with Rugrat. George, you go with him too."

Rugrat traced his route, memorizing it. "We're moving."

They jogged up to the top of the wall and Rugrat jumped off, mana wrapping around him as he threw himself through the air. George regrew his wings, flapping beside him. The others covered themselves in mana, surrounding them.

The command center was built like a square pillar, covered in arrow slits and landing platforms. People using mana or aerial beasts created a constant stream to and from the platform. Rugrat and his team landed on the large, armored tower's landing platform.

"Star emblem," a guard said. Rugrat presented his, getting a raised eyebrow at its level, before it was checked. "You're free to go in." The guard snapped to another. "Take them to the Mission Hall briefing room."

"Sir!" The other guard braced and indicated for them to follow him. They weaved through people of all kinds in the halls, from merchants and civil servants to association members and soldiers, all part of this fight, or seeking something from the command staff.

Rugrat spotted Yui. It wasn't hard to miss the stars on his shoulder or the Alvan armor.

"Briefing is through here." The guard indicated to large double doors and an auditorium with a large map on the rear wall.

"Thanks." Rugrat pulled off his helmet and Yui did the same as they walked in.

"Seems that the city is eager to press the advantage while they have it. Tear clearing mission," Yui said as they walked inside.

"Corvettes?"

"They're searching them out right now. A few hits."

"Quiet!" a man yelled, thumping the bottom of his spear on the stage.

People quickly moved to the bannisters. There were no seats in this auditorium.

Kay'Renna walked out, looking tired, but no less determined or beautiful than when Rugrat saw her last.

"I am Kay'Renna, the Mission Hall's liaison for this battle." She looked through the stands and picked out Yui and Rugrat. "Alvans, your corvettes and aerial forces headed out over the wall, what is their situation?"

Yui stepped forward. "Miss, they're scouting the area to find out where the tears are located. They move rather quickly and should be able to get away if they run into issues. May I share our discoveries?"

"Please, our mission, as most of you have guessed, is to clear out the tears in this area."

Event: Tear Clearing
Requirements:
Search and destroy Shattered tears around the city. Kill Shattered present.
Rewards:

Experience
    Mission points
    +2-star mission
    Rewards may be increased based on performance

"That is per tear you close. Experience and mission points will be given out on what you personally contribute."

The few markers on the map updated with dozens more.

Kay'Renna glanced back at the map. "Looks like we know where we need to go."

Yui raised his hand. She indicated for him to speak. "We can link the teleport formations here to the formations on the corvettes, teleport in ground forces, and give the warships coordinates to transition to."

Kay'Renna grinned. "Well, that saves us from having to ride out there."

As she finished talking, the corvette's path updated. Tear markers dotted a twisted valley. Other markers appeared to denote Devourers.

Rugrat and Yui's devices flashed with the message. "Scouting force under attack. Diverting away. Will move to observation height."

"Okay, first we'll have Mission Hall groups teleport through the Alvans' ships." Kay'Renna gestured out the moves on the map. "Once that's done, the warships will transition over and rain down mana fury upon the tears. We'll sweep through the area, then grab some beers."

There were some cheers and laughs.

"Warship commanders, talk to Dorian." She pointed to a man who raised his hand. "Coordinate the transition offset. I want you to be ready to fight as soon as you transition. Ground force leaders, you will be assigned a teleportation pad, and a given a number. Get your people organized and to that teleportation pad. When your number is called, you go through. Let's move now. Longer we wait, the more Ravagers we'll have to deal with!"

She nodded to the room and headed back the way she had come.

A woman with an Alvan Fleet patch moved with other warship leaders toward Dorian.

"Looks like the hunt is on," Yui said.

"One of the biggest hunts I've seen."

Rugrat stared at the teleportation pad, its runes inert. A dozen pads lay at the edge of the courtyard, fighters waiting, ready to sprint forward.

"Corvettes in position!"

"First Ground Teleportation!" The teleportation pad flared to life. The first Alvan took off at a sprint, the line running behind him. The sky brightened. Rugrat looked up at the warships disappearing in a shimmer of mana.

Groups ran through the teleportation formations without pausing, the whole courtyard was in motion now.

Rugrat gripped his rifle tighter.

"Seventh Ground!"

Rugrat's group ran forward, joining the rear of the sixth group.

His feet carried him forward, through the teleportation pad, into the waiting corvette's hangar. There was a moment of disorientation, but they had trained for that.

He kept running, following the white arrows down the corvette's ramp, and jumped. The corvette's weapons blazed, elemental attacks hammering her barriers. The corvette's engines flattened the forest around it, bending trees, ready to ignite at a moment's notice.

The ships that had transitioned from the city filled the skies, their attacks shaking the ground as if giants were trying to forge the land itself.

He and his group ran into the sparse forest, thinned by Shattered lines of advance and attacks. The growing whine and breath-stealing thump of mana cannons charging and firing, the rounds howling overhead, created tracks in the sky, causing the ground to shudder with impacts.

They pushed up a slight rise, coming up along the rear of the firing line getting established at the mouth of the valley.

Rugrat released his bipod, jumping between boulders and hitting the ground again, seeing more of the battlefield.

Shattered poured out from tears across the valley several kilometers wide, braced by broken mountains.

Forces were laid out on different high grounds, firing and casting at the Shattered advance. A corvette howled overhead. Whistling filled the air as bombs spread out in a line, carpeting the undulating valley, leaving a path of craters, destroying several tears.

"This is us!" Niemm yelled.

Rugrat dropped onto his belly with the others. Sticking his bipod in the ground, he enchanted his first round, seeking a target.

Those around him found targets and started firing.

Someone stabbed a formation stack into the ground, turning the handle with the sound of metal on metal. It hummed, throwing out a barrier around the hilltop.

Rugrat found a Devourer and fired, his rifle throwing up a cloud as the six limbed gorilla-like Devourer lost his front arm. Rugrat fired a second time, hitting the beast in the chest. It reared up. Rugrat's third round nailed him in the neck.

"Reloading!" The world as a cacophony of weapon fire, spells and constant communication. Rugrat kept half an ear open as he moved between Devourer attacks.

Elemental attacks struck its barrier.

"Looks like they know we're here!" Niemm said.

Rugrat aimed and fired as fast as he could. "Reloading!" He threw his magazine to the side and put in a new one, smacking away the empty cartridges hitting the bolt carrier release. He adjusted back into his firing position, aiming at groups of Shattered or Devourers as he spotted them. They were thrown back with a barrel sized hole in them, separating most in two.

The wind pressed down on him, the warship's engines down blast clearing the tops of the hills, adding their own firepower to the mix. They cut down any Shattered that tried to launch into the air. Their cannons collapsed tears and slowed the tide. They created a U in the sky as the ground forces created a mirror along the ground.

"Teleportation pads up!" someone yelled from behind.

Reinforcements passed through even faster, attackers moving shoulder to shoulder and filling in the breaks in the line as wounded were evacuated.

Devourers launched from the ground or dove from the sky to be met by aerial mounted forces or mage teams held in reserve to deal with them.

One of the green and yellow patches with a long tail and four sets of wings jumped for the sky, releasing a breath of smoke aimed at a frigate.

Let's see if you're fireproof.

A spell weaved from Rugrat's hand as he braced, aimed, and fired. The force blew the ground back around him, pushing his leg and foot into the dirt. He didn't move an inch. Three rounds hit within a nickel spacing of one another, entering the beast's chest, turning into fireballs.

The Devourer exploded, its stream of gas turning into a torch. The force killed Shattered too close and threw Ravagers aside in a forty-meter area.

"Prepare to advance!" Niemm called.

"Up and forward, fifty meters! Keep inline with the person to your right and left!"

The line pushed forward rapidly and stopped, laying in their attacks.

Several missiles dropped from the sky, hammering grouped tears and Shattered.

"Another fifty! Move!"

So they advanced, the Warships raking the enemy and thinning them before the ground forces' ranged weapons finished off what remained.

The line grew quiet, and they picked out Shattered moving in the ruins of a small town.

"Dungeon underneath it," George pointed out.

Rugrat enhanced his vision. Little remained of the town. The ground had collapsed in several places, creating a ramp into the dungeon below. More sections of the dungeon were revealed as the warships fired on the town.

"What the hell are those?" Rugrat muttered. The creatures had the same Pepto-pink skin and teeth-filled mouths that seemed to dominate their bodies. Some had horns; others were covered in bones or had hands and tentacles.

They shambled up through the breaks in the ground.

"Stollor Devourers! Three of them. Prepare to advance with spell scrolls. Aerial forces, open that dungeon complex up," Kay'Renna ordered.

The warships focused their fire on the town. It fell apart as the ground cracked and dropped open.

Dungeon monsters crashed into the Shattered, tearing them apart.

Rugrat spotted one of the Stollor Devourers, a puddle of flesh and teeth, which seemed to have been created from several creatures, but none of them its real form. The Stollor clambered forward, grabbing Shattered bodies, and melding it with their own, adding their limbs, their mouths, and other parts as it moved. A building collapsed under its weight.

Dungeon monsters attacked it. The first few attacks cut away parts of the beast before it stopped taking damage and started recovering. It hurled out spines, killing the monsters. A lazy swipe from a tentacle smashed the others flat.

It picked up the bodies that collapsed into elements.

Elemental lines dragged the power into the Stollor, which grew larger as it roared with its different mouths and pushed forward, always melding, always growing.

Mana cannons pierced the creature, but it recovered quickly and started to change form. Damage from the attacks became weaker and weaker against its new defense.

Several dozen beams fell among the village, striking out at the three twisted masses of flesh.

"They must be using the wood element." Rugrat enhanced his round with the metal element to counteract, aimed and fired. His rounds sparked as they hit the creatures and exploded. The beast started to change.

Where the hell is their weakness? Each round he fired had less of an effect on it.

We need to hit them with something they can't compensate for. Rugrat studied the armored underside of the ships. *Drills.* He slapped his sound transmission device. "Kay'Renna, our ships have mana drills on them to refuel."

"And?"

"They use every element and mana. You think those things can recover from that?"

Minutes later, corvettes came into a hover over the Devourers, nearly a kilometer up. Light twisted and shifted into a spiral of chaotic energy, barely contained and controlled by the mana that reinforced it. Mana drills descended from each corvette.

The Devourers screamed as the drill cut through them and the ground beneath. Chaotic shells and rounds struck the Stollor groups, overloading their ability to adapt. Their bodies popped, releasing a massive wave of Wood element that turned weeds into wild grasses. Trees pierced through the ground and reached for the heavens.

"Advance!" Niemm yelled as calls and horns ordered them forward.

They marched down the hills and into the flatlands, killing anything that wasn't from the Ten Realms with prejudice. Stollor got special attention, not being left to dissipate on their own. Mages burned every last scrap.

Teams moved into the dungeon, clearing through it as light warships and mounted parties spread out to track down and destroy any remaining Stollor.

Rugrat rolled his neck and found a rock to sit on. The valley was a mix of destruction and crazed growth.

Event Completed: Tear Clearing
Requirements:
Search and destroy Shattered tears around the city. Kill Shattered present.
Rewards:
+23,654,702,293,847 Experience 250 Mission points +2 star mission (4)

Warships had spread out, their dungeon cores sucking up the rampant elements in the area.

"With a bigger dungeon core, it'll be harder for the Shattered to open their tears. Win-win," Rugrat muttered.

"You don't sound so excited," Niemm said.

"Not really. There has to be what? A few hundred Devourers in the Ninth Realm to let all this happen? The Imperium keeps making plans to take the Ninth back, but until we do, the back door is open down here. If they can open one tear in the Ninth, they can open three in the Seventh."

Rugrat entered the command center where they'd been briefed. Kay'Renna stood at an arrow slit turned window. She absently pushed away a section of stone, her arms crossed, studying the fighting scarred city beyond.

Houses had been flattened, sections of the wall were being repaired. Fire smoke curled skyward.

She turned her head first, her impassive face breaking into a smile as she turned her body, resting her left hand on her hip. "Well, if it isn't the bathtub knight."

"Thought I might say goodbye. Not sure when we might see one another again."

"Got to make every minute last," she said, sadness slowing her words before she put on a smile. "I take that you and your Alvans are heading out?"

Rugrat nodded. "More missions to search out tears across the Seventh."

"I've been hearing."

"About our missions?"

"Your ships are pretty recognizable. There's nothing like them in the Ten Realms. They look *fun*." She grinned.

Rugrat laughed. "Not so fun when you have to jump out of them at speed."

"Joking aside, I've heard good things about you Alvans and your Adventurer Guild, helping out all over the realm, accelerating people's training. It's created a push across the lower realms, even stopped the fighting in the Seventh Realm. People want to join guilds to fight."

"It's surprising. I didn't think there would be so many people willing to fight for the realms. You know how the groups all look after their own interests."

"This is our home, all our homes. It was only when the humans that made it to the higher realms learned about the Shattered that the fighting between the Gnomes, Elves, and humans stopped. A larger threat than our petty troubles can put things into focus."

"Until it goes away."

Kay'Renna snorted and shrugged.

"The Stollor, what were they?" Rugrat asked.

"One of the nastier things to have come from the Shattered Realms. They cultivate by eating and reproduce at a prodigious rate. They'll eat anything living: beast, person, other Shattered. They only respect power that can destroy them, and there isn't much that can. They're Wood element users. With enough mass, they can consume parts of their body to regenerate and alter themselves."

"Like if a human had three times their stamina?"

"Right, they have three times the mass. Adapt to attacks, so Devourers, even a level one, is rated as strong as a level two."

"We need to slim down these tears. There are more every day. If you'd asked me a week ago, I'd have said we were pushing them back," Rugrat said.

"And today?"

"I'm starting to think we've lost the initiative and are on a slow decline through the realms. There are good people in the lower realms willing to defend their homes, but they don't have the power that the people in the higher realms have to deal with these—" Rugrat gestured at the town. "—kinds of things."

Kay'Renna looked out over the town again, its destruction laid bare.

"I don't know what will happen. I have heard chatter among the Imperium. The head keeps promising to take action, keeps making plans. At the same time, he is leading the Imperium across the Seventh Realm, clearing cities and tears by the dozen. He has raised thousands of Imperium acolytes up."

Her brow pinched together.

"But?"

"The Imperium gaining power doesn't worry me, but there have been more people joining the Imperium than ever before. They are accepting more people, increasing their levels, but they are barely training them. That speaks to someone gaining power, not someone creating a fighting force."

"Right now, Alva is doing the same. We have too few people that can fight in the higher realms."

"Yes, but you're training your entire military. They're only training people who ally themselves with them. They are building closer ties to the sects and clans. They have always been apart. I think the new head likes the attention. Otherwise, why would he ban people from going to the Ninth Realm?"

"Lots of information and resources up there owned by the Imperium," Rugrat said.

Kay'Renna snorted. "Well, that's something else he's got wrong, *and* the people who were attacking you and Erik. Avegaaren is for all the realms, not just for the Imperium. With the Ninth and the Tenth open, Shattered are pouring into the Ten Realms unmolested. In the Seventh Realm, the Devourers can cultivate with a small risk of mana deviation. Sixth Realm, and we're going to start dealing with mana-enhanced Devourers."

They fell silent.

"I hope we attack the Ninth, and soon. If we don't, we could lose it all," Kay'Renna said in a small voice.

"You really think that?" Rugrat looked down at the powerful, fierce woman who controlled fleets and armies with her every word.

"I do."

"Well." Rugrat sighed. "These Shattered pricks are really ruining date night."

Kay'Renna laughed and thumped him on the shoulder.

Rugrat grinned and winked. "Frigging apocalypse."

"This date better blow my mind."

"You ever had deep fried chicken?"

"What's that?"

"Have to wait and find out. Stay safe." Rugrat tossed her a needle. She caught it, looking at it.

"What?"

"My buddy Erik cooked it up." Rugrat walked away.

"How is this a master potion? It's as strong as a three star!"

"He's a really big alchemy nerd?" Rugrat shrugged.

She pressed her lips together, her eye twitching like she didn't know whether to yell at him or thank him.

She wrestled with the corner of her lips turning upward. "Get out of here and go win this damn war, else I'm liable to do something *physical* to you before your damn date!" she growled, trying to be threatening but Rugrat couldn't help but find it incredibly cute.

5

Orders

E rik and Rugrat had spent the last two weeks running from one fight to the next, trying to stem the tide of beasts pouring into the Seventh Realm. They'd gone on separate missions, working with the special teams. A concession to put their friends and commanders' fears at bay.

They'd been sent back to Alva to rest, rearm and recuperate.

The living room had turned into a kit bomb of all their gear. Rugrat had disassembled *the Beast* and was cleaning it part by part.

"Have you been working on your cultivation?" Erik asked as he checked his medical supplies, making notes on what he needed to replace.

"As much as I can. Just been doing small increases." Rugrat blew on the upper receiver, working his cleaning toothbrush into the grooves.

"Don't want to pull a metal tempering?" Erik asked.

"No. I don't want to turn into a leaky carbon metal statue. You working on your wood tempering?"

Erik rolled up his shirt. Glowing green veins spread out from the tempering needle in his shoulder, like roots spreading through soil. "I've built up some passively. When we were in the Violet Sky Realm, I'd already partially tempered. Just taking my time, but with the knowledge we gained from Avegaaren and technology." He pulled down his shirt. "With things how they are in the higher realms, don't know if I'll be able to make that next step. Whenever something has gone cataclysmically wrong, the day before everything was fine, just building up in all different kinds of ways and then—" He snapped his fingers. "—it isn't."

George burst through the front door, the two's heads snapping over as they went still.

"Another attack?" Erik stood.

"Messenger from the Imperium. Orders from their head."

Erik and Rugrat looked at one another.

"About damn time," Rugrat muttered. He slapped his rifle back together with mana manipulation.

Erik collected the gear with his storage ring as fast as it took to stand.

George held the door open as they ran out of the house. Erik flung himself into the sky, shooting toward the headquarters. Rugrat caught up as George closed the door, his wings spreading out from his back, launching with a powerful flap of his wings.

Massive skylights and a series of mirrors had been set into the Alva living floor's roof to bring in the daylight, making it feel airy and open. Towers ran up the thick support columns dotted around the landscape. Alva dungeon was in constant motion, the city that never slept, and at its center the new dungeon headquarters rose to look over the city.

Erik and Rugrat passed through guards. Yao Meng and his special team, usually on operations across the realms and in places they shouldn't be, acted as their security.

"Thought it was a message, not a messenger," Erik muttered.

"Must be coming up in the world," Rugrat said.

They passed the Imperium guards standing outside their office. Alva's guards opened the doors for them.

Erik took it all in. He had been in the room as little as possible. Large windows showed Alva beyond and below. Two desks were set back from the windows, one for each of them, and there was a seating area and a planning area.

The messenger sat in the seating area, drinking tea.

"Cheers guys," Erik said. The guards nodded and closed the doors, leaving Erik, Rugrat, and the messenger.

The man drew himself up to his full height, taller than Rugrat but thin and rakish. An administrator, not a fighter. "The Imperium requests your attendance at Cronen as soon as possible, along with all forces that you have capable of fighting beyond the Ninth Realm." The man's voice made it clear this was not a demand, or request, but an order.

Erik cleared his throat.

The man continued. "When can we expect you to be ready?"

"What's the mission?"

"Do you know what happens to people that go against the Imperium, against the war?" The man's eyes thinned as he looked down his nose at Rugrat. "They stop existing."

"That a threat?" Rugrat stepped forward.

Erik put out his hand, holding him back.

The man smirked. "Make sure to keep your dog on a leash."

Erik took his hand back from Rugrat. "Our patience has limits," Erik said. "These decisions are not ours to make. We'll need the battle plans and information on the attack to present to our military."

The man sneered. "Are you not supposed to be the leaders of this… place? Or just puppets?"

"Give us the plans or get out. What are the objectives? What is required?" Erik said.

"I knew you were primitive, but I didn't kn—"

"You want *our* help. You do not own us or order us around." Erik's command voice made the man step back, his words cracking out like machine gun rounds, leaving him no room to talk. "You will pass plans and information on the upcoming offensive, which will then be passed to our council leader and military advisors to see if we can help in any meaningful way! This information is to be presented in the next twenty-four hours. You act like a child, I will *treat* you like a child! Now, boy, pull your fucking shit together and get the fuck out of my Empire. I will ban you from my lands, not to return unless you have permission by the council leader."

The man backed away as his eyes widened. He turned in a scramble, running as fast as his legs could take him, enhancing himself with mana. His guards chased after him.

"You know the First Realm could be called your lands now," Yao Meng said.

"I think he has the mana stones to go to another realm." Erik sat back.

One of the Imperium guards returned a few minutes later with a bundle of files and papers. He stormed across the room with a grimace on his face and thrust it toward Erik. "The information on the offensive."

"You know it is the polite thing to *bow*." Yao Meng's cultivation crashed down on the man, and he almost buckled and fell. His face paled, his resistance lasting half a second as he bowed at a perfect ninety degrees, holding out the papers.

"Good stretch, isn't it?" Yao Meng said. "Sorry, sirs, seems that there are some people who need to learn proper manners in the realms still." Yao Meng bowed and moved to the side, not showing the slightest strain.

"Who sent you?" Erik asked.

"The Imperium!" The man's face was red, with spittle on his lips as he yelled at the floor. "For this they'll—"

"They'd best do nothing. They are already fighting one war and they are seriously pissing me off with this fuckery." A silence spell cut off the guard. "Who was the person that cut the orders? Who told you to act like a bunch of assholes?"

Erik released his spell.

"Captain—" Silence spell

"I can read every lie that you come up with and, honestly, I don't have much to do around here, being a figurehead and all." Erik cancelled his spell.

"The head."

"Which one?"

"The Imperium head!"

Erik looked at Rugrat.

"Clive Andross?"

"Yeah."

Erik flexed his jaw. "Not been in office for a month and he's already starting fights with others in the realms."

"Xun Liang would have his ass in the trainer faster than he could scream for his momma." Rugrat shook his head.

Erik took the information from the man. "Get the hell out of here."

The guard relaxed as the mana manipulation was released from his body. He turned and walked away stiffly.

Erik leafed through the information, sighing. "I'd hoped the Imperium was above this positioning bullshit."

"Welcome to the Ten Realms, where people care more about their position and looking good than the fact we have aliens spitting out elemental energy and entering our worlds." Rugrat shrugged. "Glosil?"

"Yeah." Erik stored away the information as Rugrat called Alva's military commander.

Erik watched Glosil and Elan leaf through the information, making their own notes. Over the last couple of years, Glosil had gained a gravitas of a leader and a capable one. His office was utilitarian, tucked into the back of Alva's command center. The decisions and position had weighed on him heavily, leaving him with early wrinkles.

Beside him was Elan Silaz, Alva's spymaster, though some called him the Director of the Intelligence Department. He had eyes and ears everywhere and in most places he shouldn't.

The two men worked through the information while Erik sat across from them. Rugrat stood by a board in the back of the room, highlighting key points about mana cultivation to George.

Delilah knocked and opened the door. Glosil and Elan glanced up and went back to reading.

Erik waved to her. She nodded and walked over to Rugrat, grasping hands as she listened in on his lecture, adding in her tips to George as well.

Erik took the time to check his stat sheet.

Name: Erik West	
Level: 104 *Race: Human-?*	
Titles: *From the Grave III* *Blessed By Mana* *Dungeon Master V* *Reverse Alchemist* *Poison Body* *Fire Body* *Earth Soul* *Mana Reborn V* *Wandering Hero* *Metal Mind, Metal Body* *Sky Grade Bloodline* *Strength of Water*	
Strength: (Base 162) +88	2750
Agility: (Base 155) +120	1650
Stamina: (Base 165) +105	4455
Mana: (Base 647) +134	8132
Mana Regeneration (Base 670) +71	475.24/s
Stamina Regeneration: (Base 302) +99	90.32/s

591,087,147,250,338/1,168,160,000,000,000,000,000 EXP till you reach Level 105

Glosil finished with the last of his papers, picking them up and stacking them. He placed them back into the folder.

Elan finished around the same time.

Delilah walked over and sat in the chair beside Erik's.

"So?" Erik asked.

"Fucking thing looks more like some academic's essay than a battle plan," Glosil growled and leaned back in his chair. He rubbed his eyes and pinched his brow. "The mission is to go to the Ninth Realm, where the Alvans are going to be used in whatever role the Imperium deems fit. They have the right to claim our warships if they think we're not up for the task. Then it gets worse." He opened his eyes. "Transition to a totem on one of those teleportation hub islands and basically, attack anything and everything that comes from the Shattered Realms."

"Okay," Erik said, unsure of the problem with that.

"That's not a plan; it's an overall objective. A plan would be, go in, hit the tears with enough mana to destabilize them, clear through the realm in sections, keep hammering the tears so they can't pull in reinforcements. From there, have the Seventh Realm forces clear out the remaining Shattered in the lower realms, assist with Devourers and then go for the Tenth. This is just... The enemy is there and we're gonna kill them. In flowery fucking language." He punctuated the last three points with his finger into his armrest.

"There's no mention of how many people are going, what order they'll be deploying in, and little break down of objectives." Glosil let out a heavy breath. "It's a fucking mess, sir."

"Not our plan." Erik shrugged and looked at Elan.

Elan checked his notes and looked up. "Meeting point is in Cronen, and it looks like whoever made this plan was trying to hide a lot in the details. I find it interesting that there are no clear objectives. Also, the wording around the tears and their destruction is *selective*."

"So?"

"So, it means that they have not specifically committed to closing all of the tears."

"They have to, right?" Delilah asked.

"That's not what my people are saying," Elan said. "The Imperium head wants to make a name for himself. He needs to make sure the lower realms don't think he or the Imperium is weak. What is better to show your power than a war?"

"So, what? Leave the tears open so they can fight in the Seventh Realm with an audience?" Delilah said.

"Yeah," Elan said.

"You can't be serious." Erik frowned.

"The Imperium is an old organization and they've been away from the public light for a long time. Those that join them are from the lower realms. While they're stronger than most in the lower realms, they haven't been able to show how strong they are.

"This allows them to show the threat of the Shattered Realms, and bring a spotlight on how strong those that join the Imperium are. We all know that the number of people that make it past the Eighth Realm is low and not just because of the trial," Elan said.

Erik slumped back in his chair. "They're using it to recruit."

"And we're the best target to help them."

"Target?"

"They've been spreading lies about us to reinforce their position. I have reason to believe they are going to use this offensive to take our equipment and throw our people into the places we can't go. We're one of the larger forces that can fight in the Ninth."

"Glosil, what are you thinking?" Erik asked.

"That this plan is a pile of crap. Too many unknowns and with our allies conspiring against us and we've got such a small portion of our forces we can deploy." Glosil shook his head.

"That good, huh?"

"Oh, it's a flaming turd wrapped in a bow."

"Your recommendation?" Delilah asked.

"We head to the Seventh, support the cities that are under siege, take out tears, have the cities stand on their own feet, or head back to key cities to gather strength and push later. Clear out the Shattered region by region. We can deploy most of our forces to the Seventh, and it'll be a great way for them to increase their overall experience. Then we could have a larger force that can go into the Ninth Realm and be effective, instead of just scraping out everyone that made it past the trial," Glosil said.

"What are the implications? I hear that the associations are moving against some of the smaller sects and clans?" Delilah pointed her question at Elan.

"They have done so, but only in extreme cases. They declared that anyone supporting the defense of the Ten Realms will be protected. They made several examples. Treated it as if an association location had been attacked."

"You think they could do that to us?" Erik asked.

"I don't think they would be that bold, but we should watch the association locations that we deal with frequently with a closer eye. We are the Imperium head's favorite bully boy."

Delilah cleared her throat, breaking the silence. "Alvans want to do more than just sit on the sidelines. I've had several key figures voice such opinions. With the rumors flying around, they want us out on the front and showing people what we can do."

Glosil shifted uncomfortably in his chair. "Emotions shouldn't dictate battle."

"I know, but I am a representative of the people and follow up on what they say. I will not put our soldiers' lives at risk unless we have clear goals, a clear mission, and a way to carry it out and this—" She gestured at the files. "—is not that. So, how can we help? Can we support the efforts in the Seventh Realm?"

"I think it's the best option. We have preliminary plans, but we need to update them for your approval."

"What is the expected fallout for telling the Imperium to piss up a tree?" Delilah said.

Rugrat snorted. "She got that one from me." He walked up between Erik and Delilah's chair and put a hand on each of their chairs, leaning forward.

"They could mess up trade relations with the association. We have backups with our allies. I suppose they could mess with our allies and start a slander campaign against us," Elan said.

"If we're fighting in the Seventh Realm, people will see that we're taking action," Delilah said. "The Imperium will look like a child if they throw a fit. Or we can make it look like they are. Elan, I think it would be a good idea to make sure the information we have on the new Imperium targeting us was to reach our allies' ears."

"You think that is best?" Erik asked.

"We need to get the information in front of them. The facts need to be out before the slander, so it falls dead."

"It could weaken the Imperium's position and they are defending the Tenth. They're the only force that can."

"And I have to look out for Alva and our people. If we have traders on the road and they are attacked because Alvans are seen as traitors to the realms, it's on my head. They want to play with lies, we give the truth. They aren't going to thank us for taking their hits. The new head started this power game, straight forward and simple, and we will treat them just like any other powerful group in the realms."

Erik felt into an uneasy silence and shrugged. "I leave the politicking to you all. Just give me a mission that isn't a load of crap."

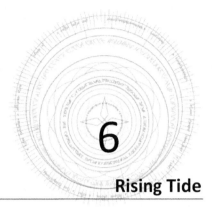

6

Rising Tide

Rekha's spells allowed her to see through the massive cavern's darkness and the horror that was the twisted four-legged armored lizard that filled it. The Devourer was ten meters long and five meters tall. Eight eyes ringed its brow line. Brown and blue scales shimmered in the spell light and attacks, backlit by the desert beyond the tear behind it. Over a hundred sworn Ravagers fought the seventy Imperium warriors that accompanied her.

More of the creatures pushed through the tear, eager to enter the fray.

Rekha slashed through the Devourer's leg, causing it to stumble. Its elemental attack fell apart, just missing Cayleigh as she hacked through Ravagers. Her quick brutal actions opened scales and skin, reaping lives from the press of bodies from the elemental tear.

"Now!"

The two backup teams near the cavern entrance, away from the melee, used their spell scrolls.

Mana spears slammed into the Devourer as Sam used a mana manipulation spell, pulling her and Cayleigh backward.

Rekha circulated her mana and elements, recovering from her fatigue and mana. The warriors jumped backward as the mana spears tore through the Ravagers and slammed into the Devourer.

"Fucking Earth Devourer," Cayleigh growled. The creature, bleeding from a dozen wounds, stood back on the leg she'd slashed through. A scar covered the wound, while its other new wounds scabbed over before her eyes.

"Hit it!" Rekha drew on her mana and elements, circulating and expending them through her hand, creating a fist sized beam of chaos. The other groups added their beams in. The ravager released a warbling cry as its wounds failed to heal. The beams pierced its hide, causing it to glow with an inner light.

Streams of Earth and Water elements spread through the cavern, like glass smashing against the floor.

The Devourer collapsed and its remaining Ravagers tried to flee the cave, some running back through the tear as it wavered and shrank, others rushing the Imperium fighters.

Sam cast a spell of compressed air and fire, cutting through dozens of Ravagers in front of the tear.

The reserve force changed their target and bombarded the tear.

Rekha and Cayleigh stepped forward with the other front-liners, hacking through Ravagers. The light from the tear disappeared as it snapped shut, splitting several Ravagers in half.

The remaining Ravagers lasted a handful of seconds before the last fell.

Rekha cast a clean spell on herself, clearing the blood off her face and clothes. Dense, chaotic elements filled the cave, trying to claw their way into her body. She pulled out an element gathering formation and dungeon core. The elements surged into the dungeon core, which then purified and cleansed the limited mana, consuming the elements.

Cayleigh cleaned herself of gore as well, raising an axe in salute to the other teams.

Each started checking on their members, then made sure the Ravagers were really dead. Unlike other creatures in the Ten Realms, they didn't have tombstones.

"Nothing but closing tears for a week." Sam stretched and rolled his shoulders. "I thought we would be heading back to the Ninth by now."

"Got to prepare. People to organize, supplies to move. You know the rest of it."

"Wouldn't have lost the Ninth if not for the Alvans," a team leader muttered to his comrade.

"The hell did you say?" Rekha growled, stepping toward him.

"They came up to the Ninth thinking they were hot shit. Well, they messed up. Lost us the Ninth." The man shrugged.

"The hell do you know? Were you there?" Rekha looked him up and down, finding him lacking.

"No but—"

"*We* were, and the Alvans paid blood right beside us. They stood shoulder to shoulder, and they were the last ones out of Avegaaren. They *saved* lives."

The man held up his hands. "Shit, what's your problem?"

"Bud, you best take a walk," Cayleigh said.

"What? I'm just saying."

Rekha's blast hit him in the chest. He hit the ground, rolling near his team. "You keep slighting my junior brothers and I'll duel your ass. Learn the truth before you start spreading your crap." Rekha turned back to Sam and Cayleigh, crossing her arms and tapping her foot. "The fuck was that?"

Sam grimaced. "New head, new policy."

"What do you mean?"

"He's new into office. Needs a win and he needs a scapegoat. Alva has been rising in position and they did show up in Avegaaren. Don't blame them, but mention they were in Avegaaren right before it fell. Weakens the Alvan position, makes some people think that it wasn't the Imperium that lost the Ninth, but the Alvans."

"Good for morale." Cayleigh pumped her fist before rolling her eyes and shaking her head.

"What the hell? So, he's been slighting the people that came and helped us?"

"Its politics, Rekha. Weaken the Alvans and the Imperium gets stronger. That's how they think."

Rekha's sound transmission device activated. She listened to the message.

"New orders. We're to head to Cronen tonight and be ready to move in three days."

"The Ninth?" Cayleigh asked.

"Back to the Ninth," Rekha confirmed.

"Goddamn cowards."

Eli'keen looked up at Clive's latest outburst. Clive shook his head, throwing the report back at the messenger, focusing his attention on the war room's central map table, leaning on its edge. "The Alvans are too scared to support us in the Ninth Realm. Shows how reliable they are as allies."

Eli'keen didn't miss the sect leaders' and clan heads' interest from their side of the room. They had become a permanent addition to the war room, which had become more like a theatre than a place of work. Clive was acting like the Shattered were just a passing problem, setting up his legacy.

The realization hit Eli'keen like a wall, halting his movements. A new horror spread through him. This was the largest invasion in the Ten Realms' history. *No, I'm overreacting. There's no way a head would use this to gain political position.* He tried to laugh off his thoughts, but it lodged in the back of his head.

"They insulted our messenger and then they do this," Clive growled, gripping his hilt and pushing it forward. "Well, if they're too cowardly to fight, we'll be happy to borrow their ships and put them to good use." Clive drew himself up.

"Yes, sir." The messenger bowed deeply and snapped around, marching from the room.

Eli'keen saw major movement at the Seventh Realm table. He walked over, watching pieces shift into position at Vehpolis. The city started on one side of the mountain, progressively turning the mountain into the city and the surrounding valley and dungeons, and it was besieged by Shattered on all sides. Remote and quiet compared to the massive tiered mega-cities of the Seventh Realm, the idyllic setting was turning into a nightmare.

The Alvans were evacuating the city as quickly as possible, but being isolated in a mountain range, they had little support. Their teleportation pads didn't have the capacity to teleport over the airships they needed to defend the city.

I bet Clive won't mention this. Eli'keen frowned as markers for the Imperium forces at Vehpolis withdrew from the battle.

"We will draw upon our reserves and dedicate everything we have to the Ninth Realm fight. Though it will weaken our assistance in the Seventh Realm." Clive agonized as new force markers appeared in Cronen. "Send out orders. We only have two days until the offensive."

Eli'keen looked between the two tables. Clive had pulled out their forces from the Ninth Realm not that long ago, and now he was talking about rushing back up there. He hadn't re-organized their forces or gathered supplies. Was Weebla right? Was Clive making decisions to grow his power instead of defending the realms? Eli'keen served the Imperium to protect the Ten Realms.

His gaze rested on the map of Vehpolis. The battle was brutal and hellish, yet the Alvans held on, dedicating personnel and resources to evacuating people, letting in only a small number of reinforcements.

It took the trust of soldiers in one another, in their leadership, who trusted them to hold while they brought up forces to help and evacuate people that they owed nothing.

Eli'keen's sound transmission device took his attention.

"Eli'keen, a report from the seer formations in the Tenth Realm. We don't know what he intends to do, but Akran has entered the ascension platform. His sworn continue to guard the fortress."

"He must be looking to destroy it," Eli'keen muttered.

"Elder, we detected the tower activating, but not defensively."

"When did he enter?"

"Yesterday. There's a time lag on the seer formations," the intelligence officer said.

Eli'keen frowned. They would get an immediate alarm here if someone was trying to destroy the platform. A chilling thought struck him. He pulled out a special formation of six ascending lights. The first one was glowing.

"Shit!" Eli'keen felt weakness run through his body.

"Elder?"

"He isn't attacking the ascension platform; he's *using* it. He's trying to ascend." Eli'keen closed off the sound transmission and walked over to Clive. "Sir, I need to talk to you."

"What's on your mind?" Clive sighed.

"Sir, it is about the Tenth Realm."

Clive tilted his head to the side as Eli'keen indicated to a side room.

"Well? Out with it," Clive said, not making a move to the side room or to use a sound cancelling spell.

Eli'keen showed Clive the ascension platform formation.

"What is this?"

"This shows if someone is attempting the ascension platform. Akran didn't go to the platform to claim it, or destroy it. He's using it to *ascend*." *And Clive let him.* He kept his features from betraying his thoughts. He reminded himself that there was no way of knowing if they would have been able to hold the Tenth Realm, though he knew the fortress. He knew the power they had prepared for generations, ready to defend against an attack like this.

Clive's eyebrow climbed. "We haven't had *one* person ascend in two *thousand* years. No way some Shattered mutt will be able to do it. Anything else?"

"Sir, he has—"

"Look, Eli'keen, I know you've served this Imperium well, but I need you to focus on things that are important. Deal with the crafters and make sure our people have clothes and potions. I'll deal with the fighting and leading the Imperium, all right?" Clive clapped him on the shoulder.

"I understand," Eli'keen grated as he felt something break inside, something key, something he had thought true all these years but had stopped this day.

Louis Gerard looked gaunt, with deep bags under his eyes. The time since he had rebelled against Edmond had not been kind to him. The light had dimmed in his eyes over the passing years as clans had left what remained of the Sha, and the Sha had gone from a power from the First Realm into the Seventh to a nearly nomadic grouping of clans that lived on their warships.

Milo LeBlanc and Lady Veltren had stepped up, working themselves to the bone to get the best for the clan. They sold weapon designs and every service possible to generate funds and support. They had carved out a place for them to settle at Kircross, in the Seventh Realm. It was a key location in the northern mountain ranges of the fourth continent. Several cities were in teleportation range of the city, smaller cities that didn't have the people or fighting power to stave off the Shattered and their tears.

Le Glaive, the once proud flagship of the Sha, had been stripped down into a utilitarian warship. Its perfect appearance was marred with the signs of hard months and battles. Most of the lower realm clans had collapsed and scattered. Edmond had gathered others and had joined the Alvan Empire, or at least connected to it.

"Report?" Louis asked the officer on watch.

"Some tears at the outer regions. The Grey Peak Sect fleet dealt with it."

Louis grunted and moved to his command chair. The throne had been cleared and a simple chair remained.

The Grey Peak Sect had absorbed the Black Phoenix Clan, subduing them. The Grey Peak Sect was part of one of the smaller cities around Kircross. They'd withdrawn their civilians, but kept their fleet in the area, ready to reclaim their home and the region.

Of the groups that had gone against Alva, their fates varied. The Willful Institute and the groups that supported them were searched out, arrested, and became Alvan prisoners, or died fighting. The Black Phoenix Clan had lost their homes, most of their fleets, and the leadership of the *Eternus* had been handed over. They were prisoners of Alva and the rest had folded into another sect.

"Warship transition," a seer officer said.

Louis checked the scrying formation feed as the first three ships appeared.

"What the hell are those?" the officer said.

Louis blinked, not sure what he was seeing. Flying ships with *wings* howled through the sky, picking up speed as two more groups of three identical ships transitioned in. Larger winged ships appeared, cutting through the air, with carved lines or armor and armaments that dominated the air with their presence.

He sighed when he saw Alva's symbol emblazed on their flanks as the forward elements exited Kircross with speed. "Alvan warships."

Flames spewed from their rears as they cleared Kircross and accelerated. A rumble ran through the air as the ships increased altitude.

"Holy shit," the watch officer said as the ships rapidly disappeared into the distance.

"Well, the Sha brought new designs to the warship. Looks like the Alvans have their own version. Where are they headed?" Louis tried to sound calm and collected, painful memories surfacing.

"Looks like Vehpolis, sir."

A shiver ran through him. Even kilometers away, one could occasionally see the attacks light up the sky and the ground tremble. Louis gritted his fist and teeth. "I'm going to see Milo. Ready our forces!"

His steps came firmer, a fire in his gut. If Vehpolis fell, Kircross would be next.

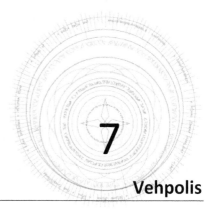

7

Vehpolis

Edmond pulled on the belts that held him to his command chair. They'd become a must with the new speed of the ships.

He sat on the flag bridge. Communications, intelligence, and seer officers brought him the latest information from across the fleet and maintained the flow of information between each ship under his command.

Seer screens showed the outside as if they weren't in the dead center of the ship. The thrum of the jet engines decreased as the fleet slowed down, closing in on Vehpolis, no longer shoving him into the back of his seat.

"Local information has tears in every direction. Some twenty Devourers estimated, and Ravagers in the hundreds of thousands," the Intelligence officer reported from her chair. "Eighty percent of the civilian population has been evacuated."

"Ground and air forces have transitioned to Kircross," Esther said, at Edmond's side. Everything in Vehpolis was being used to evacuate the people, turning Kircross into their staging area out of the enemy's line of fire.

"Okay, time to target?" Edmond asked.

"Fifteen minutes."

"Get the aerial wings out and teleport up their replacements from

Kircross. Just as we planned."

The fleet had broken into three main units named main, attack and support. Edmond commanded the main fleet directly, six corvettes, four frigates, two destroyers, and two cruisers. Back left was the leading attack fleet, with ten corvettes and supporting sparrow wings lining up off them as they launched from the destroyers and cruisers. The support fleet hung out to the rear right, in-line with the main fleet with four corvettes, five frigates, one destroyer, and one cruiser.

"Attack fleet is moving to position," Esther said.

The ships, sparrows, and Kestrels accelerated as the support and main fleet banked away from one another.

"Map updating!"

Edmond grimaced as buildings disappeared, showing rubble and tears inside the city. A section of the mountain collapsed, revealing a hollowed-out interior. The city guards were doing their best to hold back the tide of Shattered, but they weren't prepared to deal with a force like this.

The attacking fleet spread out and leveled off, passing over the city and heading to the north where the enemy was thickest. A sheet of bombs fell from their storage devices, tumbling below.

The support fleet came to a hover back from the fighting in the west. The main fleet plowed forward, dumping bombs over the Shattered as they banked above Vehpolis, coming into a hover over the top of the city's mountain.

Bombs detonated, wiping out tears and any Shattered or structures in their blast radius. Craters were all that remained.

Kestrels dropped from the main fleet as the attacking fleet banked in a wide circle around the city, raining destruction on the tears and Shattered below, breaking their lines.

"What is the Imperium doing?" Edmond growled.

"They have orders to pull back to prepare for an offensive in the Ninth Realm."

"At a time like *this*?" Edmond gripped his armrest, bending the metal.

"The order came from the Imperium head."

"Good, very good! Then we'll fight this battle ourselves. We don't need their help! Does the support fleet have their targets?"

"I… Yes, they do, sir."

The support fleet had fanned out. Frigates' missile doors opened, targeting the grouped tears as the rail cannons took on standalones. The main fleet added their attacks into the mix.

"Devourer, seven o'clock." The flagship *Resolute* shifted to the center of the main fleet's formation as it descended, accelerators charging.

The ship jolted as the first accelerator fired. The slug tore through the Devourer, the detonation evaporating what little was left.

"Teleportation pads are down. Ground forces are advancing. Attack fleet has split and they're dropping their people," Esther said.

The Attack fleet corvettes hovered above the city, opening their armored shutters as Alvan CPD units entered the city.

Sparrows and Kestrels gave overhead cover as the PDCs—Personal Defensive Weapons—lit up the sky with heavy automatic flak rounds, cutting down aerial Ravagers.

Every gun and missile port was ablaze, raining hell upon the Shattered below.

Erik ran for the teleport pad, passing through and entering Vehpolis. He and the four special teams with him moved through the teleportation point.

The city had been torn up, with tears inside the city walls and mountain. He checked his map and bearings. The ground rumbled with bombs impacting nearby.

"Let's go!"

They left the defenses around the teleportation point, spreading out as they crossed through the city. Ravagers appeared randomly. The special teams barely paused, cutting down the creatures and moving on.

They passed through a warehouse district. Erik ran up between buildings as elemental attacks filled the air between him and the group ahead. He accelerated and fired in the direction of the attacks, slamming through the wall the group was using for cover.

"Team six, team four, keep their asses pinned down. Team eight, go back and loop around the left flank."

Erik moved to a window, firing at the Ravagers running toward the fighting. He opened fire. The Ravagers dropped by the dozen. More rushed up, pushing the advance before team eight opened up with spell scrolls.

The wave of curling fire rolled down the street.

"Calling in fire support, tear!" Yao Meng yelled.

"Hold firm. Team two, get over here. I want you along our right flank," Erik ordered. He rolled to the side of the window and checked his map.

The rail cannon rounds caused the earth to jump and the rubble piles to shift.

Erik watched their next target updating on his map in real-time as Glosil coordinated their advance with the Vehpolis forces. "Roska, your team has point. Get us to objective Charlie!"

Erik stuffed his map away.

"Got it. Moving!"

The teams pushed through the ruins, hearing the distant air support raining down, spells and rifles cracking off in the distance.

They passed through previous tear locations, picking up the pace where they could.

The sounds of furious spell casting came from the other side of what had been a manor. Erik hurried toward it with Tully, team six's leader, using a short wall for cover. He glanced over the stone. Vehpolis guards were engaged in a wild melee with Shattered in the street.

Ravagers crashed through walls and jumped between buildings to reach their targets.

"Barriers up. Advance down the street and get to that carriage. Set up a base of fire there," Erik said.

"Got it."

"Roska, you're next, then Storbon, then Yao Meng."

Erik checked his machine gun.

The MG4311
Damage: Unknown
Weight: 4.45 kg
Charge: 10,000/10,000
Durability: 135/135
Innate Effect:
Decreased thermal gain by 27%
Socket One:
Ammunition storage
Socket Two:
Empty
Integrated Enchantment
Heat Exchange - Remove heat from area
Dissipate - Expel Fire element
Range: Long range
Requires: 7.62 round
Requirements:
Agility 75
Strength 45

"Ready," Tully said.

"Let's go!"

Tully and her team jumped over the short wall and started running.

"Go!" Erik waved Roska's team forward and jumped in behind the last man. Storbon and his team moved up next.

Tully and her people reached an overturned cart, the beasts half-eaten, and opened fire, cutting through Ravagers

Roska's team moved to their left flank against a building and watched another street, using spells to create trenches.

The Ravagers turned toward the death, dying in the tens. The Vehpolis guards found new strength and pushed them back from the barricades as what looked like a crab with a blood-covered maw crashed through a two-story building.

Twin manipulators on either side of its mouth released a jet of water that tore through the cart and sent it flying backward, downing two of Tully's people. Storbon punched the cart with a spell, shattering it before it hit his people.

"Devourer!" Erik fired on the beast's armored legs. It whistle-chirped as its leg collapsed.

Team members armed with anti-material rifles based off Rugrat's beast fired. The rounds stumbled the creature and sparked off its carapace.

"Need support! Dealing with a Devourer!" Erik contacted higher while he fired.

Ravagers gathered as the weight of fire slackened on them.

"Focus on the mouth!"

The beast lashed out, cutting through the street and hitting a team member. Erik hit them with triage spells to stop the bleeding. The creature lost its manipulators, rearing up.

The Ravagers turned from their attacks and charged the special team.

"Coming in low," a voice said in Erik's ear. He felt a sudden rush of wind. The street *filled* with cannon fire as a sparrow wing flew in a line just above the houses. Rounds ran down the street, tearing apart Ravagers and Devourers.

"Cover me!" Storbon yelled, already running. Parts of the buildings came down as he sprinted at the Devourer. It shook its head, dazed but getting back to its feet.

Erik shot at the beast's eyes. It cried out in pain and looked away, covering its face with a paw.

Storbon pulled a spear from the ground and jumped, shoving it into the beast's mouth. He hung from it, opening it wide enough to toss in the grenade in his hand, then dropped back down. The Devourer stumbled backward as Storbon kicked off the ground, diving into a nearby shell of a house.

The Devourer *popped* every joint and opening in its carapace, expelling what was attached. The main shell dropped to the ground with a hollow thud.

"Maintain fire on the Ravagers!" Erik yelled.

"Friendlies moving up from the rear!" A unit of riflemen pushed up from where the special teams had advanced, following the trail they'd broken.

"Yao Meng, link up with the Vehpolis people. Roska, you take point. Tully, support here, clear the four surrounding blocks, and get us security." Erik looked at the newly arriving unit, one of them dropping down next to him.

"Who's your officer?"

"Raddich, over there." He pointed down the line to a woman.

Raddich? Erik moved over to the woman. He remembered a time when he knew everyone in Alva's military. "Tully, Roska, the rifle unit will be your reserve. Use them to plug gaps." Erik patted the woman on the shoulder and crouched next to her. She looked over from talking with another soldier. "Hey, Raddich?"

"Yes, sir."

"Get your people stuck in. You'll be supporting the teams when they need you."

"Yes, sir."

Erik jogged over to the Vehpolis lines. The guards had fatigue etched into their expressions, but determination and duty held them upright.

"Thank you, sir. We used up all the spell scrolls that could deal with Devourers." One man stepped forward and bowed his head.

"No worries. My guys like to improvise." Erik dropped down into a couch against a pile of rubble that had been a house.

Storbon ran back over to his team, coordinating with Roska and Tully.

Yao Meng caught his eye and waved him over. Erik grunted to standing and jogged over.

They were using what had been a trading stall to share map information. Erik pulled out his map and touched it to the Vehpolis guard's map.

"North is the worst, where the section of the mountain fell in, nearly at the central plaza. The east and west are folding in. South is holding the furthest from the mountain. Where we are," Yao Meng said, pointing at the forces across the map. "They've been using spell scrolls as their main way to deal with the Devourers, but they don't have many strong enough to deal with it."

Erik's helmet rang with a notification from command. He held up his hand, listening to it.

"We've broken through and will connect with Vehpolis forces to the south. Teleportation formations will be shifted from deployment locations to the new link-up locations. Vehpolis locations will collapse to these southern teleportation formations. Get dug in. Bombing runs have been successful in dealing with most of the tears around the city. Whatever is inside the city is what we've got left to fight." Glosil's voice ended with the message.

Erik opened his team chat, adding in Raddich. "We're going to fortify this location. Storborn, gather up all the teleportation formations. Your team is on defense and the teleportation hub building. The rest of our units will converge on our locations." Erik looked around at the shops, a church, and houses. It looked like a Victoria suburb.

People peered out through the door of the church over pews they'd stacked at the door to block it off.

"Yao, keep talking to him. Anything we can learn, relay to higher." Erik pointed at the guard leader.

"On it." Yao turned and started asking questions.

Erik jogged into the center of the shared courtyard, his domain stretching over the ruined three-story houses surrounding it, confirming there was no one there. He fused and compressed the ground, making sure it was level, then collapsed what was left of the buildings and created several bunkers away from the street, facing outward.

"Roska, get some people to clear out those buildings to the south. They're blocking my view!" Erik yelled as he reinforced walls to create barricades from houses, pulling stone and metal from the rubble to create obstacles.

Roska and her people tore down buildings with attack spells while Storbon's team hastily erected defenses.

A flare lit up the position.

"The hell is that?" Erik asked.

"Signal to the civilians to gather here. They're all over the place," Yao Meng apologized.

"As long as it works."

Storbon's team put down teleportation pads. They lit up only a few minutes later as the Dragon Corps started pushing out.

"Yao, get me some local guides!"

Yao waved some of the Vehpolis officers over.

"You, take your people down that way. Create defenses as you go. Knock down anything between your position and ours. We can't make a solid line, but I want interlinking arcs of fire. This here is your guide." Erik waved over Yao's guides.

Corvettes from the Attack fleet howled overhead, tracking around the city, hunting down Devourers and tears.

Kestrels came into land in a courtyard to their rear, dropping off soldiers and supplies.

"Anything for me?" Erik asked.

"No, sir."

"All right. Get going," Erik said. Tian Cui, Yao Meng's second in command, jogged over to him.

"We're moving all the civilians we can back to Kircross." She gestured at the church with her chin. People were funneling out and moving to the pads as Alvan soldiers were exiting them.

"Got four in and eight out, two to one."

"Sounds good. I want some eyes around us, take five others and get alarm formations out in front."

"Already done. Team two."

"All right," Erik accessed his command chat. "Tully, Roska, get Raddich and her people to take over the defensive. Tully, Roska, I'm with your teams. Yao Meng, Storbon, you two will be together. Move to the teleportation hub. We're quick reaction now."

"Yah, Devourer hunters." Yao Meng whistled as Erik and Tian Cui returned to his stall.

"How we looking?" Erik asked.

"We're securing the southern defensive line, pushing up the east and west some. Inside the mountain is the problem. It's like a damn ant's nest in there and the Shattered are bulldozing through it while the residents are running through the streets. Units getting cut off and shit. It's not pretty."

Erik grimaced. "And if we go in there, we're just going to add to the confusion."

"Yeah, Glosil has the Tigers creating a defensive line at the mountains, something to offer the Elevenths."

"Elevenths?"

"Not of the Tenth Realm—Elevenths—Shattered, add in some spice."

Erik smiled. "Whatever."

"Good news. Well, if it is that. The people that were in the north, the civvies, are coming down here. Most of the teleportation formations were in the mountain. They can collapse those defensives. They were a meat grinder. Bad news, we're going to be quickly swarmed by people."

"Are we sure there are no Shattered in here?" Erik gestured at the area between lines.

"We don't think so."

Erik checked objective and unit locations. "That mountain is going to be the biggest pain in our ass." Erik stabbed at it with his finger. "Filled with Shattered, covered, and we're not allowed to shoot blindly."

"Why not?" Yao Meng asked.

"Something about personal property damage."

"House values are at an all-time low," Tian Cui said as another series of houses were destroyed to clear their line of sight.

Close shooting broke out as all three faced off with the noise. Sporadic fire turned into a massed rage and died with several dull thumps of explosions.

"Guys on our right flank found a group of Devourers in the sewers," Tully said.

"Got it. Thanks for the update," Erik said.

Erik ducked as an accelerator fired overhead, followed by a second, third, and a fourth. The explosions far off in the distance could be heard even across the city.

"I fucking love having superior firepower," Yao Meng said.

"Supposed to be twenty Devourers in the area." Erik checked the map. In the corner, a tally had been created. "We've got six of them in the ground."

"And fourteen wandering," Tian Cui said.

"It was a guess, and you know how guesses can be," Erik said.

"Under or over, nearly never on."

"Give the lady a prize." Erik laughed.

"Scramble, Scramble, Scramble! Devourer delta seventeen. Even teams, you're closest."

Erik checked the grid square, finding the pin. "Yao?"

"We're ready to rock and roll."

"Go."

Yao Meng and Tian Cui took off, running toward the Kestrel perched on top of the church. They ran, using the broken building and spells as stepping stones. They jumped into the Kestrel's open ramp.

The ramp closed behind the last team member before climbing up into the sky, their two Sparrow wings swooping in around them as support.

Erik watched them disappear from sight. His gaze fell on the main fleet as it positioned itself on the southern side of the mountain.

It was a race now to get the people out of Vehpolis as fast as possible and collapse their forces quicker than the Shattered could create hidden tears in the mountain or overrun the Alvan positions.

Retaking that mountain is going to be a stone-cold bitch.

Edmond got the support and the attack fleet circling Vehpolis while his main fleet floated above the controlled area of the city. The civilians had made a mad dash to the south and the teleportation pads, disappearing to Kircross as fast as the lines could move.

"Tigers gave them the strength they needed," Esther said.

"They held out longer than I thought they would. The Vehpolis fighters held their own," Edmond said.

"Takes a certain kind of person to hold out in that situation. Lieutenant General Yui is moving to position *Firebreak*."

The map updated as the line across the southern edge of the mountain shifted as one mass, flooding down through the streets.

Three, two, one.

The main fleet fired every weapon they could bring to bear on the area ahead of the defensive line. The attack fleet flew overhead just a few minutes apart, carpeting the area in bombs.

Resolute bucked as her accelerators tore through a Devourer and four city blocks.

The Alvan fleet laid down a rainbow wall of spells, and weapons fire, obscuring the ground and letting nothing past.

While Erik and his four special teams were in the southwest, Rugrat and his teams had linked up to create a defensive line to the southeast.

He lowered his rifle and looked at the constant stream of people going through the teleportation pads.

George shifted in his chair, yawning and stretching.

Rugrat went back to watching the street through his scope and the hole in the wall. "Keeping you up?"

"Just been in one place for a long time. How do you sit there all day and not get bored?"

"Practice, training, and thinking of other things. You can entertain yourself out of boredom most times."

Kestrels came into land near the teleportation pads, dropping their ramps. Medics rushed down them. The civilians halted as the wounded were teleported to the field hospital in Kircross.

"You think the Shattered are going to hide in the mountain until we leave?"

"Come on, George, don't tempt fate like that. I hope to hell they do."

"You scared they're going to get stronger and then we won't be able to take this place back?"

Rugrat paused. "I hadn't really thought of it that way. I guess the longer they're here, the stronger they'll get. Makes me wish that we could blow that mountain even more."

"What if we can't cut off the tears?"

"Then the Ten Realms will be Seven Realms real quick. We need to push them back. The lower they get, the safer it is for them to cultivate and get stronger. Up here, about one in five will survive cultivating. In the Third Realm, they can cultivate as much as they want, and they'll be just fine." Rugrat sighed, looking over his sight. "The Ten Realms is just ten planets. The Shattered Realms... not even the Elves and Gnomes knew how many worlds were connected. They use tears to get into the Ten Realms, but there are gateways all across their planets, connecting them like one messed up spider's web. There are a lot more of them than there are us."

"So why aren't we helping the Imperium?"

"You heard Glosil. The plan the Imperium had, while it sounds good to clear out the Ninth realm, wasn't really a plan. They were just trying to get control over our forces and resources."

Rugrat's sound transmission flashed with a priority message.

"Check your maps for movements in the dungeons. All forces, pull back to the southwest and southeast rally points," Glosil said.

"Shit!" Alarms were going off under the city as the Shattered used the dungeons to advance underground.

The warships opened fire, tearing through buildings, streets, and the ground below. It split the Shattered, but groups went deeper, and others moved too fast to be caught by the attacks.

The lines for transportation had shrunk in the last couple of hours. They started to shift again as units withdrew, herding the last civilians through totems and teleportation formations. A line appeared between the forces splitting east and west.

The main fleet pulled back, watching over the retreating forces, moving toward Rugrat's position. The Support fleet covered the southwestern fallback.

"Should slow the Shattered some." Rugrat watched the battle, biting his lip. "Get ready."

George grabbed his machine gun, taking position at his stone reinforced window, watching the road.

People flooded back to the teleportation pads. Some had been trapped; others had resisted until they saw the true threat they faced. Humans rarely acted upon the first noise of danger, and often reacted too late.

Officers checked their defenses again. They'd turned four square blocks into a walled base.

Rugrat saw the Shattered advance, marked with the collapse of buildings and rail cannon fire tearing apart the ground.

The last units pulled back inside the base's walls. Rugrat silently prayed for the evacuation to speed up.

"Fire in the hole! Fire in the hole! Fire in the hole!"

Charges went off in series, cutting down buildings and creating a moat around the camp. The dust cleared to reveal the dungeons below.

Machine guns opened fire as they spotted targets.

"Eleven o'clock!" Rugrat fired, killing a Shattered metal tree covered in lightning.

George's tracers cut through the group of trees as Rugrat added in his fire.

"Third company, pull back!" Niemm yelled.

Rugrat tuned out the orders, focusing on his piece of real-estate and keeping it clear. The main fleet hung in the sky, tearing through the city and the dungeon floors below.

Beasts jumped the gap between the city and the fallback location. Rugrat and George killed some, but there were too many of them and the weight of fire from the other buildings had slackened.

"All remaining units, prepare to pull back as one. Execute spell scrolls on my orders. You will be pulling out via corvette!" Niemm yelled. "One minute!"

Rugrat tapped a spell scroll on his carrier and fired, flinging a Shattered back. He fired as fast as he could pull the trigger on the next three.

"Reloading!" Rugrat tore out his old magazine, smacked in a new drum, and looked through his sight. "Shit, got a Devourer." He shot as he talked. "Back in!"

It looked like a demon, humanoid, horns, tail, and three sets of hands with metal and lava falling from several wounds.

The demon flinched from the rounds but continued to run, even as George brought it under fire. Spears shot out of a house. The side of the building and roof were shredded with thousands of metal shards, the barrier stack complaining and filling the air with the smell of hot metal and ozone.

"Use your spell scrolls and pullback!" Niemm yelled over the howl of corvette engines as the first dropped down into the center of the camp.

Rugrat pulled on the tab of the spell scroll on his vest, quickly aiming it. Spell formations appeared across the moat. Destructive spells of every element and color detonated.

He grabbed the barrier stack formation, pulling out one shard and stabbing in another. He turned the handle, locking the stack into place, and *hurled* it through the broken house and into the moat. He turned as George jumped out the back of the attic. Rugrat followed him out, dropping four stories to the ground. He took the impact with his legs and ran after George. Fighters and soldiers flooded out of the buildings as the first corvette took off, a second coming into land with its ramps already down.

Soldiers ran up the ramps and into the ship's vast hold. Rugrat moved to the side, smacking people on the back as they drained into the ship and ran through the teleportation formation inside.

The ground cracked and shifted.

"Shattered underneath!" Rugrat yelled, following the last man up the ramp, seeing Niemm running up another ramp.

"Get us up!" Niemm yelled. The corvette's ramps started to close as the ground began falling away. The corvette slid backward and down as the square came apart.

"They're coming up!" Rugrat yelled as PDC's fired, revealing the Shattered-infested ground.

A Devourer hit the ship's barriers, causing it to jerk to the side as it started to climb and tilt away. The demon Devourer got a face full of jet thrust, tearing its body apart as Rugrat tumbled forward, losing his grip on the grab bar. George yanked him back by his carry handle, grunting as he held onto a standing strap with the other hand. Rugrat clasped his arm and the grab handle as the ramp doors sealed them in red light.

The corvette leveled off and Rugrat let gravity take him, hitting the ground.

He grunted, rising to his feet. "Thanks, bud." He nodded to George.

"You know how heavy you are?" George muttered, rubbing his shoulder.

Rugrat rolled his eyes, looking at the seer screen as the main fleet dismantled their fallback position with prejudice. Missiles and rail cannon rounds pounded into the camp, collapsing the surface into the dungeon below and deep into the underground.

"You good?" Erik contacted him first.

"Was just gonna check in on you. Everyone got out." Rugrat moved to a drop chair, pulling it down from the wall and sitting.

"We got the corvette express and cleared out. Looked like they were trying to pull your ass back down to hell."

"Yeah, it was a close one." Rugrat felt that jolt from the Devourer attack in his bones.

"Main fleet is going to stay here, mop up as many tears as possible. We're going to get based in Kircross. Attack and support fleet are going to merge into the second fleet and go tear hunting."

"Who are we going with?" Rugrat reached up and pulled his faceplate off to rub his face.

"Two special teams with each fleet, other four on standby. You want to take the first shift?"

"Yeah, you're better with all the hand shaking and smiling crap. Give me and George a fight any day."

George took off his helmet and pulled down the drop seat next to Rugrat, grinning.

"Got it. You'll be with team three and five."

"Nice." Rugrat shifted his head, stretching out his neck. "Any word on the attack to retake the Ninth?"

"Nothing yet. I'm not sure if they've headed off yet."

"Yeah, we need to close these damn tears." Rugrat recalled his talk with George. "If we don't, we're going to get buried under Shattered."

8

Avegaaren

Rekha checked her gear for what had to be the fifteenth time. They had been called back to one of the cities controlled by the guilds and turned into one of several dozen rally points for the Imperium forces aiming to retake the Ninth Realm.

"You're going to wear out your storage ring." Weebla smiled and carried on knitting with her metal threads.

They were waiting in the back room of a bar. The owners were familiar with Weebla and with enough teleportation pads and routes to the bar that it wouldn't draw any undue attention. Or alert the new head of the Imperium.

Drink lay in casks against one wall, the rest given over to crates that had been piled to create chairs and a table.

Rekha let out a breathy laugh as she played with her fingers. Her worries seemed to be burning a hole through her stomach.

Cayleigh checked the sharpness of her axes. They all looked up, even Weebla, as Sam walked over.

Rekha grimaced at his expression.

"What did they say?" Weebla sighed.

"Plan is really easy, actually. Go to the Ninth Realm, bloody their noses, close down the tears in Avegaaren, then group together and figure out our next moves," Sam said with forced ease. "Well, you know, other than the fact there's no damn plan. That's literally it. We go into the teleportation hubs, we teleport into Avegaaren, spread out, kill Shattered and tears. Call in the warships for support and push through the city."

"Doesn't seem that bad," Cayleigh said.

Weebla's look made Cayleigh's head retreat into her armor. She stored her knitting away, her actions lethargic. "Stay close to me."

"What's wrong?" Rekha asked.

"While the Imperium controls the academy, the fighters are mostly in groups. Instead of planning this out like an operation, its being treated like a mission the mission hall might give out. How many party leaders do you have in your sound transmission device? Do you know the parties we're going in with? You know where your wounded are supposed to go, if you have to deal with it, or call up a healer, or send them back to a healer?"

Rekha frowned, starting to piece it together as Weebla continued.

"Small gaps, small problems when you are dealing with five, ten groups, but there are hundreds if not thousands of groups, and few that have worked together before. We have our mission, and little else. Now, if you'll excuse me, I have to make some transmissions."

Weebla took out her sound transmission device and map.

Rekha sat back as several old Gnomes and Elves arrived in their corner of Cronen. Gnomes, given to frowning, dry humor, and having a stiff upper lip, looked older quicker, but the older they got the more ingrained they became with the natural world. The air around them was refreshing and calm, the ground becoming level and smooth with their passing. The elements greeted them as one of their own, and their wild hair styles and eyes reflected the elements they had mastered.

Weebla's own knitting, while innocuous to most, weaved not only metal, but the elements, creating three-star level gear.

Old Elves, well if an Elf ever looked old, they had to be closing in on millennias of age. Their beauty products were legendary across the realms. Eli'keen had a forty-three-step program every morning to retain his youth, and he was seen as older, but not old in the eyes of Elves.

Sam and Cayleigh straightened and moved from their positions as they approached. Cayleigh grabbed Rekha and pulled her to the side.

Standing so close to the Elves made Rekha feel like she was standing at the entrance to a small cave, yelling into the darkness beyond and losing her voice to the abyss.

They both bowed their heads, Rekha joining.

"Hah, this your granddaughter, Weebla? Must be hell on two legs. Two axes! Not a mighty battle axe."

"I'll give you a battle axe, Grog," Weebla muttered.

Cayleigh snorted, a smile on her face.

"Give us a minute, you three." Weebla sighed, sliding off her crate and spreading her map on it. The rowdy Gnomes and benevolent Elves gathered around the table.

An Elven woman put her hand on Sam's shoulder.

"Mom?"

"You missed our last family dinner," she said. A true beauty with a smirk on her face, she exuded grace as she looked to Cayleigh. "It's good to see you, Cayleigh."

"Miss Avariose." Cayleigh bowed her head with perfect pronunciation over that little tongue twister.

"Stay safe. Seems the old battle axe is in a mood. Mustn't keep her." She hugged Sam. "Ah, you grow up so fast."

"I'm thirty-two, Mom,"

She sighed. "It took that many years to have you."

"Didn't hurt for trying." Another elf threaded his arm around her and waggled his eyebrows.

"Oh, councilman Avariose, keeping up the Elven grace," she muttered, age old love in her eyes as she kissed him on the cheek.

"Maybe we should try for our seventh?"

"Ughh, we'll leave you to your talks." Sam grabbed Cayleigh and pulled her away.

"I do so love grandchildren," the councilor said.

"Dad!" Sam increased his pace.

"Councilor, general." Rekha bowed to them both, unable to keep the smile from her face.

Sam's mother pulled her up into a hug, stunning her. "The family dinners aren't the same if you're not there," she said, tightening her grip on Rekha.

Something caught in Rekha's throat as Sam's mother released her and her husband smiled.

"Our home is yours. Don't be a stranger."

"I'll do my best," Rekha said.

They tilted their heads with knowing smiles.

"Xun Liang was a brilliant man and as proud for you as the daughter he never had." Sam's mom squeezed her shoulder, and they headed to the crate surrounded by vagabonds, ruffians, and legends of myth.

Rekha composed herself, joining Cayleigh and Sam along the wall.

"Looks like the old battle axe is making an appearance." Cayleigh's eyes shone, a grin threatening to split her face.

"Battle axe?"

"Gran's old nickname. She has an old battle axe my granddad made for her. She wielded it to become one of the four Gnome generals in the retaking. Now she's one of two left. Grog is the other."

"Grog was a general?"

"Appearances aren't everything. The Elves and the Gnomes still have a few legends and secrets up their sleeves."

"Why do they have generals still?"

"They do work for the Imperium, but nothing is for sure in this world."

"What are they going to do?"

"Plan a battle." Cayleigh sighed. "Not many Gnomes and Elves left anymore. Got to make sure that we don't waste one life."

The hours counted down as humans entered the back room, including several warship admirals. Rekha, Sam, and Cayleigh patrolled the bar, and outside the bar.

With just a few hours to go until they headed for the Ninth, the Imperium forces moved toward the totems that would carry them. The meeting under Weebla's direction wrapped up.

Sam's parents hugged him and headed off, all with grim expressions, preparing their minds for the fight ahead.

Rekha and her group moved to Weebla who reviewed her map one more time.

"Messy." She shook her head. "Get your maps updated."

Rekha did and reviewed the changes, showing a rough battle plan and positions.

"Once we enter the realm, we're going to have several groups move into defensive positions around the teleportation islands. We will teleport in as close as we can to the admission hall. There aren't any gardens, training areas or anything special there, so Shattered haven't been in the area as much and shouldn't walk in randomly. Clear the area, set up a base of operations, call in the warships and push forward." A whistle cut through the air, three times. Weebla stored her map and pulled out a scarred battle axe mounted on a worn wooden handle, wrapped with beast hide. "You three are my guards, which means you'll be watching my back. Everyone has details of your sound transmission devices. Pass me reports as they come in and update the map as needed."

Rekha felt a new weight settle on her shoulders. One missed message could mean death for others.

"I see you're scared by that. That's good; it'll keep you alert. Let's get moving."

They walked with Weebla, surrounding her unconsciously.

Cronen's mission hall and streets had been turned over to the Imperium. Tens of fleets lifted from the ground and moved toward the totems, ready to transition.

They were close to the front of the totem line when the war horn blared across Cronen, shaking windows and Rekha's heart.

The line moved forward as the totem flared with transition. It seemed like she had breathed and that she had been there forever, thoughts of death and destruction, anxiety swirling in her gut.

They drew their weapons at the ready as Weebla activated the totem and they arrived at one of the teleportation islands.

"Move it! Clear the totems!" a man yelled, repeating himself as they jogged clear of the totem. People flooded across the ground, leaving the totem defenses and heading to the teleportation pads. Weebla led them, checking her map and sending a sound transmission.

"Away we go into the fires of hell." They stopped on a teleportation pad. Weebla entered a location, and they appeared in the admission hall. The massive cathedral-like building, with chairs that were normally filled with nervous friends and family, lay empty. They came out of the teleportation pads that would have taken applicants to the arenas to test to join the academy.

"Wake up, you dolts," Weebla yelled. The statues around the room opened their gem-filled eyes and stepped down from their pedestals, shaking the ground.

"Defend the admission hall."

Gnomes, Elves, and humans ran out of the admission hall teleportation pads and spread out. Weebla took them through side doors and a lift.

Light flooded in as they reached the top of the building and looked out at Avegaaren beyond.

The landscape was foreign to Rekha. The ground had been churned over in the fighting, buildings smashed into oblivion. The city beyond Avegaaren's front gates looked like a forest after a firestorm had swept through it. There were roars in the distance—Shattered issuing challenge as they fought one another.

Tears dotted the landscape, revealing a dozen other visions into the Tenth Realm.

The statue golems stepped outside of the admission hall, creating a wall around the building. Fighters took up positions in the hall.

Weebla checked her map. "Cayleigh, get Grog. Sam, updates on defenses," she called out. "Rekha, the ships, call them in, say you're assisting the Battle Axe."

Rekha used her sound transmission device. "Orders from the Battle Axe. You are good to transition to admission hall. Sending coordinates." She added it to the message relayed through the teleportation pad and totem to the warship.

Several seconds later, shadows passed over the admission hall as corvettes appeared, then frigates and destroyers, cruisers and a battleship.

Rekha coordinated with the fleets, getting them to spread out.

"Grog, you take the first three fleets and head out when you're ready." Weebla paused. "Yeah, I know about the dungeons. Just get your strongest in there. I don't care what they say. Blow the shit out of anything hiding a tear and get me my Devourer pelts. Advance into the south. Avariose, your group will head to the North."

More ships appeared over the admission hall. Fleets shifted away with ground units underneath, spreading out.

"Forces at the arena are being pushed back," Cayleigh said.

"Ah shit," Weebla cursed.

Rekha checked her map. Their groups had spread out sporadically at the totems around the arena, each pushing out in their own direction. Warship markers were dotted overhead. She cast Far Sight, seeing the warships raining down hell on the ground.

"City is turning into a mess," Sam said.

Rekha turned in that direction. The second wave of warships appeared in the sky, coming under fire as they did so, not having the time to even put up their barriers.

She looked over at the flash of weapons to the north. Grog's warship engaged tears as his people brought their power down upon Shattered. Devourers surged out of the ground and flocks of aerial beasts diverted toward his ship.

"Tell Grog and Avaroise to do as they see fit. Rekha, have the warships gain altitude and prepare to head into the city to support our forces there. Cayleigh, get the incoming forces to gather and organize into units. They're going to head into the city."

"The head is ordering you to send forces to the arena," Sam said.

"Tell him they're engaged. If they push out of their positions now, we'll lose the admission hall. I have a group heading to the city to link up with our people there. We're the closest."

The fighting increased in ferocity in the north and south as the armies advanced. Rekha checked that they were advancing above ground and below at the same pace, maintaining a united front.

A floating island plummeted from the sky, coming apart before it smashed into the side of a hill in a plume of dirt and rolled apart.

"They're targeting the islands. Hey, Peli, move the damn island over the admission Hall," Weebla ordered. "Yeah, I know. Call in fleets to cover you."

"Situation in the city, Rekha?"

Rekha scanned the map and checked the city with spell-enhanced eyes. "Units are all over the place. The warships are fighting it out, but the ground fighters are getting wiped out. There're reports of Devourers all over the place."

"Cluster fuck. Got it."

"Some units are pulling back."

"Dammit," Weebla muttered.

Rekha answered a transmission.

"This is Ferlin. Third unit is ready to move."

"You are to head into the city."

"Understood."

The newly arrived units organized by role marched out of the admission hall, mixed races, warships moved with them.

"Where the hell are they going?" Weebla grabbed Sam and pointed at four fleets that had been holding around the admission hall that were now heading into the academy.

"Head gave them new orders."

"Seriously?" Weebla shook her head and hit the back of her axe against the ground.

More fleets appeared above the admission hall. Most of them headed off as soon as they arrived.

"The arena has been lost," Cayleigh said. "The units there are falling apart."

An explosion tore through the city. Rekha braced against the wind, looking at where a warship had detonated. The city collapsed beneath it, revealing the dungeons below, stone turning to lava.

"Get the word out to *stop* going for the city," Weebla barked.

Rekha saw shadows moving through the clouds. They broke through to reveal a teleportation island surrounded by several fleets, their weapons firing into aerial Shattered.

The air flashed as another fleet appeared, formations flaring to life as it shifted into position.

"Fucking Admiral Peli," Weebla said in admiration. Rekha stared at her. She had never heard her swear once in her life.

Weebla had the grin of a hunter. Another part of her soul ignited as she looked at the mad fleet barging their way through the aerial Shattered, laying a barrage of fire into the city along their flank, closing tears on their way to the admission hall.

As fleets appeared over the hall, many powered their formations and charged toward the heart of the academy. Elven, Gnomish and human fleets shifted to assist the three ground units.

Gnomish warships dove into the ground, which parted around them like waves, to support the forces in the dungeons.

Elven mana canons spun white light across the heavens, cleaving through Shattered as they came from every direction.

The realm's ground boiled with Shattered, thousands jumping into the sky, flitting shadows blocking the sun.

"We're engaged with Devourers currently," General Avariose, Sam's mother, reported in Rekha's ear.

"Devourers have engaged the northern unit."

"Have formed units head out to support the north and south. Get the officers in the admission hall to shake out any of the new forces that appear."

The teleportation island, being flown like a warship, cast a shadow over the admission hall as it moved to the open area facing the academy. The covering fleets spread out, moving to reinforce defenses and push out to the three armies.

Shattered poured out of the ground or tunneled through it toward the admission hall.

Peli's fleet laid down attacks with a vengeance, laying open the dungeons below. Explosions tore up the ground as the Gnome warships made their presence known.

Two warships from the fleet rushing into the academy lost their barriers and their flight capability, dropping toward the ground as the fleet piled on more speed to get out of the fighting.

"Get those ships to start teleporting their people out now," Weebla used her sound transmission device.

The corvette and destroyer plowed into the ground, leaving dark lines in the ground as they smashed through buildings, finally coming to a stop.

Rekha listened to General Ferlin's sound transmission. "General Ferlin says that the city is a mess, above and below ground. He's going to set up a defensive and send warships to destroy any tears they can find," she said.

The noise of battle rolled over them all, somehow familiar. Rekha's fears, anxieties, and even her own body, had evaporated. In the heat of battle, there was a singular focus on the tasks ahead of her.

"Shattered." She pointed past the crashed warships on the academy side. Shattered crawled out of out of the ground and ran across the hills.

"Dammit," Weebla growled.

Rekha checked the different areas. Ramps led down outside the admission hall into the dungeons below. Powerful spells and attacks had ripped open the ground, revealing several fights that went from above ground into the dungeons, and the inner workings of the earth.

The first two units to form up were making the greatest progress. Fleets of fast-moving ships flew further afield, destroying tears and supporting the fight against Devourers.

"Cover one another and fall back to the Seventh!" Clive's voice came through their sound transmission devices, in an anxious yell.

Rekha looked at Weebla who was looking at her map, murder in her eyes. *That doesn't sound like a leader of the Imperium.*

Weebla activated her sound transmission device, connecting to all her leaders and Rekha's party. "Peli, make sure no more are coming through the totems. Clear out the people up there and get altitude. Once the ground forces are gone, you and the fleets take the island to the Abarrath mountains and hide it there. I'll coordinate the hall's defenses and set up the undead formation. Grog, Avariose, Ferlin, your ground forces will pull out first. Collapse your lines and withdraw, use the Golems."

"Ma'am," they chorused and set to their tasks. Weebla threw out formation pieces that spun in front of her, using mana manipulation to slot them together and a metal fuse spell. The formation glowed as she put it on the ground and threw out a dungeon core. It floated into the middle of the formation. The lines of the formation turned blood red, filling the air with the smell of iron.

A ripple of power shuddered out of the formation and spread out.

An unholy cry came from the depths of the dungeon. A dead Devourer, missing half its face and one leg laid upon the ground, shuddered and shifted. The dinosaur Devourer rose, gathered its power, and charged its old allies, tearing through Ravagers.

"Undead formation?" Cayleigh asked.

"It'll cover our retreat and be a pain in the Shattered's asses. With all this elemental energy, the core can grow rapidly and should spawn dungeon beasts to defend this place."

Units ran up the ramps and across the ground into the admission hall, pulling back.

Weebla talked to the officers inside the admission hall as the golems around the hall ran out to engage the enemy.

The units flooded back through the admission hall. The undead increased their ranks as the golems crashed into Shattered, element and claw meeting metal and blade, locked in combat.

The warships pulled back behind the last of the ground troops, linking up with the fleet around the island.

"Come." Weebla led them downstairs. The admission hall defenders ran back through the teleportation pads. Rekha's group were the last through.

The island and the surrounding fleet accelerated away from the academy on a new heading. The other ships teleported to the lower realms, thinning the sky.

The wind was fierce upon the island. Rekha looked over the side. The academy looked nothing like how she remembered it. Its perfect gardens and stately buildings were now ruins and gaping maws into the heart of the world.

Dungeon creatures battled Shattered. The air thick with elements and mana stirred to a frenzy. Mana and elemental spells flashed among buildings. Sparse, isolated battles in the streets and fields.

"What do we do now?" Rekha asked against the wind.

"We head back to the Seventh and plan a real attack, not this mess. Hopefully, we haven't lost our only chance." Weebla led the way to the totem.

Rekha grabbed her sword, impotent rage running through her. She wanted to punch, to hit and hurt something. She hadn't been able to do anything.

And what the hell was everyone else doing?

Eli'keen kept working sound transmission devices, trying to link groups together so they could pull back in order. He kept an eye on the forces under Weebla in the admission hall, but they didn't need his help.

The Imperium war room was filled with voices of the generals and admirals of the Imperium.

"The Nor'esk Island is under attack by Shattered aerial forces! We're losing the totem position! We need warship support!"

"This is fifth fleet. We have to retreat! We are unable to assist forces on the ground. They're heavily engaged with Shattered. They are covering our retreat. We lost another frigate!"

They'd rushed forward into battle and the Shattered, in much greater numbers than expected were swarming the eager forces.

They're targeting the totem islands.

"Cut that off!" Clive hissed.

Live sound transmission channels went dead, the silence even more oppressing

Eli'keen's body was cold, his heart in his chest. The battle had turned into a complete rout. Worse was that the teleportation and totem islands that floated around the realm were being hunted down by the Shattered.

"We need to destroy teleportation and totem islands." Eli'keen raised his gaze from his map. The room became silent as people turned from him to Clive.

"If we take those out, then we won't be able to use them for a counterattack," Clive spat back, as if he was explaining to some youth uneducated in the ways of war.

"The Shattered control them now. They have already activated some to access the Eighth Realm."

Clive screwed up his features, preparing a verbal deluge.

"If we don't destroy them, then the Eighth Realm will be lost and their incursion in the Seventh Realm will reach a state where we can't deal with it. We must cut off the routes or else we will have lost those battles before we can reorganize our forces. We need time to mount a counterattack, time that the enemy will use to swarm into the lower realms."

"We need those totems and teleportation pads open to get out our people!"

"They're already lost." Eli'keen's voice was cutting. "Anyone that retreats through those locations is being torn apart. Have them retreat to the islands and warships that we control."

Clive focused on the map of the Ninth dominating the main table. "If we only had more people." He muttered.

If we'd only had a real plan. Eli'keen bit back the remark.

"I will heed your advice, Eli'keen, but the lives we lose of those that won't make it to the lower realms are on your head." Clive looked up at him with accusation in his eyes.

"I do everything I can to save people." Eli'keen activated his sound transmission device. It would add more chaos and slow down the retreat, but at least people would be able to get to the lower realms instead of being slaughtered just as they thought themselves close to a totem.

The force at the admission hall had retreated. The only ray of hope was Peli's fleet guiding away the teleportation island, getting free of the Shattered.

We're going to need them in the coming days.

As the other islands fell, the remaining forces funneled through this island and Peli's ships.

Groups across the Ninth Realm were surrounded and getting killed without any support or way out. He could only watch and listen to their pleas for support and help.

"Those damn Shattered were ready for us!" Clive leaned on the war table. "Get me Weebla—*now!*"

Clive looked at the maps and went through the information, talking to his advisors as the Ninth Realm information slowly stopped updating.

Weebla walked into the war room with a grim expression. "Head Clive," she said in a grave tone.

Eli'keen stiffened. This was not going to go well.

"Come with me. Eli'keen, you too."

"Sir—"

"Now!" Clive walked down the corridor.

Eli'keen shot a look at another elder who nodded and started using his sound transmission device. They still needed to get people out of the Ninth Realm.

Clive flung the double doors to a conference room open and stepped inside.

Eli'keen trailed after Weebla. Something was different about her, something older, something familiar. He closed the doors behind him.

"I know that you don't like me, Weebla, but what in the hell was *that?*"

"The mission was to enter and clear the Ninth Realm. That was what I set out to do."

"Set out to do!" Clive's laugh was short and ugly as he smacked the high-backed chair around the conference table. "You put the Elves and Gnomes into units, like *you* were the head."

"You could have ordered us to do it." Weebla's words contained an undeniable edge, an unwavering steel.

Eli'keen stood straighter, studying her.

Clive snorted. "You think that I haven't heard the rumors that you're preparing to have Rekha take my position? A woman that sacrificed her entire family to the Tenth Realm to gain her power?"

"You know that's not true!" Eli'keen admonished.

Clive reared on him. "What is true is that the Elves and the Gnomes are working together again. What's next—a purge of the lower realms?"

"Purge the lower realms? You say that as if we were the ones that led the fight in the Ten Realms." Weebla shook her head. "You humans and your short memories."

"We all know that Rekha killed her family, cleaned house and the clans that took in her sisters. Then she went to the Tenth Realm, returned several months later, and rose to the peak of Avegaaren. She used her request to trade for power. Maybe she used her family as the price. Maybe it was something else, but she killed her *family*. Who would trust such a person?" Clive sneered.

"I will take attacks on my character, but I will not listen to you slight someone because you lost a battle."

Clive's expression became even uglier. He stepped to Weebla, towering over her, the veins in his neck popping out. "You went against my orders! Are you trying to lead a revolt against the Imperium? Trying to take *my* position?"

"Look, boy, I've been doing this a spell longer than you. Us Gnomes and his Elves have *seen* what the Shattered will do to a planet. We drove them out of the Ten Realms and nearly *all* of our people died in the act. Eli'keen has been the advisor to seven Imperium heads. I've led fifteen campaigns against the Shattered."

"Are you the head of the Imperium? You might have got the power back from Xun Liang, but you didn't get his office. A waste to give that much power to some broken old Gnome!"

"Clive," Eli'keen raised his voice.

"You fucking elves and Gnomes think you're better than the rest of the realm. You think that this Imperium is your own nation? It's not, and it hasn't been for two millennia! Get that through your skulls. I will lead us to victory. I will create the Imperium anew, better, stronger, respected. Your undermining of myself, of the Imperium, is what led to today's loss. There is no unity. You only work with one another! You are hereby stripped of your offices and your positions! If I ever see you again I-I'll—" Clive gnashed his teeth, slapped his scabbard, and walked to the door, unable to give words to his rage. "The higher realms are for the fighters, the warriors among us. Not the *crafters*." He looked back, sneering at them. He tore open the doors and left the duo.

Eli'keen waved his hand. Mana shut the door and a sound cancelling spell covering them both. "Looks like we're both out of a job."

Weebla raised an eyebrow. "And when has that stopped us?"

Eli'keen sighed and rubbed his temples. "He held off attacking the Ninth for as long as possible to drive home the point to the people in the lower realms that the Imperium is strong, and now it's come to bite him in the ass."

"It's covered in tears and there are Devourers everywhere. I haven't seen anything like it before." The tremor in Weebla's voice stilled Eli'keen's hand. A shiver ran down his spine.

"He left the tap running and now it is a flood. Question is, can we shut off the tap?" Weebla asked.

"Akran is trying to ascend."

"What?" Weebla's eyes widened.

"He is at the ascension platform and ascending." Eli'keen took out the platform's linked formation, the number of lights had increased. There were only three lights left.

"Why the hell didn't you tell me?"

"It is the head's decision to make."

"Not all heads are made equally, Eli'keen. Xun Liang was a great man and there are few like him. The only reason our people weren't slaughtered in the Ninth is because I called the old generals and admirals together to fight at the admission hall. Clive didn't have a plan; he had a propaganda mission. He doesn't know the scourge of the Shattered; he's only had a taste!"

"I know that now," Eli'keen ground out. "Who else is going to save the Ten Realms?"

Weebla started pacing. "If we call on the Gnomes and Elves, we can pull a fighting force together. Has Akran moved his sworn out from around the platform since they arrived?"

"No, they opened tears, so there are even more Shattered moving around and going to the lower realms. It has one of the largest concentrations of Shattered in the Tenth, acts like a way station into the Ninth Realm."

"You got a map?"

Eli'keen pulled out his map and put it on the table. Weebla looked over it, moving it around.

"Nasty business. That's a lot of Shattered and Devourers, even with our people that's too much for us to handle. We can ask the Alvans for their support," Weebla said.

"Are you sure they'll help us?"

"They don't care about titles and accolades. They care about protecting their people and doing the right thing. We can't rely on the Imperium. Clive might be strong and have connections, but he doesn't have any skill or understanding of battles on this scale."

"Are you sure? Clive and his new advisors have been slighting them this entire time." Eli'keen winced.

"That's certainly not going to help. They have their own pride, but if they have a mission, one that has a clear goal and a good reason, they'll fight tooth and nail beside us."

"It's a dangerous precedent."

"I've already had the Gnomes and Elves fighting side by side. We were the only group that took ground, held it, and advanced. I don't care what the head says. I care about the Ten Realms being free for my granddaughter and my great grandchildren. Isn't that why you are—*were*—the advisor to the head of the Imperium? Hmm, *Major*?" Weebla fixed him in place with a look.

"That was a long time ago." Eli'keen's eyes flashed up to meet hers.

"You were a tailor for much longer than you've been a soldier, and it's time for you to come back to the fold."

"If the Elves and the gnomes united then the rest of the realms—"

"Eli'keen, you underestimate yourself *and* the people of the Imperium. Clive might be the head, but we are the blood and bones of the Imperium." She held his eyes. "Get over your damn feelings and pull yourself together. I know you've put a lot into the Imperium, but isn't the reason you joined the Imperium to make sure the realms were safe? We must fight with whatever we can to end this."

Eli'keen's heart was confused and bitter. He'd worked to make the Imperium a force to deal with whatever threats came their way, and upon the eve of their testing, they collapsed.

"Use what you can, not what you hoped for." A smile spread across Eli'keen's face as he stood up straight. The meek tailor seemed to melt away, a fire in his eyes. Even if he had to spill his own blood, lay his broken body on the battlefield, he would defend the Ten Realms.

"Alright, General Battle axe. What do you need? There are a fair few things that the Imperium head might have missed." If he was going to make a clean break of it, he might as well go all the way.

"Talk to your Elven Conclave and I'll go smack some Gnome heads together and reach out to our allies in the Imperium. We'll come up with a plan and take it to the Alvans. We should get enough skeletons out of the closet to put up something of a fight and we go to the Tenth Realm and kick Akran's ass back into elemental energy. Not cause it's the pretty thing, or the thing that will get us position, but because it's what we need to *do*."

Eli'keen sighed, closing his eyes. When he opened them, he felt the change, like putting on an old set of armor. His expression slackened, and his eyes grew cold.

"There's my Major Eli'keen. Time to go raise your hell riders."

"They're a little out of practice."

"Well, there are plenty of Shattered to fight in the Seventh Realm to warm them up."

9

Across the Realms

Glosil studied the Adventurer's Guild leader, Blaze, Admiral Edmond, and lieutenant generals Kanoa, Chonglu, Pan Kun, Yui, and Domonos.

They'd just finished reporting on each of their units, states of readiness, and training. They were the combined staff that he had wrestled from the front lines for this briefing.

Elan Silaz was with them in his role as intelligence director.

Glosil sat back in his chair. "All right. First, any problems?"

No one made to speak.

"Well, that's good at least, because the realms are full of them. Elan?" He swiveled in his seat as they all watched Elan.

"The attack on the Ninth failed in a spectacular fashion. It seems clear that the Imperium plans were just delaying tactics to get public opinion on their side. Now they don't have the public opinion and people are evacuating into the lower realms. The Adventurer's guild has ballooned in size." He tilted his head to Blaze. "People are scared in the Seventh Realm and are looking to blame someone or get out of the way of the fighting. The Imperium head continues to say that no one is allowed into the Ninth Realm and higher."

"Scared that we might do the job for him?" Pan Kun shook his head.

A month ago, Glosil might have cut him off with a look, but he was saying what they were all thinking.

"How are we doing on increasing the number of people that can pass the Eighth Realm trial?" Blaze asked.

"We should have all the people we need to command the fleet," Edmond said.

"About a third of our standing army could go. We're also raising lower realm units to fight in the Sixth Realm," Glosil said.

"You think it will come to that.?" Elan asked.

"We're losing cities and can't cover all of the Seventh anymore. People are getting stronger from the fighting in the higher realms, ours included. Most people just want to be safe, not fight. Tears are appearing with increasingly regularity in the Seventh Realm and there are reports of some opening in the Sixth Realm. Blaze?"

"We moved all the Sixth Realm forces. We have engagements every few days currently, but they're becoming more frequent. We're having to shift Seventh Realm guild members down to support them." Blaze grimaced. All the officers in the room looked grim, like they had come to the same conclusions.

"Even with all those people, it's a small army compared to the Devourers. We go up there and poke the nest, say we kill a few of the tears. The Imperium is gunning for us. They'll use this to come down on our heads," Chonglu said.

"Has that rumor been confirmed?"

"Yes, the head is not a fan of Alva. Doesn't like how much power we have. Seems he likes the spotlight."

"Would explain why the hell they went in there without a fucking plan," Domonos said.

It was criminal to lead a group into battle without a plan, and Glosil knew the others in the room agreed with him.

"What's done is done. Elan said there was something you wanted to share from the Ninth?"

"So, there was *one* good thing that came out of the Ninth Realm. A group of Gnomes and Elves are working together. They did some good work and activated an undead formation. Like the one in Vuzgal. It's still running. The undead and dungeon creatures are fighting the Devourers right now. The formation uses a dungeon core, making it really expensive."

"Trade a warship for an undead formation," Edmond muttered.

"In an element dense area, if there are Devourers around or high-level dead," Yui countered.

Glosil's sound transmission flashed. He answered it. "Glosil here, go."

"Commander, we have a report from Kircross. they're under attack. There are tears opening across the Seventh Realm in larger numbers than before."

"Understood."

Glosil tapped the table, and it turned to a map, highlighting Kircross. Markers swarmed across the mega city.

Defenders stood along the walls, while enemy groups and tears appeared beyond the city. Sensing formations picked out tears opening one after another. Warships fired on the tears, closing many, while Ravagers from tears beyond the warship's range continued to spread out. Tears appeared in the air, on the ground, and in it.

"Domonos, get your people ready to move. We're heading to Kircross immediately to assist. Edmond, organize your people. You'll act as a strike force, taking out tears further afield. Thin them out and stem this tide as best as possible," Glosil said as they all stood.

Two of the fleets with Chonglu's Crows were hunting down tears across the Seventh Realm. *If I take them from their task, we'll only have to deal with more tears sooner.*

"Pan Kun, have your people on alert in case someone tries to raise trouble in Alva. Elan, get us information on what the Imperium is doing. Domonos, your people will be on the wall. I'll get in contact with the Mission Hall liaison."

"Sir," Domonos nodded.

"Yui, your people just got back from the fighting. Make sure they're rested. Only day passes. All overnight passes are cancelled. Keep them close in case we need them. I want them rested and ready to fight, not strung out."

"Yes, sir," Yui said.

"All right. Domonos, you best get moving."

Erik and Rugrat tagged along with Domonos. People moved out of their way, sticking to the walls as they marched through Kircross, their helmets hanging from their vests. Half a special team walked behind, leaving a path through the command center.

Kircross was a massive city sitting on an ant hill of dungeons. Most of the fighting was happening on the main level, but defenses had been erected underneath the city in force. The city council had mined a number of dungeon cores, creating defensive dungeons under the city. Getting through those would be harder than through the main wall.

The command center was a hive of information and movement. Runners dropped off messages. Others relied on communication devices. City guards opened the doors for them as they walked in.

The side room they were taken to was massive. There were several large map tables, each with staff around them.

"Where there's a fight, there're Alvans." Kay'Renna stood up from the map table she was looking at. Erik didn't miss her gaze settling on Rugrat.

She winked, making Rugrat grin. "Hey there, lover boy."

"We were told to report here for our mission?"

"Right." She waved them to the map table.

They flanked it as she zoomed it out.

"We were able to blunt their first attack, but they've been adding in more and more attackers. The Devourers are getting smart. They're holding back, gathering and sending their sworn to test our weaknesses. I don't like smart Devourers." She circled a section of the wall. "This is yours. I could really use your ships doing… What was it you called it?" She made a motion with her hand over the map and looked at Rugrat.

"Bombing run?"

"That's it. Scorched earth, mother fucker."

Erik looked at Rugrat, grinning out the side of his mouth. *I wonder who taught her that?*

"I want to hit their tears. There are too many of them. We need to slow the bleed. This here is a secondary command center." She circled another building and looked at Domonos. "It's all yours."

"Thank you. Support?"

"You're the Alvans. We usually come to you for support." She grinned and looked around, her tone dropping as she used mana to talk to them. "The Imperium might show up here. I've put in a word with the city leader to get them on the other side of the wall from you."

"That might be for the best." Domonos checked the map one more time.

"They don't have the healthiest attitude," Erik said under his breath.

"Don't have to tell me. I got reports from some of the people at Avegaaren. What a shit show." Kay'Renna waved over a guard. "Take them to sub-command center three"

"Yes, ma'am."

"I'm beginning to think this war is going to keep me from that date you were talking about." Kay'Renna stared at Rugrat with a playful smile.

"War's a right bitch, isn't she?"

Erik's thoughts moved to Rekha. Right after the attack on the Ninth failed, he'd contacted her, to check she was alright. He told himself it was because they shared the same teacher. *But that would be a lie.*

He followed the others out of the room with the guard leading. Domonos worked their sound transmission devices, organizing the Alvan army. Rugrat caught up with them a few minutes later as they reached the teleportation pad.

"I need to get that damn date. Fricking Shattered."

Domonos gave a slight grin, shaking his head as everyone donned their helmets.

They broke apart as they got to the new command center. Command staff filed into the tower already. Erik led the special team and Rugrat away.

"Looks like they're letting us work together again. Must be a limited time thing," Erik said.

"Well, can't keep us apart forever."

Erik looked at the wall. Large staircases wide enough for five men side by side ran up three floors to the top of the wall with a landing for the second floor into the wall where the mana cannons roared.

Watchtowers, in Chinese style, covered in tiles, lay evenly spaced across the top of the wall. It stretched across the breadth of Kircross, just one wall of five that enclosed the massive, tiered city.

Erik looked up, spotting their fleet.

Corvettes created the outer arrowhead formation. Frigates flew behind them, creating an inverted arrowhead, forming a diamond with the corvettes. The fleet's flagship, a cruiser, was positioned in the middle of the formation.

They flew at an altitude of five thousand meters. Aerial beasts were still a threat, but they remained at less than a kilometer above the ground and it would take them time to reach five times that high. Time that the fleet could easily winnow their numbers and evade with engines or teleportation.

Erik checked the map again, looking at the walls, and the sea of red beyond. "Just how many Shattered are there?" Erik muttered.

"Thousands upon thousands." Rugrat's sober tone hit Erik hard.

"How the hell are we supposed to win against that?"

"Cut off their tears, kill them all, and purify the hell of the place. They might have thousands, but we do too."

Kircross' population measured in the hundreds of millions. One only had to look at the warships floating above the main wall. They were floating weapons platforms.

"Are those dungeon cannons?" Rugrat pointed at blue steel cannons floating above a white, glowing platform.

"Dungeon cannons?"

"Yeah, they use dungeon cores to control the cannon. Like if you converted the power of an Earth grade dungeon core into pure destructive power."

"Damn."

"Yeah, I've wanted to build one for a long time, but no one will let me use a dungeon core."

"We both know how nasty those chaotic warheads you theorized are. Might be for the best."

"They're nasty bastards. I hope the frigates packed heavy."

Edmond checked on his fleet of four corvettes, three frigates, and his own cruiser.

He viewed the map of the land below. The city ended at nearly ten kilometers from the wild mountains and valleys. The ground had been cut up by farmers into squares, bordered by trees, fences and roads. Roads spread from Kircross through the mountain and valley passes, linking towns and villages that had been evacuated.

Kircross stood at the mouth of these valleys, creating a natural trading point for the surrounding towns and a choke point.

The Shattered were gathering beyond the range of Kircross' defenses.

High level Devourers moved through the mass, chivvying the Shattered into position, dominating the weaker members. *They're planning out their attack.* Edmond forced himself not to grit his teeth, unable to do anything to change the situation.

Smoke rose from the towns, villages, and hamlets that the Shattered had crossed. They continued forward, massing at the edge of where the mountains and valleys met with the fields.

"We have tear targets," Esther said.

Edmond pushed himself out of his chair and went to the map table. Everything in his new warships was made for functionality, only gaining form if necessary, but they were missing some of the character his old warships held. After fighting with the new ships for nearly three months, he found he didn't care about the frills. Each of his warships was worth seven of his old ships.

"There's a lot of them," he said as Esther joined him.

The tears continued to pop up as they came into range of their sensing formations.

"Have the frigate captains pick out their targets along this line of attack." Edmond drew a line on the map, tracing over the enemy forces and backing up to the lines they held, facing Kircross.

"Yes, sir." She relayed his orders as Edmond pressed a button. The map extended out of the table, showing different groups at different elevations across the battlefield.

Five minutes later, the frigates had all submitted their fire plans. Edmond altered them minorly and gave the corvettes orders.

"Begin the attack."

The frigates disappeared under the missile exhaust as tubes fired and reloaded as fast as possible.

Edmond focused on the seer screens showing the ground.

Missile flares cut across the screen, elemental attacks striking some, diverting their path or turning them into fireballs. Most survived, glowing as their destructive formations activated just seconds before impact. Plumes rose from where they landed, the blasts obscuring the targeted tears.

Edmond studied the map as the chaotic warheads crashed into the terrain, wiping out the gates and changing the topography. The vacuum of elements annihilated one another, and the force of that reaction tore apart tears outside the chaotic warhead's blast radius.

Devourers had scattered after the first warhead arrived. A goddess of vengeance was released upon them. The chaotic missiles struck one after another at groupings of Devourers. Sworn were thrown into disarray and some of the remaining tears closed.

Rail cannons fired on automatic. Their warheads were smaller and picked out outlying tears and Ravagers.

The fleet banked, the missile tubes firing as fast as they could be filled, leaving barely a handful of tears remaining.

"Secondary targets," Edmond ordered.

The frigates changed their targets as the corvettes spread out, coming on an attack vector across the enemy lines.

Devourers remaining on the battlefield charged toward Kircross out of a sense of preservation instead of a coordinated attack. They descended into the fields.

"Kircross is attacking."

Spells and mana-powered weapons lit up the wall. Spells arrived first, their formations raining down attacks on the Shattered. Mana cannons' swirled shots of light crashed on the ground like the sea upon rocks, unleashing a deadly spray.

Holes opened in the Shattered ranks, eagerness and fear driving them forward.

"We'll come along the entrances into the Kircross plains. Corvettes, ready for bombing run."

"Brace for hard bank!"

Edmond grabbed onto a bar. Others checked their belts or adjusted their grips as the message repeated through the ship and fleet.

"Banking." The fleet banked back across the Shattered lines, low and fast. The corvettes opened their bays, dumping bombs as cruiser and frigate teams opened the slits under their ships, sticking storage rings through and dumping out the bombs stored in the rings.

It didn't create the carpet at the speed of the corvettes, but the simple modification created a wave of carnage in their path.

PDC's opened fire, shredding aerial Shattered making attack runs on the fleet.

"Get us back to altitude," Edmond said.

"Sir," Esther said. The fleet's engines accelerated them upwards and higher, out of reach.

Dungeon cannons flashed, releasing blasts across the open ground, targeting Devourers and groups of Ravagers.

The Shattered raced toward the wall as both sides attacked the other with whatever could reach the other, turning into a wild melee of energy.

Kircross' barrier blazed with impacts, a curtain of glass against the maelstrom.

10

In Service of the Realms

rik turned his head, looking through the flagship *Le Glaive*'s porthole at a nearby frigate. firing missiles into the air. Specialized Falcon scouts picked out targets. Alvan missiles were the only weapon capable of reaching out far enough and with enough destructive force to harm the Devourers.

By the time night arrived, the fighting had died down. The Shattered were regathering. Their reinforcements didn't come through tears but from across the realms instead.

How many tears are open in dark little corners across the Seventh now? With the loss of so many cities and without eyes around the realm, the Shattered could descend with impunity.

He went back to reading his book on body chemistry. Ever since he had made potions from his blood, he had thought of the interactions of chemicals within one's body. With the developments in the field of elemental alchemy, it took his ideas in a new direction. *Just a sentient pill forged by the Ten Realms cauldron.* He snorted at the absurd thought and kept reading. He was stationed with two special teams. The other teams were spread out, trying to complete their missions as quickly as possible to reinforce Kircross so they could lead a counterattack.

Erik turned a slip of paper in his fingers, a note no bigger than a sticky note and written upon in hurriedly scrawled ink.

He looked at the note, reading the words again.

It was from Fred and his party, who were continuing to operate out of Cronen Mission Hall. Reports confirmed that Cronen was under attack now. The third major city in the Seventh Realm with a population measuring in the millions.

Cronen. He rested his hand on his forehead, looking at the bunk above. He was staying on one of the cruisers, ready to teleport with the special teams to wherever they were needed. Thankfully, he'd gotten officers' quarters, only having to share with Storbon.

There were a thousand such cities, but if they lost one, the whole region would be without coverage. In his mind, he saw a map of the Seventh Realm with cities falling and the Shattered spreading like an infection.

Erik flicked the paper with his forefinger and looked at the second part of the note, an update.

They now knew why the Devourers and Shattered targeted warships with such aggression. "Dungeon cores. Eat them up like beasts eat monster cores. Christ." Erik flicked the paper as if hitting it would remove the truth.

"No oversight. Advancing without us knowing where the hell their tears are or where they're coming from. Creating hordes more intent on killing us than one another." Erik closed his eyes. "Fuck." *Every dungeon core they consume on their path, that's fewer dungeon beasts to attack them, more elements released and purified.*

He looked at his book, but his frustration had built to the point where he couldn't read it. He dropped his note, holding his hand to the bed in frustration, letting the book down on his stomach as he leaned his head back and groaned. He was barely holding himself back from punching the bunk above, knowing he'd dent it, and then he'd need to fix it so Storbon didn't have a metal fist print in his back when he was sleeping.

A knock on his door pulled him from his thoughts. He tucked away the note in his book. "Come in." He stood, grabbing his carrier.

The door opened to Storbon, and Erik released the shoulder straps. *Not a call out.* "Why did you—"

Storbon moved to the side, gesturing to two people in the corridor and stood to the side. Eli'keen and Weebla pulled down their cloaks.

Erik bowed his head to Weebla.

"You think you need to do that around me, boy? You been keeping up with your training?" She smiled and stepped into the cabin, Eli'keen following.

"Yes, teacher," Erik smiled. "To what do I owe the pleasure?"

"Bit different." Eli'keen looked around the cramped room.

Storbon closed and sealed the door.

"Room is at a premium. I've got a window and a desk. Pretty roomy compared." Erik's smile weakened.

"Sorry that we haven't been able to see one another. You've been off on your missions and I on mine. The Ten Realms are filled with stories of the Alvans' fighting," Weebla said.

"I've heard about you in a few places, too. The Imperium is all over the *Seventh* realm." Erik couldn't keep the bite from his voice.

"I agree with you too much, and we come to you with a request."

"Request?"

Weebla made a tell him gesture to Eli'keen. He cleared his throat and sighed.

"We're here with a request and a mission."

"Another suicide run to the Ninth?"

"No, nothing as stupid as that. A suicide run to the Tenth Realm." Eli'keen smiled.

Erik frowned, looking at Weebla. "Am I missing something?"

"He pissed off the new head, got fired. He's just a regular unemployed elf now."

"Fired?"

"Yes, it has been rather nice." Eli'keen's expression tightened. "Erik, I am sorry for the rumors and lies the Imperium has been spreading. I have seen the reports. You and your Alvans have been working tirelessly in the Seventh

Realm to save lives and get stronger so that you can fight in the higher realms. You have my respect." He bowed deeply.

"Okay," Erik said.

Weebla took the chair at his desk and sat down, taking out her knitting. "Good, now that's out of the way, tell him about the mission and what the hell is going on. You might want to take a seat, Erik."

Erik sat down on the bunk bed and looked up at Eli'keen.

"This attack was not random. It was planned and executed by a very old and very smart Devourer by the name of Akran. A possible level five Devourer."

"Every element."

"Every element," Eli'keen confirmed. "He led the attack, but his purpose was not to just break into the Ten Realms. His target was the ascension platform."

"Big stone tower stuck in the ground up into the clouds. Massive, made by ascendants. You get through the platform, and you can become ascendant," Weebla said, straightening out her yarn and continued knitting.

"Akran entered the platform. At first, we thought it was to destroy it from the inside. Then this happened." Eli'keen held out a formation. "This shows how far someone has gotten through the platform."

Four of the six lights were lit up.

"That's not good. What happens if he ascends?"

"If Akran ascends," Weebla said, "then the Ten Realms are lost. We need to kill him, or destroy the platform, and we can't do it on our own." She didn't look up from her knitting as if it was the most normal thing in the world to discuss, like the weather, or what was for dinner.

"Ascending! Shit, we can't let that happen. If he makes it—*can* he make it?" Erik asked.

"Shattered are basically beasts and people that have consumed the elements instead of mana in unregulated ways," Eli'keen said.

"So yes. Damn, if he becomes an ascendant—"

"We won't have anyone to stop him, and he will control the Ten Realms," Weebla said.

Erik rubbed the back of his neck, bouncing his leg. "Well, okay, so kill him or destroy the thing. What are we looking at?"

"The biggest grouping of Shattered and Devourers are in the Ten Realms. Hell, maybe in the Shattered Realms." Weebla looked up with a grin.

Erik's whole body went cold, hyper-focused. "Are you kidding me?"

"Nope, and they are in one of our defensive structures, one of the strongest. It's damaged, but even in ruins, they're impressive."

"Akran controls the most sworn out there," Eli'keen said.

"And sworn are like... Shattered that follow him?" Erik raised an eyebrow and crossed his arms.

"Sworn are Shattered that he has dominated and taken command over, like how Ten Realms contracts are made, except these are made in blood and elements. He has dozens of Devourers, all of their Ravagers, and thousands of his own under his command. When you kill the leader of the sworn, the binding is broken, and they are free again. Most will flee to maintain their freedom and grow their power to dominate others. It will cut off the tears they're holding open for others and the main line of reinforcements into the realms."

"So sworn are elementally bonded slaves."

"Essentially."

Erik grew quiet, playing the information through his head, frowning as scenario after scenario passed through his mind, a dozen different angles.

"I don't think that's anything we can do."

"You won't be alone. The Elves and Gnomes will be going, along with our allies from the Imperium and whoever else we can pull together." Weebla paused her knitting. "Erik, I know the Imperium has treated you like... Well, a bunch of bastards. From when you were in school to slighting you to look good in front of others. I won't apologize for that because it wasn't me. I'd rather like to take Clive over my knee and teach him some damn manners." Her words came out in a growl. She sighed and recovered. "Erik, we need your help. We need you and your Alvans, not for some mission of wealth and glory. There is no gold, or mana stones here, only death and destruction. Sacrifice, honor, to fight for tomorrow. But if we don't stop Akran, the Ten

Realms are lost."

"Even if we kill him, the Ten Realms are falling. It's slow, but it's slipping, slowly and surely." Erik smacked his hands on his thighs. "The tears have been open too long. We shut ten tears, they open forty. Tears open across the Tenth and the Ninth realm are unchecked. The Seventh is holding on for now, but the small cities, the remote ones, are falling. In the hidden corners of dungeons and the lost cities, tears appear and more Shattered gather. Next, it will be the mid-range cities and the large cities. Some forces can deal with two-star Devourers, a few three stars."

"If we defeat Akran, his forces will collapse," Weebla said. "His sworn are keeping tears open to the Shattered Realms and the Ninth. Opening tears to the Tenth Realm takes a lot of power. Only level two Devourers can open a tear into it from the Shattered Realms."

"So they can run to another corner and open more tears. And aren't they going to be strong as hell being in the Tenth for so long? Mana and all."

"Too much mana for them to take in. They can't cultivate there because the elements are so thin. It's like someone from the First Realm going to the Tenth and someone from the Tenth Realm trying to cast a spell in the First Realm in the same person. They use their elements, it's gone, and if they cultivate, the density would be so high as to tear them apart. Devourers stay in the Tenth Realm for as long as possible and then go lower. We can take out their forces at the ascension platform. It will cut off the flow to the Ninth Realm, which will cut off the flow to the Seventh Realm. Tears, Devourers, and clean up the Ravagers."

Erik crossed his arms. "When?"

"Three days," Weebla said.

"Based on his rate of advance, Akran will pass through the platform and ascend in five days. Three days gives us the time we need to attack and insert a force into the platform, and gives them two days to catch up with him and kill him," Eli'keen said. He drew in a breath. "In the last two thousand years, thousands have entered the ascension platform. Not one has ascended, and none of them have come out of the tower."

"So it's likely a suicide mission." Erik pressed his lips together, taking in a slow breath through his nose.

"The Imperium head might have fired us, but there are many within the Imperium's ranks and among our own races and in the mission hall that we can call on for support. We will not be going alone," Weebla said.

"We're fighting a war here to hold the city. If we pull out, there's no guarantee that Kircross will hold." Erik quirked an eyebrow.

"I spoke to Rekha. She commands the Imperium forces here." Weebla smiled at Erik's change in expression. "Your attacks had a devastating effect and hit the Shattered where it hurts. We need to press that and move down their lines of advance, bomb the hell out of their rear-lines and give them something to grind their forces down. Could you spare mana and element gathering formations? I hear Alvans are the best in that area."

"Yes, I can get them, but what for?"

"Good, and we'll need to use your ships, but not just for attacking. No, they'll have a much more vital role."

"What are you thinking?" Erik asked.

"The Ten Realms has its own ways of fighting off attackers." She smiled. "You are a dungeon lord, thinking about machines and technology, yet you missed the basics! Should give Kay'Renna and Louis Gerrard the advantage they need to hold Kircross."

"What about the Imperium head?"

"What about him? If he attacks the people that went into the Tenth Realm to fight the enemy head-on, how would that look? He cares so much about his outer appearance. You think he would commit social suicide?" Eli'keen raised an eyebrow. "The Imperium is run by a great number of people, and many are losing faith in him quickly."

"What are you planning?" Weebla's eyes narrowed.

"The head of the Imperium doesn't need to be someone that cares about what the Imperium does, but they need to care about the Ten Realms and the people in it. I think we might need a new head."

"Who?" Erik frowned.

"Why not Rekha? She's young, but she's strong willed and while she has little love for the associations and sects. She does have two supportive junior brothers that have a strong say in the lower realms. She has grown much in the last three months. Working together with sects and clans where she would have ignored them before, defending their lands," Eli'keen said.

"She's seen the other side of them," Erik said. The last few months had been eye opening for him as well. The mighty sects and clans had banded together to defend their people and their homes. The Seventh is highly competitive, but there was a balance that wasn't there in the lower realms. Its political sphere was as brutal as any Fourth Realm battlefield, but their wounds were in shame, pride, greed and money, not in lives.

"In the end, people desire peace and stability," Weebla said.

"I will say what I said to the Imperium messenger. I'm just a figurehead, and I'd like to keep it that way. I can send a message to the council, and they will make the final decision."

"I'd be scared with you and Rugrat deciding policy too," Weebla said.

"Hey, we got it started just managing a few million people, thank you." Weebla snorted.

"Thank you." Eli'keen bowed his head as Weebla jumped off her chair.

"You send your messages. Briefing tomorrow at ten in the morning," Weebla said.

"I'll get those gathering formations. What do I need them for?"

"To create our own dungeons."

Delilah used a chilling spell on her coffee, spiked with a stamina formation to help clear the fog from her mind as Glosil finished reading the message from Erik.

The full council had gathered to read it, with the exception of Blaze, who had provided a sealed letter, giving his support of the proposed plan.

"Thank you, Glosil. Elan, do we have an idea of what the Imperium head plans to do?" Delilah asked.

"He plans to increase the power of his forces by recruiting direct from the Mission Hall and Associations who have been fighting in the war. He was looking to reclaim the academy and fight from there. We took significant losses, and our forces are spread too thin across the realms to contain the Shattered. I hoped that we could slowly grind down the Shattered assault, corral our forces, and push through the Divine and Celestial realms meter by meter. Akran changes everything."

"And what does Head Andross think about your plan to deal with Akran?"

"He doesn't believe anyone can ascend, let alone a Shattered. No one else has achieved it since the Ten Realms were founded."

"Three years ago, people would have said it was impossible for a First Realm empire to fight in the Seventh Realm," Elise said.

"Just because it hasn't happened in a long time, doesn't mean that it won't happen again," Delilah agreed. She took a deep breath, warming her hands off her cup as she looked at the papers in front of her. She turned her gaze to Glosil. "Commander, what do you make of the plan?"

"A lightning raid into the Tenth Realm to kill a powerful enemy opponent before he can enter the battlefield isn't without risks. We can only take around fifty percent of our forces into the Tenth Realm. We will be able to man and bring the entire fleet in support. They will be going into a dense group of Devourers and Ravagers, all sworn to Akran. His army, by itself, is a major threat. If we can shut down the tears in the area, we slow the forces pushing into the lower realms. They have been holding them open for weeks. Most tears remain open for a few hours or days, and the Devourers and sworn pass through to the Ninth Realm." Glosil sighed. "It comes down to two things: do we think Akran will be a greater threat in the future or not? If he will, we need to do everything we can to kill him."

"I need to say it, but we aren't the protectors of the Ten Realms." Elise leaned forward, raising her hand to forestall arguments. "We are the council of the *Alvan* Empire. It is not our job to defend all the realms. That said, if we *don't* defeat the Shattered in the higher realms, then it will eventually reach us down here. We can't turtle and hide in our dungeons anymore."

"This Akran is a level five Devourer, a walking cataclysm." Jia Feng's eyes darted to Momma Rodriguez, who had remained stoic throughout the meeting. "Erik, Rugrat, Rekha, her teammates, Sam and Cayleigh, Weebla and Eli'keen need to ascend through the platform and kill Akran. I know Erik says he trusts them, but they are our *emperors* and our strongest fighters. The Special Teams should be in support."

"It would be a blow to our fighting force, but they've agreed to whatever we order," Glosil said.

The room grew silent. Delilah's gaze fell on Momma Rodriguez, then out of the window, watching Alva move on by, unknowing what decisions, what turmoil hid behind her window, a world apart.

Her hands shook, and she rubbed them as if to warm them. She forced her attention back to the table with a smile that betrayed one's heart teetering on the edge of the abyss, hoping, wishing to not fall in, while feeling the lack of anything below.

"Those two would never forgive themselves if they were pulled from the fighting just because they gained some title. Oh lord, I hate it. It burns me up something fierce." She blinked against watery eyes, forcing her smile up to the surface as she blew her nose. "I'm their momma and I want nothing more than to wrap them up in a hug and protect them from the world, but they're grown men. It's their life to make, their decisions. They're *good* boys." She tightened her fist and shook it, shaking with the tension that ran through her.

Delilah exhaled and put down the mug on the reports.

Momma Rodriguez blew her nose again and looked out of her window, her free hand rubbing the cross on the chain around her neck.

"I agree with the proposed plan put forward by Eli'keen. Commander Glosil, make it so."

"Yes, council leader."

Stay safe, Storbon. Delilah knew it would be a long time before she was able to sleep fully again.

Erik and Rugrat stood with the Alvan officers, led by Glosil. Every military unit had completed their missions and reported to Kircross.

Beside them was the Imperium group led by Rekha's team, and Weebla, and Eli'keen with various officers. On the other side were Kay'Renna and her Mission Hall representatives. The last group around the map table was the city's fighting force. Louis Gerrard, once a member of the Sha military and now Kircross' admiral, stood behind General Korani, a powerful scaled demi-human and leader of the city's fighting forces.

Korani cleared her throat, bringing the room to silence.

"First of all, I would like to thank you for gathering here. Kircross is grateful for your support." She bowed her head and raised it with a fire behind her eyes. "Now, General Battleaxe and I have discussed a plan to push back the Shattered and give us some breathing room. General?" She stepped back as Weebla conjured the stone under her feet to rise to meet their height.

"The plan is simple. We advance with our strongest ships to dungeon core locations. Using the Alvan mana drills, we carve out the dungeon cores, program them, and use them to augment our own lines. The cores will convert the mana and elements into dungeon monsters to fight the Shattered." Weebla tapped her map to the table and several purple markers appeared. "These are all known dungeon core locations of various grades. They need to be gathered and combined to make dungeons strong enough to support such an endeavor. There was a fear of dungeon collapse with collecting cores before. Now that the dungeons have been cleared, we don't need to worry."

She used mana manipulation to circle locations. "Dungeons will be placed in these key choke points to slow or cut off the Shattered advance."

"Pick up the cores, combine them, drop them off, and let them fight it out with the Shattered?" Kay'Renna said.

"Correct. We'll program the cores with some blueprints, formations, and the like."

"And if they get taken?" Korani asked.

"Formations will be added to destroy the dungeon core if it is at risk of capture. The resulting detonation will be sizable, thus why the locations for the new dungeons are spread out," Weebla said.

"How far do you intend to extend this?" Glosil asked.

"As far as we can. Scouts will find the dungeon core locations. The warships will transition to them, drill out the cores, and retreat. We put together the dungeon bundles, bomb out an area, place the dungeon core, and fire it up, get out of the way and let them do their thing. We start with the dungeon cores that are located outside of the city's walls. The warships will hunt the dungeon cores that aren't near the Shattered as much as possible, speed up recovery. We have three days to carry out this mission."

The briefing wrapped up quickly. Erik and Rugrat moved to the side with Rekha, Sam, and Cayleigh.

"So, I heard that we're going into the platform," Cayleigh grinned.

"That's the plan. What's the layout?" Erik asked.

"Information is sketchy, but it seems like it'll be a series of trials that one must pass before they can ascend," Sam said.

"No one has finished it and recorded it. When the first ascendants emerged, thousands had died trying to ascend. They found that one ascendant helping another greatly improved the process. They created the platform to recreate what they did," Cayleigh said.

"What happens when someone ascends?"

"They can command the Ten Realms. The elements and mana are an extension of themselves. Some say that they have the power to destroy and create worlds or remake them anew," Rekha said.

"Just call me Zeus." Rugrat grinned.

"You don't even have the metal tempering," Erik said.

"I can magic me up some fine lightning bolts, though."

"How are things with the Imperium?"

The trio shifted uncomfortably. "Tense. Factions are starting to show themselves," Rekha said.

"The Elven and Gnome leadership banding together made the rest feel insecure. The head has been muttering about them banding together to go against his power. He's talking out of his ass, but people listen to someone with that much power." Sam shook his head.

"I don't know how he got into power," Cayleigh said.

"Friends in high places and he seemed competent. Been rallying against

Xun Liang for years."

"Xun Liang was twice his age, but he wasn't going to give his position to someone like that," Rekha said.

"You thinking of making a play for the leadership?" Erik asked her.

"I'm too young to be the head of the Imperium and we need to bring the Imperium together and fight the Shattered. That is our duty, to hold the Tenth Realm. Clive doesn't seem to get that. He cares about accolades, parties, and honor. Accolades don't keep people safe and alive."

Erik looked into her eyes. She was steady and calm with everything. He smiled and looked away, his heart twisting in his chest.

Rugrat tapped Erik on the shoulder. "Looks like we have to go."

"At the platform, we'll see just who's more determined," Cayleigh said.

Erik grinned. "We'll have to see. Rugrat and I can be stubborn bastards when we want."

"That should be good." Rugrat looked through the formation ring of the cruiser hovering above the ground. He stood on a clear platform above it and the larger drill baseplate.

The cruiser stilled and Rugrat made sure everyone was away from the drill.

"Drill is clear and good for firing." He flipped a breaker with his mana manipulation and the ring formation fired up. "Activating drill."

The drill base plate activated, drawing in elements and mana. It twisted and directed the energy into the ring formation that further compressed it as it spiraled into the ground, tearing through it like a laser through paper, too fast to even blacken the edges of where it passed.

It went on for several minutes before Rugrat felt the energy of the drill being drained away. He flipped the breaker as the energy dissipated and the formations dimmed. Rugrat reached out with a mana manipulation spell, traveling into the hole bored through the ground.

"There you are."

> **You have come into contact with a dungeon core.** With your title:
> Dungeon Master, new options are revealed.
>
> **Do you wish to:**
> Take command of the Dungeon
> Remodel Dungeon
> Destroy the Dungeon

He pulled out the dungeon core and deposited it in the cruiser's side hangar, usually reserved for the airforce's birds.

He waved the notification from his vision. It would disappear within a few minutes. Leaving the dungeon as is was part of the agreement they'd reached with the Kircross leadership.

Rugrat checked a screen, looking out at the Alvan warships dotted across the landscape, mana drills boring through the ground as they mined dungeon cores.

The cruiser's engines were already moving them toward the next dungeon core location, aiming for the strongest and deepest dungeons.

"You think they'll let us keep any? Could do with some more warships," Roska said, on Rugrat-watching duty.

"Agreement was to mine the dungeon cores. We get Mission Hall missions for them, experience, and points. The cores remain Kircross property, but the formations and everything, those plans remain ours. Just lending them for the fight," Rugrat said.

"Just something to keep us busy, huh?" Roska grinned.

"Plentiful employment!" Rugrat raised his forefinger to the ceiling.

"Employment? Hell, with all the loot, I've got one hell of a nice retirement fund."

"Gonna be looking forward to beaches, beers, and some barbecue after this." Rugrat stretched as the cruiser started to slow. He felt the twist of elements in the area, drawn in toward the dungeon core.

"Back to work." Rugrat looked through the scrying screen, aiming the mana drill beneath his feet.

"Shit, just looking at that thing gives me the chills."

"You jump out of birds hundreds of meters up," Rugrat said, connecting to the helmsman. "Bit to the right."

"Sir." The helmsman's voice played through the room.

"Yeah, I jump out of them before I think I'm jumping. Once I'm in the air, I'm all good. It's just seeing the drop and not wrapping myself in mana." She shook her head and shivered.

"Bit forward." Rugrat snorted. "And people say I'm weird. Stop there."

The ship came to a stop. Mana reacted to his thoughts, flipping the breaker.

"Activating drill." The drill bored through tree, grass, dirt, and stone. "Kind of weird. like, I know I'm talking to the helmsman, but the whole big, massive ship just moving to what I say. Never had this kind of pull in the navy."

"'Cause you'd always be ordering it back to port for a few more beers?" Rugrat chuckled.

"Damn, are there some stories about shore leave."

The pack of Ravagers ran off through the forest the Shattered advance had churned up.

Slowly, Special team One materialized from their hiding spots.

Erik saw every blade and every bug with his domain as they swept forward. They fanned out, weapons sweeping the area as they crossed the opening the Shattered had rested in and into the small creek, following it to the cave it originated from.

They entered, rifles leading as they exited the stream and moved down a side cave, coming to a dead end.

"Deni, you cover here," Niemm said, using his sound transmission device

"Sir." She and four other team members moved to the side cave entrance.

Niemm nodded to Erik.

Erik reached out, moving the walls back and stretching out the cave, lengthening and deepening it.

"This should be it." Niemm checked his map and marked the ground with a wet X.

Two team members secured their weapons. The rest were facing the entrance. They pulled out sections of a massive stack formation a half meter wide and a meter tall, connecting and locking them into place. Two others secured mana storing formations and cornerstones to one wall.

Erik took out mana gathering formations. He checked his map and placed them around the main formation. Three sections had been fused, leaving the center empty.

He took out the remaining section. The dungeon core within glowed as he put it into the middle of the massive stack formation.

The formations across the stack flared as they fused, an interconnected whole.

Erik took out a blueprint and put it to the stack formation.

Do you wish to apply this blueprint?
YES/NO

He selected yes. The blueprint burned up as changes spread from the dungeon core, like a spreading spider's web altering the ground and ceiling.

Elements thick enough to create thin mist trails were absorbed into the dungeon core until it couldn't handle anymore. Dungeon beasts rose from the ground, formed from swirling elements, and headed out through the compressed stone halls of the updating dungeon.

"Good to go?" Niemm looked around. "All right. Good. Deni, we're heading back to you."

Erik activated the last blueprint.

Compressed stone filled the chamber, metal weaving through it like tree roots.

They'd eventually cover the dungeon core and its formations, creating a hardened sphere the Shattered would need to break through to disable the dungeon core.

Erik nodded at the closing room, turned, and jogged back through the stream. Two of the special team members lagged behind him.

"Ready for pickup," Niemm said as they reached a clearing, fanning out to provide all around security.

They lay down, waiting. Their ride announced its arrival on a flap of wings.

"Get on!" Niemm hissed.

The group ran up the ramp into the Kestrel. The chief counted them all before the ramp closed and they shot off into the sky. Erik opened his vision, seeing through the world, its hues of elements and manas filling all things and coloring the air, drifting everywhere.

He could easily pinpoint the elements and mana gathered at the dungeon core.

Gathering formations arranged around the valley by other teams activated. The power in the valley shifted, drawn into the formations, and shot through the ground. Dozens of streams of mana and elements intersected at the dungeon core.

Erik watched as the ground around the dungeon core changed, creating golems row upon row like a terracotta army.

He closed his eyes, returning to their bright blue as they flew back toward Kircross around the enemy.

Erik woke with a start as they landed in Kircross.

"Morning, sleeping beauty," Deni said.

"Still looks like night to me."

"Well, everything is a morning when you wake up."

He followed the team down the ramp and into the crafter district. The district had been working through the night. High level teams accepted formations and headed out to plant them across the lines of approaching Shattered.

Other teams brought in their prizes—dungeon cores ready to be combined to create Sky level cores and inset into Alvan stack formations.

Materials poured into the different workshops in a steady stream. Aerial mounted forces carried the finished products off, all under the watchful eye of the Alvan, Imperium, and Kircross guards.

The team reached the largest crafting workshop in the middle of it all. There were several layers of guards blocking off roads and turning the area into a fortress.

Erik rubbed his face as he presented his passes to the last checkpoint before being allowed through.

Formation masters of the master and expert grade, even two starred formation masters, carved, shaped and filled formations in dozens of workshops. Erik studied them as they passed. They were working on the components of the formations they had placed around the dungeon core.

They were checked again before being allowed into a central workshop filled with Alvans. It was here that stack formation components from across the realms and the workshops were fused together and assembled.

"Back again? You'll have to wait a minute!" Julilah said as she finished checking a formation. A man was waiting quietly, watching her every movement. "Good to go. Just watch out for the metal. It's starting to strain to the limit, but will be fine with a temperature regulating formation."

"Yes, miss." The man bowed his head and took her place to start working on the changes. She walked over to Erik.

"Hey, Julilah," Erik said, hugging her.

"You're wet," she said, looking at him.

"Little walk in the river." Erik smiled. "Looks like you've got things well in hand here."

"The outer workshops are making the storing and gathering formations. Also, trap formations. Alva has a dozen factories working on the components. Qin is there doing quality control. Mostly, we're just adding in any necessary alterations and fitting the dungeon core."

Erik looked at a stack formation that was coming together. Several masters worked on the different plates, adding it to the large hexagonal tube.

"It's like our dungeon headquarters, but miniaturized."

"Exactly, and we have a building and dungeon to put all that into back home. Here, we've got a metal pillar. It's coming along, though. The assembly lines are pumping them out, but there's a slight time lag."

"You've done well. This is incredible." Erik patted her shoulder.

"Miss Julilah?" a woman asked, giving Erik a nod as she interrupted.

"Duty calls. Stay safe out there." Julilah hugged him and walked off with the woman.

She's certainly changed from the little girl that lurked around Tan Xue's forge wanting to learn how to smith.

He felt like those days were a lifetime ago, an easier time. He looked through the workshop, seeing people he had watched grow into their element over the years.

Erik sighed. *I wish Tan Xue was here to see all this, or Tanya, or Gilly, and Bai Ping.* Erik shook his head and cleared his throat. It had not been an easy road, but they continued to forge a path forward.

"Your gear is ready over here," a man said, guiding them to a table with formations identical to the ones they had placed.

"All right, switch over groups. Two will be on security and one will place the dungeon," Niemm said.

The team gathered the formations and broken-down stacks into their storage rings before heading out to waiting Kestrels.

"We're heading further west this time. Everyone, check your maps." Niemm briefed them as the ramp closed and the Kestrel launched itself into the air. A Sparrow wing moved around them for protection.

Rekha stretched, popping her back. "All right, get some rest, food, and a shower while you can," she said to her team and the two other small teams that she'd linked with. All night they had been placing mana gathering formations for the dungeon defenses and element gathering formations to thin out the elements in the area so tears were harder to form closer to the city.

They headed off into the command center and on to their own quarters.

Cayleigh kissed Sam goodbye and followed Rekha back to the room they shared.

Rekha took off her armor, cleaning it. It had been slimmed down and was more utilitarian and easier to pull on and off, modelled after Alvan armor. It was also a lot easier to care for and don than her older armor that needed at least one person's help or her mana manipulation to pull on.

"So, when did you start liking Erik?" Cayleigh asked.

"Wha—huh. What do you mean when?" Rekha squeaked, nearly falling over as she took off a boot.

"So you do like him?"

"Who said that!"

"You didn't say you didn't like him."

Rekha glared at her.

"Who would have thought that of all the people you could like, you go for an emperor?" Cayleigh waggled her eyebrows.

"He's a few years older than me, but I feel younger around him."

"So, do you like him, or do you want to date him?" Cayleigh dumped her armored vest on the floor and flopped onto her bed, her booted feet hanging off the end.

Rekha looked at her and put her armored vest on a rack to air it out.

"Got it, dating it is. Not one to play around, are you?"

"You didn't," Rekha said.

"You don't know," Cayleigh said.

"You've had a crush on Sam since you were children and you've been going out with one another since you were teenagers."

"You should see the things I've taught him." Cayleigh grinned as Rekha groaned.

"He's my friend. I don't want to know!"

"Don't worry, I bet Erik knows a few things. He's from Earth, after all, and he's older." Cayleigh turned on her side, grinning. "So, what are you going to do about it?"

"I don't know. I'm not sure what I should do. I've not… you know. Well, I've never had someone that I've really thought about this way."

Cayleigh nodded.

"Every guy I saw when I was younger was sizing me up as a wife, someone to carry their children and little use beyond that. In the academy there was less of that, but there were still a lot of people that just wanted to get in my pants."

Cayleigh grunted. "Yeah, you went out with some idiots in your time."

"Thank you, Cayleigh."

"No worries. I call it as I see it, but Erik, he could be a good fit. He's all over the place, always trying to do something. He's adventurous like you. Comes down to a few things. Does his lifestyle match up with yours? Are you attracted to him? Does he fit your needs and if you are together? Instead of it being three plus three, it is like three *times* three. You both do your own thing and together you inspire one another to do more."

Rekha was struck by the seriousness in Cayleigh's voice.

"Sam meets all of that for me." Cayleigh snorted. "Even got me to try out some vegetarian dishes his mom makes."

"Well, you can't really refuse his mother. Remember that time we went over there for a week and she beat us black and blue for a month?"

"That's what I said." Cayleigh laughed. "Remember when Xun Liang showed up?"

"Yeah, he tried to escape when he found out she was training us, but she challenged him to a duel. Every day for a week they fought. They were so tired no one saw them for a month." Rekha sniggered, her features softening. His loss was recent, but she realized he had made his choices and she needed to respect them, honor them. She'd gained a sense of inner peace and rolled through her memories of their time together instead of focusing on his loss.

A knock from the door startled them both.

"Who is it?" Rekha asked.

"Weebla!"

Rekha opened the door.

"Welcome back." Weebla smiled as she entered their room and Rekha closed the door behind her. A sound cancelling formation made her ears pop as she trailed Weebla.

"Move thy ass, granddaughter."

"She's on the warpath again," Cayleigh warned and moved her feet. Weebla gave her the stink eye and sat down on the bed.

Rekha grabbed a chair and straddled it, crossing her arms over the back, and resting her chin on them.

"Well, it looks like we've gained some attention. The Alvans are making their dungeon pillars for other nations and Clive's eyes and ears are flooding the city. They've always been here, but they're more active now."

"Do you think he knows?" Rekha asked.

"I think he suspects something, but I'm not sure if he knows that we're intending to go to the Tenth. I think he's thinking that you are making a play for leadership."

"Why would I do that?" Rekha frowned.

"Because you're young, strong, you fought for Avegaaren and there are many people who saw you leading the defenses there. You have been fighting across the Seventh Realm hunting down tears without care for accolades. You are Xun Liang's student, and you have both the Elves' and the Gnomes' backing while Clive is losing their support."

"Can he lose their support?"

"Of course he can. The Imperium is a just a place that we work. Its purpose is to defend the Ten Realms. He seems to have forgotten that and is using it as his own plaything to gain people's favor."

"Is it really that bad?"

"Not yet, but it wouldn't take much more. He's in a bad situation. Xun Liang is a hero in everyone's eyes. Clive has been blaming the Alvans for all our troubles, but the Alvans have been out in front time and time again. While they carried out impressive attacks, evacuated cities and more, the Shattered got into the Ten Realms on our watch. We lost ground across the Seventh Realm and the Ninth Realm attack. It's struck fear into the rest of the realms and the people in the Imperium are losing faith in our leadership." Weebla took a breath. "But that is not your problem. I just wanted to say, watch what you say and where you say it, just in case his eyes and ears hear you. Two more days and we'll get back to the simpler things in life."

"Kicking Shattered ass," Cayleigh said.

Weebla raised an eyebrow and looked at her granddaughter. "So much like your grandfather." She side hugged her, and Cayleigh hugged her back. They released one another and Weebla smiled. "The dungeons have gathered enough power and the first ones are powering up. They're attacking the Shattered around them already.

There was a rapid knock at the door.

"Who is it?" Rekha yelled.

"Eli'keen. Weebla, you need to see something."

Rekha opened the door. She quickly got out of the way upon seeing Eli'keen's expression. He was always quick with a smile; she had never seen him like this.

"He just passed another level." Eli'keen pulled out an old formation with several lights on it.

Weebla took the formation and slid off from the bed, taking in a sharp breath. "Shit."

"It's weakening the mana in the Tenth Realm. There are more tears now. Level one Devourers have been able to open their own."

"Inform the others. We move tonight. We cannot wait any longer." Weebla passed the formation back.

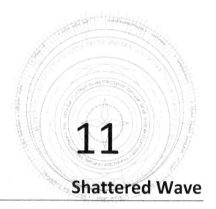

11

Shattered Wave

"They are pouring in from the higher realms. Way more than we thought," the Kircross commander reported.

Kay'Renna gritted her teeth as she studied the map table. A spread of red crossed through the lands around Kircross. Golden emblems marked the dungeons that had been already setup. The surrounding areas were clear of Shattered, though a few were still getting past.

We thinned their numbers, but we haven't stopped them.

"Thank you, commander," Korani said. "Man the walls and focus on emplacing dungeons across the final line. Any additional dungeon cores are to reinforce the city's warships and dungeon core."

Kay'Renna's eyes tracked the dungeon line—a series of locations picked out around the city that were in range of the weapons on the wall. The dungeons would act to fight and thin the Shattered while those on the wall would smash them with their attacks.

With larger dungeon cores, the city's ships will be able to charge faster, moving quicker and firing sooner.

Kay'Renna looked at the marker in the middle of the city. The main dungeon core was a replication of what the Alvans had done at Vuzgal, turning the whole city into a war machine beneath the surface.

She looked over at the Alvans who were talking to the Imperium forces and walked up to the group. They grew silent at her approach.

"You need to get your people ready to move," she said. "You can't stay here, or you'll get bogged in. The longer the fighting goes on, the harder it will be to withdraw. Use your largest ships to mine the strongest dungeon cores. I want the corvettes and frigates on bombing missions. Create as many dungeon pillars as possible and go." She looked right at Rugrat.

"Yes, ma'am."

Corvettes howled overhead, heading toward the advancing enemy. Units marched through the street to their positions. Erik and the special team landed on their Kestrel, where a group was waiting for them.

"All the materials are inside, and a map on the dungeon line," the man yelled, passing Niemm a storage ring, then running away.

"Take us back up," Niemm yelled, pulling out the map and tapping it to his own, then sending it to everyone else. Erik adjusted the map band on his arm, looking at the ring of dungeons right around the city. Their targets were outlined in a specific color, showing the position of the different formations.

The Kestrel took off again. Niemm grabbed the handles on the ceiling to walk between the team members like a drunken sailor. He took out formations and passed them out, giving them their missions one by one.

Erik glanced out of the Kestrel. There were flashes in the distance and rolling clouds as the fast attack craft met the Shattered lines.

"Hoped that we'd have more time before shit hit the fan. What happened?" Deni, who sat beside Erik, asked him.

"Akran went up another level. He's only one level away from ascending."

"Shouldn't we be going there like now?"

"We'll be heading out tonight, but each level takes longer."

"If each level takes so long, why do they think we can catch up to him?"

"We're from the Ten Realms. He's not. Every time we've ascended from the First to the Tenth Realm, the realm changed us with experience. Gave us a path for elemental and mana cultivation."

"Well, there are hundreds of different ways to increase your cultivation. What path?"

"The way that mana and elements change our bodies. The Shattered, they cultivate the elements first. Really, they're just stuffing energy into themselves. They have to create ways to use that power. Some create elemental cores. Others grow large bodies, or appendages, to hold that power and then later use it. That's why two Shattered that are from the same race and cultivate the same element can look so different from one another."

"So the Ten Realms has been what, imprinting a plan on how our bodies should create a solid mana core, elemental core, or a mana heart say?"

"Exactly. Formations are like a blueprint for an extension onto our bodies as we go up through the realms, while the mana and elements are the building materials we use to create the extension."

Deni leaned her head back against the hull. "So, how does that help us inside the platform?"

"The platform builds upon the Ten Realms, so we should be able to progress smoother than Akran. His body will be undergoing these changes for the first time. He got through the first few levels and then stopped. His progression has only slowed. This was a surprise," Erik said.

"And why is it making it easier for them to get into the Tenth Realm?"

"The platform uses a massive amount of energy, decreasing the density in areas further away."

Niemm made his way down to them.

"We've got three dungeon cores. Need two more to complete our setup." He transferred the components to Erik and shifted to Deni. "Deni, you've got attack formations."

"Nice." They transferred as well, and Niemm moved opposite and sat down.

"Hello, everyone." Egbert's voice filled the air between the trio.

"Hey, man," Deni said.

"They let you out of the basement?" Niemm chuckled.

"How's setup?" Erik asked.

"Good to see that you are all in good spirits. I am connected to the city's dungeon core. So cute and small."

"Too used to the dungeon cores back home," Erik said.

"Oh well. We'll make this one work. I'll be linking the main dungeon up to the dungeon line. Wanted to let you know I'm online and if you need anything, just yell."

"We got teleportation now?" Niemm asked.

"No, not like in Alva. Kestrels and walking for you."

"Been aiming to slim down."

Erik snorted as they started to lose altitude, heading for their landing zone.

"Well, have fun burying cores. Rather ingenious, I think. We'll have to take some for the Tenth!"

Edmond spent the day watching the maps around his bridge.

"Corvette wing two has returned," Esther said beside him.

"How is loading going?"

"We have Chonlgu's crows loaded on all ships. Weapons are maintained, restocked, and ready. We got another shipment of ammunition from Alva. All magazines are full, and we have plenty in storage."

Edmond took in a deep breath and released it. The corvettes moved across the sky on approach to the fleet, decreasing their speed and allowing their hovering formations to take over.

Imperium and Mission Hall fleets had been moving around all morning. Under the surface, the Tenth Realm attack force had moved off the wall, handing it over to allies remaining behind.

Forces from across the realms had gathered at Kircross.

"If Clive didn't suspect anything before, I have a feeling he might suspect why there is so much fighting power in Kircross now."

"Sounds like a personal problem." Esther smiled, cracking her professional veneer.

Edmond leaned on the map table with a smile, finding Louis Gerard's ship.

"I can't believe they gave him command of the warships," Esther said.

"He is a fine officer and a great fleet commander. He treats his people well and looks after them." Edmond sighed and stood up. "He was doing what he thought was best for his people. Might have been too trusting, or too paranoid. He did what he thought he had to do for his family. I can't fault a man for that, but to kill his second in command, a man who was like family to him?" Edmond shook his head. "Even if it wasn't him, he will hold that death over his own head for the rest of his life."

Edmond looked at Esther. He held her own father's death as a failure of his own.

"Do you ever regret it?"

"Regret what?"

"Joining Alva?" Her words were quiet, curious over conspiratorial.

"I like leading fighters, but I am not well suited to lead people." Esther nodded at his words. "I was suited to be the Marshal, not the leader of the Sha. Your father would have done a brilliant job. As good a job as your brother, I am sure."

Esther grimaced and looked away.

"I think the people and soldiers of Alva are brilliant and for the first time in a long time I can relax, in a way. I can do what I am good at. The ships might be a little less refined—"He smiled. "—but the crews are the best I have worked with. They fight for one another and they stick together. They have the community that I had hoped to see with the Sha and what we had at the beginning. So no, I have no regrets. You?"

"I don't have to wear a dress anymore for gatherings, I get to command one of the strongest warships in the Ten Realms, and I have access to fully automatic weapons. What's not to like? And the food! Not even the banquets you had could compare."

"I always missed the food once we got into the higher realms. Cooks were so underrated."

"Sir, ma'am." An officer approached the table, making them look over. "Commander Glosil has taken command. We have passed him our readiness report, and he has ordered us to continue to phase one."

"Very well. Have the fleet prepare for immediate transition. Just as we practiced. Let's go ruffle some Shattered feathers," Edmond said.

The man saluted and talked into his communication device.

"What do you think about Kircross?" Esther said.

"I think that we've given them one hell of a defense. The Shattered are pouring in. The dungeons can slow them, but we don't have the density to stop them."

He watched the areas where the dungeons had been placed. Elements curled together to create dungeon beasts that charged into the fray, focusing their attacks on the Devourers. Like Xun Liang's incarnations, they would use all of their power in their attacks.

Attack formations would activate, calling down attack spells as fast as they could charge while the dungeon cores labored to purify the elements kicked up in the fight.

Rugrat looked around the destroyer *Damocles'* hangar. All eight special teams were gathered, as well as Egbert, Erik, George, Davin, Weebla, Rekha, Sam, and Cayleigh.

Eli'keen walked into the hangar wearing elven armor.

"You coming with?" Rugrat asked. "Heard you were a crafter."

Weebla snorted. "You're a crafter too."

"I didn't mean they were mutually exclusive."

"Been a long time since I used a sword for anything but training," Eli'keen said. "I put it up a long time ago when the associations were made."

"I forget how old you are."

"Thank you." Eli'keen's words fell flat as Rugrat rubbed the back of his head.

"If you haven't been fighting for a long time, are you sure you're any good?"

"You've seen Kay'Renna fight. Seeing as I taught her, I think I can handle myself."

"You know Kay'Renna?" Rugrat perked up.

Eli'keen worked his jaw, amused. "She's my daughter."

"Your what?"

"Daughter," Weebla said, patting Rugrat on the chest. "And don't worry, he's only one of the best swordsmen in the realms. Xun Liang wasn't able to defeat him."

"Ah, yes, okay." Rugrat forced a smile to Eli'keen's arched and examining eye.

"Transition in fifteen. Get ready," Erik said, saving Rugrat as he turned away, keeping Eli'keen in the corner of his eye.

He didn't feel distinctly safe around him anymore. He's her dad? They're nothing alike! What's her mother like?

Rugrat edged over to Weebla.

"Come to get protection from Eli?"

"Kay'Renna's mother, is she…?"

"You mean Vice Admiral Var'keen? The Lightning Wraith. A woman that makes Xun Liang look tame in her training and is about as emotionless as a block of iron when she's commanding? She's in charge of the fleet heading to the Tenth," she said lightly. Her grin spread across her face.

"Even my mother said to not get on her bad side. Loves her children, and she's one hell of a fighter," Sam said.

"Sam's mother is General Avariose. She was in the planning meetings."

"Why do you all have legendary freaking parents?" Rugrat grumbled.

Rekha, Sam, Cayleigh and Weebla stilled.

"What? Is someone behind me?" Rugrat turned around quickly, but no one was there.

"Your mother is *the* Momma Rodriguez," Cayleigh said.

"Mayor of Alva, general badass?" Rekha said.

"She's just my momma," Rugrat said.

"The legends of Momma Rodriguez are famous across the realms," Sam said.

"What, no, that can't be—really?"

"Why you think Kay'Renna is so nervous around you?" Rekha asked.

"*Nervous* around me? Are you kidding?"

"Rekha's about as blind as a bat when it comes to relationships and love, but even *she* saw it," Cayleigh pointed over her shoulder with her thumb, her face plastered with a get a load of this look.

Rekha smacked Cayleigh, blushing.

Rugrat surreptitiously turned, seeing Erik talking to George and the special team leaders, while Davin was chowing down on meat pies and talking to some of the special team leaders in the background.

He turned and looked back at Cayleigh, who grinned and nodded. Rekha glared at her, hitting her again, and looking away as everyone turned at the noise, turning beet red.

"Well, I wish you the best of luck." Rugrat winked as Rekha tried to effectively turtle into her armor.

Rugrat spotted Egbert and Eli'keen talking. Egbert quickly took out a bundle of books and passed it to the other, disappearing in a flash. The two smiled and nodded to one another.

Were those... Egbert's private collection?

Eli'keen must have felt his eyes on him and looked over, his smile blanching as his eyes went wide—mortified. Egbert clapped him on the shoulder and waved at Rugrat.

Rugrat stiffly raised his arm, turning and walking away.

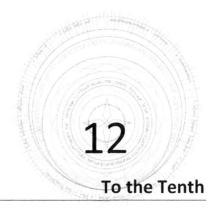

12

To the Tenth

G losil stood in the command center of the cruiser *Meokar*.

"Edmond reports all forces are ready for transition," a communication aide said.

Glosil looked at his screens. Kanoa was on the *Zahir* while Chonglu was on *Le Glaive*. He checked the reports from the different forces that made up the Tenth Realm Fleet, then activated his sound transmission device broadcasting across the fleet. "Today we are heading to the Tenth Realm. For some of you, this will be your first time there. We go to the Tenth to wage war and destroy those that intend to destroy our way of life and our people.

"The Shattered do not negotiate. They only look to consume and grow. We will teleport to the Tenth Realm, where we will engage their main army. We will force closed the tears that so threaten our realms. We will destroy their leader, Akran, to secure the safety of our realms.

"You stand next to Elves, humans, Gnomes, and demi-humans. People of the Ten Realms joined in a singular purpose. Follow your orders and fight for the people beside you. Fight for the people of the Ten Realms. United, we can work to defeat whatever lies in our path. Prepare for transition in thirty seconds."

He closed the channel, a lull in movement before people gathered themselves and moved on.

Glosil looked at the warships of the fleet, dozens of different styles. They floated above the city totems. There were the gigantic dreadnoughts of the Gnomes and their stubby tunneler ships, battle fleets of the Imperium. Elven Cruisers, shaped like fine blades, with sects, clans and roving Mission Hall ships creating their own vagabond fleets. The gun-metal grey Alvan fleets with their black emblems and white outlined hatches.

A wing of Alvan corvettes disappeared.

Glosil checked the map. The gnomes and Elves had given them the ability to connect through the totems and teleportation pads.

The corvettes spread out, accelerating away, and circling the area of their targeted totem.

"Scouts report the location is all clear," an officer said.

"Send the first phase," Glosil said.

Dreadnoughts appeared on the Tenth Realm map, powering their massive formations; accelerating away from the totems, creating an advancing line four warships long. A fifth moved out of the path of the fleet, watching over the totem.

Phase two followed afterward. Corvettes appeared, accelerating out of the way, as they disappeared from Kircross and moved into position around the dreads.

Ships transitioned in rapid order, taking up position off their behemoths.

Meokar shifted. The wave of mana felt like he'd just stepped into a sauna, instantly comfortable as it poured in through his mana gates, clearing his mind and revitalizing him after days of concentrated planning and organization.

"Last of the ships has transitioned over. Rear guard is holding position." A fleet of the least mobile warships remained over the totem.

Glosil could only imagine the sounds of marching through the streets of Kircross as thousands passed through the totem.

As they arrived in the Tenth Realm, they moved to the teleportation formations around the totem and laid out new formations, holding them in place, ready to be called forth.

Aerial mounted fighters were ejected from their warships, creating clouds of roving wings. Fast attack craft and their mounted aerial support broke off from the four main fleets, their targets anything near the tears.

"Edmond says we should arrive at the enemy's location in three hours at current speed."

"Very good."

Kay'Renna looked through the formation, seeing clearly across Kircross. The walls brimmed with fighters from across the realms that had come in support of their defense.

The army heading to the Tenth marched through the totems, while they gathered away from Kircross, descending from the forests and rugged mountains, coming down from the lost lands, once proud cities.

"I hate it when they get smart."

"The Head of the Imperium is demanding to know where the fleet went to," one of the aides said.

"What about the city and the Imperium forces?"

'The city isn't saying anything and the Imperium people either don't know or aren't saying."

"Good, keep it that way."

"Is that wise?"

"They're fighting in the Tenth Realm for us while he's hiding in Cronen, demanding to know where people are instead of worrying about the fighting. You think I have time to give a shit about some pumped up twat in another city?"

"No, commander."

"Good. Now get back to your job."

The man quickly turned and left.

She gripped a necklace under her vest, a protective charm her father and mother had given her when she had announced she wanted to join the Mission Hall. She desperately wanted to be in the Tenth Realm alongside them. She was needed here, to hold the city so that when they succeeded, there was something to come back to.

"They're charging!"

Kay'Renna moved to the map, seeing the Shattered like a tide, rushing across the ground, weaving toward the city.

Dungeon cannons blazed, their piercing shots targeting Devourers as they came into range. Attack formations for the city activated with a barrage across the Shattered mass.

Most had four or more limbs pumping as they galloped forward. Each and every one of them was a hunter. There were Ravagers as large as carriage trains, and Devourers comparable to homes came on.

Aerial Shattered weaved through the air, flapping their wings as they angled forward, gaining speed.

The warships hovering above the main line struck the Shattered ranks with a rolling barrage.

Dungeons changed colors as they activated, the underground Shattered meeting the formed dungeons, stopping their advance dead.

Even under such slaughter, Shattered made it through. Few in number, but still alive. They exited the forests and into the long-grass fields surrounding the city, tripping and falling. Kay'Renna's snarl turned into a wolf's smile.

Just bladed iron. Those Alvans are nasty.

The fields had been replanted with concertina wire just a few inches above the ground, threaded with one another like a fishing net across the ground. Shattered fell upon the wire, allowing the Shattered behind to advance further on their bodies before they too were snarled up in the wire or fell to attacks.

It was slow, but steady.

"The level two Devourers are remaining at the rear," one of the officers said.

"They're looking to see how the first groups do. Don't underestimate them. If they have a common goal, they'll work together. They're as smart as you and I. Just grew up in a savage place where death is more common than life."

It's as mother said, a war of attrition, of their numbers against ours.

Kay'Renna had read books about the years before the Ten Realms were created. She had read about the number of Shattered killed and the number of Elves and Gnomes that had died in the first few years. Their populations had been larger than the humans, but declined to just a percentage of their numbers when the Ten Realms were finally formed.

"Control the flow of Shattered. Close off every advance possible. Their true weapon is their hunger. They're driven wild by the need and want to consume to become stronger." She repeated her mother's words, chewing on her bottom lip.

From now on, all excursions beyond the city walls would be stopped. They would have to defend against whatever the Shattered brought to bear.

The guns of the forward ships went silent, leaving the ground pock-marked with impacts. Several Devourers and their sworn lay dead, their tears to the ninth closed off.

The fleet continued onward. Rekha checked the map. They swept across the Tenth, leaving a path clear of all Shattered. The fast attack craft had cut off dozens of tears and gathering Shattered in the surrounding area.

"We're clearing the mountains," the helm called.

The fleet had been flying high to get over the mountains between their transition point and the ascension platform.

Rekha's brows pinched together as they crossed the mountains.

The pillar of the ascension platform had been visible for nearly an hour now. Coming over the mountains, she saw where the thin white line bisected the ground, giving her a sense of just how *immense* the structure was. It rose from the ground to stab into the heavens, glowing with powerful runes.

Her chest tightened upon seeing that the runes along the side of the tower had reached three quarters of the way up. She checked the map again. The entire area around the base of the platform and the air above it was swarming with creatures from the Shattered Realm, passing through to the Ninth Realm.

The defenses' perfect lines had been smashed apart. The twin star defensives breached. Golems lay scattered across the ground, broken soldiers.

"Looks like the teleportation formation at the base of the platform is still working," Eli'keen said.

"Now we just need to draw the enemy far enough away from it that we can get past them and into the platform," Weebla said.

"That's why we brought an army," Erik said.

The fleet continued to push forward, gaining the Shattered's attention. Aerial Shattered were met with spells that shredded them apart.

The fleet started to slow. The two dreadnaughts in the middle and their surrounding fleets pushed forward as the first and fourth fleets slowed to create a blunted arrowhead.

Warships continued their advance. Rekha could feel the tension in the air.

"Fleet two and three, open fire," Admiral Peli said.

They shuddered under their own fire, cleansing the ground below, grinding it away under their advance.

Alvan ships fired missiles, targeting tears and the forces under the ascension platform.

Anti-air spells and flak colored the air, meeting with the aerial Shattered as the fleet waded forward. Corvette wings accelerated, opening their bay doors and releasing streams of bombs that went off like a string of fire crackers, obscuring the ground.

Accelerators fired, clouds of dust lit from the inside by escaping chaotic energies boiling outward.

Tears snapped shut as the Devourers led their counterattack. Elemental attacks met spells and weapons. Devourers led their sworn forward as the fleet came to a halt in front of the ascension platform.

Gnomes dropped to the ground like fish returning to water. The ground started to fall away from inside as defensive walls shot up under the fleet, creating a camp as teleportation formations activated within.

Soldiers that had been holding at the Tenth Realm totem marched out, dropping more teleportation formations for follow up units to use, then rushed for the wall's defenses.

"Come on," Rekha said, looking at the base of the ascension platform. Tears were falling apart under the strain of attacks, the Shattered moving to engage the new threat, but several Devourers and their sworn remained.

"Better than we thought," Eli'keen said.

"Time we headed down," Erik said.

They left the bridge and entered the hangars.

Rekha looked at Erik, catching him staring at her. He smiled and nodded. She did her best to return it. *What if I...* She cleared her head. Now was not the time. She needed to make it through all this before she could move on with her life.

The doors opened to the rest of their strike team.

Sam walked up to her. "How are we looking? By air or teleport pad?"

"Teleport pad, I think."

"All right, everyone, get on your pads. We're heading out as soon as we get the all clear," Weebla announced.

Everyone checked their gear and moved to the teleportation pads. Following the teleportation circle, half kneeled, the other half stood, facing outwards.

Rugrat and Egbert checked a formation that was resting on another formation. It was a large, thick disk of metal.

"Strike force, you are good to go," Commander Glosil's voice came through the hangar.

Egbert stood on top of the formation. "See you on the other side." He saluted and disappeared in a flash of light. The lighthearted undead fit right into the fabric of Alva.

Rekha secured her helmet and drew her sword as Rugrat ran to his teleportation pad, pulling on his helmet. She looked around, spotting Erik, and calmed upon seeing him.

The second group disappeared from their teleportation pad. Four seconds later, the third group disappeared. Then the world altered around Rekha. Spells flashed out from the close-ranged fighters as they tore through Ravagers. The area around the teleportation pad was burned black, metal fragments and dead laying across the open ground.

Rekha advanced from the teleportation pad, moving to the fighter's line. Cayleigh howled and charged into the line. The formation on Rekha's armor activated, boosting her attributes through Alva's conqueror formations.

Light flashed around her, appearing inside the fortress, just two hundred meters from the entrance to the ascension platform. A large door opened into a corridor that led to the teleportation pad that would allow them to enter the trial.

Alvan weapons fired, the groups advancing in bounds, creating a corridor to the entrance. Rekha unleashed spells and ran forward.

"Devourers!"

"Mine!" Egbert blasted one with a pillar of chaotic light, piercing through its chest and out its back.

Weebla threw out what looked like several knitting needles. They stabbed into another Devourer's neck. The rainbowed metal surged, lines connecting them. They flashed, connecting to one another *through* the Devourer's neck, cutting it into pieces. The Devourer faltered, slowing as its life blood poured from its neck.

"Buffs!" Cayleigh and Eli'keen ran forward as Sam and Rekha covered them in buffs. Cayleigh went low, attacking the Devourer's legs. The lizard-like creature opened its mouth, gathering mana as Eli'keen's sword flashed, making it reel in pain as he cut through the creature's iron scales and *danced* in the air. His sword flicked out, enhanced with mana, leaving devastating attacks on the creature. They worked together and ground the beast down.

"Last teleportation team!" Erik yelled.

Shattered and Devourers, learning about the attack, were turning and heading back over the walls and through the breaches.

"Push for the platform!" Weebla yelled.

A Devourer roared, streaming in from the sky.

Egbert yelled as Davin ballooned from cute imp to demon lord. George expanded, hurling stone from the ground as he exhaled flames from his mouth, as large as the oncoming level four Devourer. They crashed into the Devourer as Egbert flashed around, sending attacks into its hide.

The group disengaged, running for the hall that cut through the platform.

Two level three Devourers charged from the sides.

"I have the right!" Weebla turned and charged. A group of gnomes followed her as she drew her battle axe.

"I have the left!" Eli'keen charged the other Devourers.

They reached the entrance into the ascension platform. Rekha ducked from the elemental attacks that struck the corridor ceiling, just three meters above her head.

"We'll hold here. Get it done, sirs." The special teams created a line across the entrance to the hall into the ascension platform. They raised the ground, creating firing positions as they fired into the approaching Shattered while others fought off the high-level Devourers.

"Come on!" Erik yelled, his voice echoing through the corridor. There were just five of them left.

They ran down the hallway which was fifteen meters across, and five meters tall, periodically lit by mana lights. Formation script ran down the walls like lines from a tattoo.

Rekha saw the platform ahead and tightened her grip on her sword. They ran out from the corridor. Erik and Rugrat scanned right and left. The space opened into a circle and rose far above, a single mana light shining down on the formation.

"Dev—" Cayleigh was cut off with the sound of metal cutting metal and the forced exhale of someone being hit.

Rekha spotted the Devourer that had been hiding in the wall as it landed. It looked human, except for the chitin armor and the scorpion tail that had thrown Cayleigh to the side.

Erik and Rugrat fired first, their rounds targeting its face and chest.

Sam poured out his mana into a chaotic beam, tearing through the side of the beast.

Rekha's chaotic blasts hit the creature as chunks were torn from it and it backed up, being pounded into the ground. It released a wave of elements as it died.

Rugrat scanned the area again. Everyone else ran for Cayleigh. She was clammy and sweating, her veins a decaying brown. She held her shoulder. She had been able to turn, and the attack had gone through her right shoulder instead of her heart.

Erik pulled out a needle and stabbed it into her neck. She groaned as Sam dropped next to her, his hands shaking, not sure where to put them.

"Put pressure on her wounds." Erik took out gauze, moving Cayleigh's hand and stuffing it on top. He put Sam's hands on hers, staining them with her blood.

Erik gave her three more needles and several healing spells, drawing out poison through mana manipulation.

"Going to flip her." Erik turned her. Sam held the gauze on her front. Rekha felt weak, seeing the wet hole in her friend's armor and back.

Erik cut off Cayleigh's back plate's leather ties and tossed it to the side. He pulled out a pink sheet and put it on her back. It tightened to her back and fused, a lighter skin tone than Cayleigh's.

"Okay good." He rolled her back onto her back and held his hand above her exit wound. His eyes glowed and his fingers moved like a puppeteer as a murky gas released from Cayleigh's wound, burning up in a ball of flame as he tore open her sleeve.

"I feel so cold," Cayleigh said.

"Blood loss, don't worry, you're fine. Just dumped poison into your system." Erik got the needle in her arm. He checked the bag and hooked it to Sam's armor, then pulled out a needle and put it into the valve, injecting it into the clear liquid. "With the wound and the poison, and the conqueror formation increasing your strength at two hundred percent, your body is a mess. You're out of the fight." Erik looked at Rekha.

"Sam, you stay here. Make sure she's okay," Rekha said.

Erik nodded, working as he talked. "You can get a casualty point for the people at the front defending set up."

"But—"

"She needs someone to look after her, Sam. Give her these two needles—one every five minutes." Erik put the needles on Cayleigh's stomach. "You have her IV stuck on your chest. Keep that above her heart and you're good."

"I've told the group at the front. You get her sorted out?" Rugrat said. "We've got to move."

"But—"

Rekha grabbed Sam's shoulder. "Look after her. We'll get it done."

"Be safe." Cayleigh coughed, putting her hand on Rekha's leg.

"I'll be fine." Rekha patted her hand and returned it to Sam's. She stood up, moving with Erik and Rugrat. Erik reloaded his rifle, checking it.

They stood on the formation.

Do you wish to participate in the Ascension Trial?
YES/NO?

"Yes." Erik said and disappeared in a flash. Rugrat and Rekha followed suit.

Rekha arrived on the teleportation formation with the other two. A wave of heat wrapped around her. Magma roiled, surrounding the platform, lighting up the massive cavern. There were no human touches other than the formation she stood upon.

A normal person would have been burned up instantly by the heat.

Ascension Trial
You have reached the Ascension platform, laid down by the ascendants that created the Ten Realms. This trial is not for the faint of heart. Complete the trial to control the forces of the Ten Realms. Fail and you may lose your life.
Requirements:
Pass through the ten trials
Rewards:

"Mana is thinner here." Rekha tried to get a feel for it.

"Mortal grade, like the First Realm. Lots of the fire element. Seems to be the same amount you'd need to get a low tempering of your fire element," Erik said, muffled by his helmet.

"Formations aren't working.

"Dammit." Rugrat shook his rifle and then slapped it. "Mine either."

Rekha checked her sword. The formations were dull. Same with the formations on her armor.

Erik and Rugrat pulled off their face coverings.

"Well, this should be interesting. No tools," Rugrat muttered, putting away his rifle.

"Free sauna—what the hell is tha—" Erik dodged to the side as a floating cloaked figure wearing a broach of flames hacked at Erik with a claw of shadow.

Erik threw a punch. It passed through the cloak as if it was a shadow. Its hands scratched at his armor.

Erik frowned and used different elements before using fire. The creature collapsed into smoke around the stone spears. "Broach contains its power. Use the fire element to defeat it." Screams came from the surrounding area as they gathered their mana and faced outward.

Two charged Rekha. She slashed forward, a blade of mana tracing her path as she used the reverse motion to carve a second line at the next.

The creatures collapsed, but more cloaks and skulls wreathed in flames ran toward her. She stopped relying on her physical senses, utilizing her domain. Erik and Rugrat were laying into the cloaks as she advanced, attacking, and defending one another.

The trio worked together, coming from common routes. Just like training with Xun Liang, they hardly talked and functioned as a single unit.

"Fire element feels like it's increasing," Erik said.

"Mana too," Rekha said.

The cloaks stopped appearing, fading into the smoke.

The formation they'd arrived on glowed, adding three formation circles in the middle and turning green.

"The hell is that?" Erik asked.

"It's an impression formation, same as the formations in the totems." Rekha said.

"Well, all aboard?" Rugrat said.

They stepped onto the formations, new screens appearing.

Ascension Trial
You have reached the Ascension platform, laid down by the ascendants that created the Ten Realms. This trial is not for the faint of heart. Complete the trial to control the forces of the Ten Realms. Fail and you may lose your life.
Requirements:
Pass through the ten trials (1/10)
Rewards:
Ascend

Do you wish to ascend?
YES/NO?

"Everyone good to go?" Erik asked.

"Yup."

"Wish I had my gun back."

"On one—three, two, one."

They appeared on another floor, similar to the first, with less fog but hotter and denser mana.

"Guess those are the cloak's big brothers." Erik fired shaped mana bullets, hitting one of the smoke-black armored knights. They wore black cloaks and with unhelmeted skulls of flame.

Their swords ignited in flames as they turned toward the group and charged.

13

Defenders of the Realms

ead, a fleet from Kircross has transitioned somewhere," one of the aides said, drawing Clive's attention from Cronen's map table.

"What do you mean, *somewhere*? Why didn't we know about this before? Who is in the fleet?"

"It looks like it was done in secrecy. There were five dreadnoughts and a few hundred smaller classes of warships from Imperium, Elven, Gnome, Mission Hall, and Alvan forces."

Clive shook with range, the muscles in his face shifting as he hit the table. "Get me the Gnome and Elven leadership—now!"

The aide winced and looked at the ground. "The Elven and Gnome leadership have stated that they are fighting for their home cities."

"I don't care. I want them here now. Make it an order!"

"We can ask them to come here, but they're not actually part of the Imperium."

"What?"

"There are many Elves and Gnomes in the Imperium, but as a whole, they are not part of the Imperium. They're like everyone else and have to complete testing and swear oaths to join the associations and the Imperium."

"But there are so many of them." Clive's brows pinched together. He was sure they fell under the Imperium. Elves and Gnomes controlled a significant amount of the associations. He had always been jealous of their positions in life.

"The Imperium was made by their forebearers and ancestors. They live for a really long time, so—" The aide bowed his head under Clive's withering stare.

"Get me the leader of those Imperium forces. I want to know what the hell they think they're doing!"

"They're carrying out a priority Ten Realms mission."

Clive hammered the table. They had clearly planned this to make sure they couldn't be recalled. Someone that was on a priority mission from the Ten Realms could ignore orders as long as they were actively working to clear their mission," Clive hissed, "I guess the Mission Hall people are the same way?"

"Yes sir," the aide said.

The other commanders and aides were quiet, listening in, not wanting to draw Clive's ire.

"This is Weebla, Eli'keen, and those damn Alvans. Nothing but a meddling thorn in my side." Clive looked up, a flash of inspiration hitting him. "The Alvans are separate, and we know where their home is. Are there forces in Kircross still?"

"There are, sir."

"Good, question them. If they don't cooperate, send a delegation down to the First Realm to get out the location of the fleet from them."

"Yes, sir." The aide bowed and left.

"This is why we have to control the lower realms. If we don't, it creates dissent in our own ranks," Clive said to his commanders.

"Sir, I have reports on that wave of Shattered."

"The one that traitor warned us about?" Clive snarled.

"It was bigger than he expected. Three more mega cities in the Seventh Realm are under attack, and it looks like the Sixth Realm was infiltrated by more Shattered than we thought. Sects and the associations are reporting that they've lost contact with some of the smaller towns."

"Tell them to consolidate their positions and hold. We've been telling them to do so for weeks now."

"Sir, they have those orders, but the level two Devourers in the Sixth Realm can cultivate mana and increase their power over time. The Sixth Realm is a realm of schools, they are even less prepared to fight a war than the Seventh Realm."

"The Shattered will decrease with time. They will run out of forces. Send the Imperium forces we can spare and give the Sixth mission halls increased rewards to clear tears."

The commander cleared his throat with an awkward expression on his face.

"What is it?" Clive growled.

"There are no mission halls in the Sixth Realm, and all our Imperium forces are actively fighting."

"Then thin their ranks here so they can deal with the stragglers."

"Sir, last recorded, there were one hundred and fifty-three Shattered Realms," an elven aide hissed.

"Watch your tone, boy."

The elf scoffed. "A child with power. You made so many think that you knew what you were doing, but you just wanted the attention. Eli'keen warned you, came to you with offers of help. We all did."

"Get the fuck out of here," Clive roared.

"By your orders, *Head.*" The elf gave a sardonic bow and left. Clive shook with rage as the first aide walked over and bowed at the waist.

"What?"

"Our forces in Kircross are being evicted from the city. The city rulers have sent a message to stop messing with their city. They have said if we are willing to work with them, they will welcome our assistance. Otherwise, they will defend their city themselves."

"Good, very good! Order all of our forces out and all our resources, including all of our association members. Let this be an example to others!"

"Is this the time for petty games? We're under *attack*!" One of the commanders slammed his hands onto the table, glaring at Clive. "This is war, not a fucking popularity contest. I'm going to lead my forces to defend Cronen. The Imperium was made to defend the Ten Realms, regardless of what people thought about us."

The commander hit the desk again, turned, and stormed out. "You'll have my resignation when I'm dead from fighting the Shattered, or this war is over." He marched out in the path left by the elf before him.

Clive looked at the other commanders and aides in the room. They averted their eyes from him. "Incompetents, the lot of them! I will bring the Imperium to be the strongest in the realms. This is a test. We can win. I can lead us to victory.

"We need to figure out how to support the Sixth Realm."

The Seventh Realm losing a few arrogant sects will make it easier for us to control the realms."

Erik jumped on the back of an armored Earth worm, which tried to throw him off as he climbed up. It made to dive back into the ground. The floor was covered in dirt and dark red stone, filled with caves and warrens.

He punched the worm, forcing back the earth that made up the creature. He spotted the glowing green gem within and grabbed it, infusing it with the Earth element. The elemental core stone cracked, the armored worm hitting the ground, but instead of going through it, it collapsed into clods of dirt.

Ascension Trial
You have reached the Ascension platform, laid down by the ascendants that created the Ten Realms. This trial is not for the faint of heart. Complete the trial to control the forces of the Ten Realms. Fail and you may lose your life.
Requirements:
Pass through the ten trials (4/10)

Rewards:
  Ascend

Erik slid off the beast, smacking dirt from his shirt. "Well, I think I know what is happening with these floors. First, we had the fire floors and mortal mana. This floor has Earth element and Earth grade mana with armored Earth worms. So much Earth."

"Each floor increases the mana and the elements, tests our cultivation and sends creatures to attack us that can use the elements," Rekha said.

"This is going to be fun because none of us have completed our cultivation," Rugrat said.

"Good thing that I cultivated to the Water level and you both have your acupoints opened," Erik said. "We can help one another with cultivation. Though these creatures are going to be a pain in the ass to fight."

"They're testing our mastery of the element. We have to use fire to defeat the fire creatures, earth to defeat the earth creatures. Show that we have a greater mastery and understanding of the element," Rekha said.

"Wished that it was just a damn written test." Erik walked to the formation.

"I don't," Rugrat grumbled.

Rekha looked at the formation. It had turned gold and had greater detail than the first green formation and the second purple formation. This one created a triangle of secondary formations around the first circles.

"Three two one, ye—" They ascended to the next floor, the metal floor.

They arrived on a platform in what looked like ancient Roman ruins with pillars and grand buildings made of metal, dull grey and rusted. Statues filled the streets, stuck in poses as if they were trying to escape the teleportation formation.

One of the statue's heads snapped up, looking at them with metallic eyes.

"Ah shit," Erik grunted.

"Gonna need a minute," Rugrat said as he hit himself with a needle and coughed. "Bit more Metal element than I've dealt with before."

The statues came to life, their expressions of horror turning to hunger as they ran at the trio.

Erik reached out. Three statues slammed together and compressed, their elemental core stones popping. He opened his hand. The metal shattered into darts, cutting through several nearby, filling his domain.

"Lightning!" Erik yelled.

Rekha cut down a statue with her blade, the smell of crisp ozone filling the air as lightning arced from the sword, running through the metal shards and statues, causing dozens to collapse.

Erik compressed the metal into spears, killing two more. Iron rose to his side. A statue dented the metal as the sheet wrapped and compressed. Erik ran forward. Lightning coursed through his body as he weaved through the statues. His fists and legs no longer growled. The force of his attack *boomed*, striking his target. The wave of force following afterward blasted them away.

He sensed their elemental core stones and targeted them with surgical precision. His Finger Beats Fist hurled the stones from their bodies, turning them into statues again as they collapsed forward with holes punched through them.

The ground rumbled as sheets of sharpened metal like a sculpture's interpretation of sea coral spread out from Rugrat's hand, piercing through statues. Mana surged through his construct, killing the trapped statues.

Erik destroyed three more before he realized that the statues were running away. They froze, some toppling.

Ascension Trial
You have reached the Ascension platform, laid down by the ascendants that created the Ten Realms. This trial is not for the faint of heart. Complete the trial to control the forces of the Ten Realms. Fail and you may lose your life.
Requirements:
Pass through the ten trials (5/10)
Rewards:
Ascend

"Looks like mana does work. It's like the elemental test. You have to show a greater control over mana."

"Why didn't you just hit them with mana blades?" Erik moved back to the teleportation formation as it shifted from gold to blood-red in increasing complexity.

"It was a test." Rugrat groaned, sitting down and pulling out a healing potion. "Didn't want them to tear me apart if it went wrong."

Erik grunted and looked at the area Rekha had been fighting in. Statues lay bisected, fresh shining metal amongst their rusted exteriors.

"Let me check you out." Erik knelt next to Rugrat and scanned him.

"Did I say yes?" Rugrat grumbled.

Erik could see the metal element entering Rugrat's body, tempering as his body fought to recover and compensate for the changes. "That's not what I expected." Erik examined Rugrat's elemental core.

"I love it when doctors say that."

Erik remained silent, comparing Rugrat's core against his own.

"Will you tell me what the hell you didn't expect? Am I growing a fourth arm or something?"

"No, no, just... your elemental core is increasing, too."

"Yay?"

"It's increasing everything," Rekha said.

"Body elemental and mana cultivation," Erik said, dismissing his scan spell.

"Translated?" Rugrat asked.

"Means that the first two realms were mortal fire. We tested our cores, our fire tempering, and raised out elemental cores to the mortal grade. Earth grade and Earth element floor must have done the same thing, but we all have Earth grade fire and Earth elements."

"Metal floor, Sky grade elements and mana heart test," Rekha said.

"Newsflash. I haven't finished tempering my metal body. Erik, you don't have all your acupoints. Rekha, what are you?"

"Working on my acupoints and my Wood tempering. My elements are lagging behind right now."

"That means you're the furthest ahead of us all. How in the hell are we supposed to get down to kick Akran's ass?"

"We don't have time to stop on every floor and consolidate our gains." Rekha held her forehead and walked around.

"Body as a pill," Erik muttered, frowning.

"What was that?" Rugrat asked.

"Body as a pill. Alchemy, grow, harvest, prep, and concoct, and then there's a fifth stage—the most important—consume. The pill enters the body and changes it."

"What does my Viagra have to do with this?" Rugrat groaned. The metal elements were turning patches of his skin black, and his veins silver.

"Dammit. I was hoping to not bleed mercury."

"It's what all the cool kids are doing," Erik said, a smile spreading across his face.

"That's a I have a stupid ass plan and I'm going to test it on Rugrat smile."

"I've known you too long." Erik rolled his eyes and raised metal behind Rugrat, who leaned back.

"Feeling is mutual, *hombre*, thanks for the chair."

"Okay, so the ascension platform is basically checking to make sure we've completed our temperings, and mana elements. No wonder Akran slowed down. He's going through the same thing. Just like a damn pill.

"Thankfully, we've got an edge. We know the elements and mana increase with this place as we go. Half of a tempering pill is about making sure there's enough in the pill to bump up your cultivation. Without needing to worry about that, we just need to focus on recovery concoctions. Well, I might not know how to make a bunch of tempering potions, but I know how to make healing and stamina potions."

Erik pulled out his cauldron and withdrew ingredients, tossing them in. None of his formations worked, so he would have to do it the old-fashioned way, as he had done with the Lidel leaves so long ago. His elements danced inside the cauldron, creating a potion. He passed it to Rugrat, who drank it. He laid back and closed his eyes, tempering his body with the aid of the potion.

Erik barely stopped, working on the next concoction, a series of pills. He continued making concoctions, preparing for the challenges ahead as best as he could.

Rekha assisted him where she could and watched the area to make sure nothing snuck up on them.

Several hours later, Rugrat sighed and opened his eyes as Erik fished pills out from his cauldron, storing them in a bottle.

"Welcome to low-grade metal tempering." Erik smiled. He had been watching Rugrat's progress through his domain.

"Well, I feel like smashed ah—" Rugrat was cut off by the influx of metal element as his elemental core drew it inward. His grey veins and charcoaled skin faded back to his naturally tanned complexion.

"Wooh, that feels better,"

"Wish I had an elemental core when I was tempering the metal element." Erik stood and stretched.

"Good elemental core." Rugrat patted his chest.

"Here are your concoctions. Metal tempering pills to assist the growth, then Water and Wood." Erik passed over the different concoctions to Rugrat, who stored them away.

"Rekha, here are Water and Wood tempering pills. These pills are meant to help you recover from the raw elements that these floors are pumping out. Now, your acupoints."

Erik raised a section of the floor to an examination table.

"On you go." He waved to Rugrat.

"What now?"

"Don't worry. Just want to stab you a half dozen times."

"Zero stars. Worst bedside manner." Rugrat jumped on the table.

"Zero stars, idiot."

"Hey." Erik pushed his head down and scanned Rugrat in greater depth.

"What are you doing?"

"I'm going to open his acupoints."

"Opening one's acupoints is a delicate and time consuming—"

Erik stabbed a needle into Rugrat's knee.

"Ow!"

"Stay down, will you? You've lost a leg before. Little needle ain't going to do anything to you."

"It is with you on the other end of it!" Rugrat frowned. "That sounded weird."

"Will the patient shut up and circulate their mana?"

"Frigging medics." Rugrat did as he was told.

"Formations don't work here, but mana does, and some formations we made just direct mana." Erik injected his mana into the needle, and through his vision, he watched it spread out slightly, then stop. Rugrat's mana circulated through his channels.

"See, when we started up, we opened all our mana gates."

"When did you?" Rekha asked, suspicious.

"Over the first couple of realms. Now a kid born in Alva gets all of their mana gates opened."

"You say that like it's a casual thing. I was lucky to have so many open when I was a child and Xun Liang paid a lot to have my other mana gates opened.

"Yeah, if you don't use mana that is pure enough, then it can cause blockages. That is why it's best to do it after tempering the body some so it can filter the impurities or have concoctions. Oh, yeah. Drink this." Erik held out a potion above Rugrat, still studying his knee.

"Best to not smell—"

"Holy hot garbage! This is worse than a dip bottle that got stuck in a truck in Iraq under a seat for a month!"

Erik's stomach had a visceral reaction to that little description. "Just drink it, will you? Couldn't get it tasting like a strawberry milkshake."

"I hate this job."

"We don't get paid. It's not a job."

"Is that worse or better?"

Erik shrugged. "We own a city?"

"True." Rugrat threw his head back and drank the potion, shuddering and jerking as its contents went down his throat.

Erik finished his inspection and held out a sweet.

Rugrat shoved it in his mouth and sucked, trying to rub his tongue clean with the sugary sweetness.

"It tastes worse than it smells," Rugrat said.

Erik laughed.

"You're a monster."

"Thanks. All right, so I can't punch a hole through your acupoints like with your mana channels. There's nothing connecting them to your mana channels, so you're going to have to connect them." Erik pulled out paper, wrapped it on Rugrats leg and started sketching, seeing his mana channels and his acupoints.

"How in the hell do I do that?"

"With your will."

Rekha made an appreciative noise. "You can use your will to change your body, just like the Shattered."

"Give the lady a prize. So, Rugrat, you're just changing the blueprint of your body. You can change your acupoints, spread their mana connections out to your mana channels, but don't connect them. Get to the last levels and you can open them. The mana will be dense enough that you can open them in series. The dense mana will complete your tempering."

"Okay."

"And I'll guide you to make the right routes. Rekha, I can work on yours afterwards."

"What about you?"

"I'm altering them already."

"Why the hell didn't you need foot soup?"

"Stamina. It takes a lot to create and change your mana system."

"You mean I could have eaten twinkies instead of foot garbage?"

"You'd need like a tractor trailer of them."

"Ohh, you just watch me."

"Do your past times include marshmallows and chubby bunny?"

"Ain't no one that can defeat me."

"All right." Erik guided Rugrat, creating nearly complete routes from his acupoints to his mana system.

They did everything they could think of to prepare for the upcoming floors, purposefully changing their bodies within a hair of the possible changes they would undergo, stocking up on potions and even eating the same ingredients Erik ate to create his Revival blood.

"Okay, let's do this thing." Erik clapped Rugrat on the shoulder.

Do you wish to ascend?
YES/NO?

"On one?"

"Three, two, one. Yes."

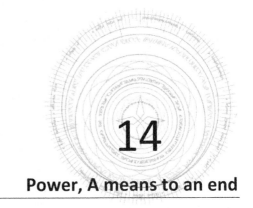

14

Power, A means to an end

GIosil watched as tears popped up across the Tenth Realm, leading to a myriad of worlds. Many exited into the Tenth Realm and immediately headed lower for more comfortable realms. Some Shattered shifted their attention to the fight at the ascension platform and charged, heading for the fleet and their ground defenses.

"Rotate!"

The Alvan warships turned to present their fresh broadsides. The fleets fired as fast as they could, but the Shattered were still reaching the defensive camp below. Bodies were piling up under the onslaught of spell and tracer.

"Shit."

He had played his hand. Everything was committed. He had no more reinforcements to call on. The ships could only eek out a little more before the guns started to melt and formations began failing.

Come on guys. It's on you now.

Louis watched the Shattered line advance as his ship rocked, only pausing their shooting to rotate the ship and bring more weapons to bear. The Shattered had continued to rush Kircross, wearing them down hour after hour with a seemingly endless supply of Shattered.

The concertina nets had been torn apart through spell and elemental attacks, covered in *shattered* bodies. The new push came across these patches, speeding up as they spread across the ground. They came onward, running the gauntlet.

Good. Louis sighed with relief as Shattered tumbled into the broken ground below a series of caves and warrens tens of meters tall.

Dungeon beasts roared, charging out of the depths of their dungeon to fight the new arrivals.

They're advancing faster than we thought. There's more of them than even our worst estimate.

Erik flew across the icebergs. Large purple octopi, with intelligent eyes as big as a man, shot out of the water to join others that were fighting him, their tentacles lashing out with water blades.

He kicked out with flames, turning the spells into mist, then congealed it into water and sent them back out in spikes. They hit the surrounding creatures, several dropping to squirm on the broken icebergs below.

He shot toward the closest octopus and touched it, drawing the water from its body. The creature shriveled and collapsed.

Erik dropped to the ground, arriving back at the formation pad.

Rugrat twisted his hands. The icebergs shot out as chains, wrapping around the creatures as he fired bolts of mana into their bodies, destroying their core stones, one beast per mana bolt.

They dropped to the ground as golems of ice rose from the icebergs and jumped into the sea.

Rugrat was covered in buffs, pale and sweating. "That should do it," he said as more of the beasts jumped out of the water.

Erik kicked one back into the sea, punched another, missing a water whip, and pierced three more with water attacks from behind.

"How do you figure?" Erik fought to keep his balance at the twin explosions from underwater.

Ascension Trial
You have reached the Ascension platform, laid down by the ascendants that created the Ten Realms. This trial is not for the faint of heart. Complete the trial to control the forces of the Ten Realms. Fail and you may lose your life.
Requirements:
Pass through the ten trials (7/10)
Rewards:
Ascend

Rugrat groaned with the increase of Water element, leaning against an ice boulder. He pulled out leaves and chewed.

Beast bodies floated to the water pools between the iceberg sheets.

"Damn, this is a crap way to increase your cultivation," Rugrat muttered.

"How are you feeling?" Erik asked, moving to him.

"Like I just ran for a week, only to find out that I don't get to sleep for another week, *and* I get to run some more."

"I'd suggest taking a pill or a potion, but the more we have in a short period of time, the less effective they'll be." Erik said.

"So best to use it when we really need to," Rugrat looped his thumbs into his carrier, lifting it to get some more air and pushing his shoulders back.

The formation changed from silver to orange.

Do you wish to ascend?
YES/NO?

Rugrat pushed up from his boulder and drank from his canteen. "All right, no time like the present."

Erik looked at him and shared a glance with Rekha.

"You sure?" Erik asked.

"Yeah." Rugrat moved into the formation. "Let's do this."

Erik stepped onto the platform, Rekha on his right and Rugrat on his left, making a triangle facing out.

"Three two, one. *Yes.*" They all said the last word together.

Erik blinked against the heat that tried to dry out his eyes as if he'd opened the oven too fast.

"At least it's warm!" Rugrat growled as they appeared on a small island surrounded by other islands.

"Down!" Erik yelled as a *fire* attack lanced over them. It detonated as the stone around the platform shot at them.

Erik jumped out of the circle, punching through the stone appendages, seeing the origin of the attacks—a man with one broken horn and the other curling around his head. His skin was scaled in five colors.

Quest: Akran the Devourer
Akran intends to ascend the Ten Realms and command them. Destroy him before he can.
Rewards:
+10,000,000,000,000 EXP +1,000,000 Mission Points Rewards may be increased based on performance

Five Star.

Erik opened his eyes, his insides feeling like they had liquified. The animalistic part of his brain warned, *screaming* at him to run away from this thing as fast as possible.

"Akran!"

Creatures started to rise from the water—robed monks hidden in their hoods, with tusked snouts and tentacles that extended from the bottom of their robe into the water below.

Erik cried out, circulating his elements and mana, raising his body to its peak condition. Ice gathered under his foot, shattering as he pushed off from it, the elements and mana around him reacting on an instinctual level as he shot toward Akran.

Akran let out a roar and charged, the elements materializing into attacks around him.

Rekha yelled, her sword flashing as Rugrat counter-spelled. Erik reacted, dodging, diverting, and attacking.

The fallout of their attacks tore apart the island, creating a storm. Rugrat used the energies. A tornado ripped into the approaching monks, tearing through their ranks as he pulled apart the elements' components. Pure elemental and mana attacks hacked at Akran.

The elements moved around Erik as if they were a part of him, reacting and acting like they were an extension of him.

A wall of water slammed into Erik. He grunted with the impact and shot to the side as fire spears passed him, exploding. Instead of being thrown aside by the motion, he used it to accelerate, punching through the follow-up attack. Spears of sand and water rose to his command, and he hurled it all at Akran.

Rugrat grunted as he fought off elemental attacks, and the tusked monks entered the fray.

Rekha covered her blade in water. She caught lightning upon it, taking control and diverting it. The water containing the lightning turned to ice, and she struck a monk with it, turning them into an expanding cloud and sending several others spiraling with the crack of thunder.

Xun Liang had taught them to use the environment to their advantage and to take away the enemy's. Akran had a greater control over the elements, so their only advantage was their understanding of mana, imbuing it and their will into every attack.

Erik and Rugrat continued their attacks as Akran shifted to focus on Rekha. She was like a war goddess. Her face was nearly expressionless, seeing her opponent as a problem to be resolved. Erik threw out a powder that carried on the wind. Akran hit it away absently. the powder expanded into smoke, decreasing the mana and elements in the area.

Akran roared and shot out of the smoke. The elements rose into his hand, and he created a spear from them and stabbed and attacked Erik.

Erik was in full retreat as he fended off the attacks, taking hits to the shoulder, to the legs, and side. Akran attacked Rugrat and Rekha with the elements at the same time.

Erik saw a fresh attack coming from behind just seconds before it happened. He braced himself as the monk's attack hit him in the back and threw him at Akran.

Akran stabbed forward as Erik accelerated faster than he had ever done before. He felt his body tearing as he turned, the spear hitting him in the arm. Elements charged through his body as he stabbed his hand at Akran's head.

An explosion detonated between them, tossing them backward.

Erik screamed, his arm a pulped mess. It wasn't regenerating as it should.

"Cauterize it!"

Rekha paused for a half second. "Sorry." She sliced off the arm. The burn and smell made Erik groan, and he gripped his arm above the clean cut.

Akran roared, growing in size, a cut across his left cheek.

Rekha charged into the fight. Erik wanted to charge with her, but she was stronger. She had fought Devourers for longer and had been Xun Liang's student for years.

What use is power if it can't be used to help others?

"Ten Realms! Take my power and kill Akran."

This request cannot be carried out.

"Ten realms! Hear me. Take my power. Give Rekha my cultivation."

Your power will be used to empower Rekha Xun to raise her cultivation.
You may only make 1 wish to the realms. This will use up your wish. Do you agree?
YES/NO

"Yes!"

"Erik?" Rekha yelled as Erik felt his power leaving his body and shooting toward her.

"Beat him, Rekha! You're the only one who can." Erik grunted as his cultivation plummeted. The elements and mana weighed upon his soul. He grabbed a tourniquet and wrapped it above where it had been cut off, tightening it as he felt his strength leaving him, becoming just another human as the pressure of the trial forced him to the ground.

"Ten Realms, buff all of Rekha's stats," Rugrat said, on his knee, coughing blood.

Power poured from his body as it had poured from Erik's, gathering around Rekha.

Rekha groaned as power flowed through her body. Her mana cultivation advanced, opening her acupoints. A wave of force threw back Akran and swept the island clear, tossing back the monks as she drained the water element from her surroundings.

Her body shifted with the new element, like a dam breaking as the elemental energy flooded through her body and into her elemental cores. She twisted, feeling like there were roots spreading from her elemental core to the rest of her body.

She looked inward, seeing the Wood element entering her pores, entering her muscles, her tendons, and moving deeper through her organs.

Rugrat's power fell upon her clothes, her sword and helmet. White runes of power lay upon her skin and glowed brightly as she reached another level, above and beyond what a cultivator of mana and elements could ever hope to achieve.

She gnashed her teeth together at seeing Erik and Rugrat on the ground, holding back their pain, as weak as lambs in that place.

Akran's charge pulled the water with him like a wave. She charged him, her sword flashing, killing the remaining monks, her sword wind slicing through the water itself.

She flung herself forward, drawing the water up in her wake.

Ascension Trial
You have reached the Ascension platform, laid down by the ascendants that created the Ten Realms. This trial is not for the faint of heart. Complete the trial to control the forces of the Ten Realms. Fail and you may lose your life.
Requirements:
Pass through the ten trials (8/10)
Rewards:
Ascend

Hang on.

She clashed with Akran. The waves behind them smashed backward, breaking their momentum.

The water depressed and shot back as Akran lashed out, his attacks meeting with Rekha's sword. The clarion clear ring of her blade turned into a high-pitched whine from the repeated attacks, too fast to see clearly.

Mana and elements threaded into one another, feeding and supporting. Each moved enough to cleave mountains and broke the sea underneath them. The islands around them cracked, breaking apart and being thrown to the side as the water was pushed up into a bowl by the fury of their attacks.

Rekha's blade danced, tearing through and deflecting elements as she cast with her free hand. She slid through his guard, cutting open his side. Blood and elements were freed under her blade's attack.

Good thing the elemental leech is an innate ability.

She accelerated around, meeting his spear thrusts, while his elements attacked her from every direction.

Their eyes glowed as the ceiling of the floor turned into spears of stone and metal. The water beneath became whips and blades as air crashed into one another.

Flames turned islands to glass to be broken into pillars and shot at one another. Water burned and boiled, used as ice arrows. Rekha returned lighting along their path, stunning Akran for a half second as she aimed an air blade, thinner than a hair and harder than any diamond, for Akran's neck. He lowered his horns into the path. Elements shot out in a beam between his horns.

Rekha moved like a ghost caught in the wind, carried away upon the currents of mana as the chaotic beam annihilated everything in its path, burning through walls and leaving a path through the islands and water.

She charged Akran again, pushing beyond any limits she had known. Elements and mana forged together into a spell she had only thought of.

The six-sided spell appeared around Akran like a cage and *pulled*. A mana and element gathering formation forcefully tore through the power within. The spell activated around Akran, *ripping* power from him. He roared in pain as it was drawn out of him, just as it had been pulled from Erik and Rugrat.

Rekha's hands flew around a miniature spell formation in her hands as her domain collected the rampant energies she'd torn from Akran.

He broke the stasis field and smashed through the spell formation like glass.

She released her gathered chaotic energy upon him, hiding him from view.

He burst out of the destruction, his scales bloodied and broken, his eyes filled with anger as he charged.

Akran left behind his pretenses as he expanded into his true form. His eye, as large as Rekha, filled with the elements. His wounds cleared as he stood upon four legs. He had the head of a minotaur, the body of a lizard, and five tails, one for each element.

His tails shook the elements and erupted toward Rekha. She weaved through the attacks as Akran released a beam of deadly chaotic energy, carving through the floor once again.

She sliced through his side, dodging his tails and dancing through the eddies of the elements. They were thick around him as she lashed out again and again, leaving wounds across him as the power upon her weakened, her speed decreasing as the near misses started to hurt.

Akran hit her with a blast of water. She used mana to dodge the fireballs and collapsing ceiling along her path. Attacks coming from behind penned her in as Akran charged her.

His body was leaking elements from all over. *I'm this strong and I still can't kill him.*

Rekha yelled and charged. She dodged what she could and took the hits she couldn't, wrapping her blade in a chaotic mass of energies. She cut Akran's maw and removed his horn. He roared in rage as elements poured out from the wound.

He hit her. She felt something shift and other things crack as her sword spiraled away. She slowed herself before she crashed into the wall. She shoved herself out of the dust. Reaching out her hand, she summoned her blade. It whistled into her hand.

Akran let out a roar and charged. "Weak human!"

Rekha yelled, clashing with him head on. They collided with one another, leaving wounds upon one another, faster than a person could follow.

Rekha's enchantment broke as Akran bled from dozens of wounds. He whipped his metal tail at her. She dodged and cut it off, hurling her sword into Akran's side, discharging the twisted energy along the blade.

She reached out her mana, the blade spinning into her hand as elements gathered in her domains, lashing out at Akran. Their domains were outlined in spheres where they intersected. Everything beyond turned to a wasteland under the wrath of two gods.

Akran charged upon a wave of annihilation, detonating elements behind him as his claws broke through the last of her power and sent her flying backward. His claws pierced her armor, leaving three bloody and ragged marks on her chest, torso, and legs.

Rekha had never felt such pain before. She skipped across the tempest of waves, crashing over an island, and slamming into the ruins of another before coming to a rest. She was barely conscious, her body working to repair the elements invading her body, impeding her recovery.

She took out a healing potion and poured it onto her face, spluttering and coughing. She could feel Akran like a storm cloud approaching.

She hissed as she pulled a spell scroll inside her armor, using all her emergency healing spells as her body started to unfold itself, reversing the damage.

She screamed in pain.

She had worked for her power, grueling, spending months in the Shattered Realm tracking down tears and closing them with her team. Xun Liang had put her back together more than once as she went through her brutal pursuit of power—power that allowed her to control her own destiny.

She knew she couldn't fight anymore, and that Akran would kill her as soon as he reached her. She had achieved what she had set out to do when she left her family. She had the power to ascend, the power to stand at the top of the Ten Realms. There was no one in the Ten Realms that would deny her power.

Her mind flashed through Weebla, Eli'keen, Sam, Cayleigh, their families, Xun Liang, Erik.

She opened her eyes.

"I want to see what you can all do." Xun Liang's last words rang through her head. Tears filled her eyes as she gripped her fist. *I wonder what Teacher would have thought about a united Ten Realms?*

She couldn't waste the power on herself.

"Ten realms, hear my request, take my power and give it to Erik and Rugrat."

Just as her teacher, as her junior brothers had done, instead of holding on to power, she gave it up.

Your power will be used to empower Jimmy Rodriguez and Erik West to raise their cultivation.

You may only make one wish to the realms. This will use up your wish. Do you agree?

YES/NO

"Yes."

The power fled her. She cried out. Her body continued to repair, but she had been nearly ascendant and the toll on her was massive. She screamed out, hearing Akran's approach, feeling death close.

He gathered his elements, not taking a risk, preparing his strongest attack. A shot rang out, sending the attack into chaos.

Akran let out a pained roar, the pressure of his presence moving away.

She gasped as healing spells ran through her body. Needles slid into her arms, spreading warmth through her.

She looked up to find herself floating, spells moving around her as Erik manipulated the elements within her body. The whites of his eyes had turned black around his bright blue pupils. The elements spread through his body.

She was in the presence of a god, while the rest of the world seemed to be blocked out apart from the sound of fighting in the distance as Rugrat clashed with Akran head on.

Rekha reached up, touching his face. She pulled him down and kissed him. "Go kill that fucker."

"Yes, ma'am." Erik lowered her to the ground and shot into the air.

Quest Completed: Body Cultivation 6
The path to cultivating one's body is not easy. To stand at the top, one must forge their own path forward.
Requirements:
Reach Body like Celestial Iron
Rewards:
Strength, Agility, Stamina, Stamina regeneration increased by 50%   +100,000,000,000 EXP

Quest: Mana Cultivation 6
The path to cultivating one's mana is not easy. To stand at the top, one must forge their own path forward.
Requirements:
Open your 72 acupoints
Rewards:
Command over Mana   Mana, Mana Regeneration increased by 50%   +100,000,000,000 EXP

Quest Completed: Bloodline Cultivation 3
The power of the body comes from the purity of the bloodline.
Requirements:
Form a Divine Grade Elemental Core with 4 elements
Rewards:
Divine Grade Bloodline
+10,000,000,000,000,000 EXP

Quest: Bloodline Cultivation 4
The power of the body comes from the purity of the bloodline.
Requirements:
Form a Celestial Grade Elemental Core with all 5 elements
Rewards:
Celestial Grade Bloodline
Command over the elements
+1,000,000,000,000,000,000 EXP

You have reached Level 110
When you sleep next, you will be able to increase your attributes by: 30 points.

Title: Rooted in the Ten realms
You have tempered your body with Wood. Wood has become a part of you, making your body take on some of its characteristics. Tempering in every element, the elements accept you as you have accepted them. You have gained:
Legendary Wood resistance.
Control over Wood mana.
Physical attacks contain Wood attribute.
Can completely purify the Wood attribute in mana.
Physical Domain
Elemental domain

Title: Mana Reborn VI
You have fused with mana as you have accepted it, it has accepted you.

Legendary Mana Resistance

Control over mana

Physical attacks contain mana attribute.

You can channel the Ten Realms mana through your body.

Mana domain

Title: From the Grave IV

You've died and come back to the land of the living not just once, but three times. You sure you're on the right side of the grave?

Rewards:

+2.0 modifier to Stamina and Mana Regeneration

+2.0 modifier to Mana and Stamina Regeneration

Quest: Ascend

You have gained the foundations needed to ascend.

Requirements:

Mana of the Celestial grade

Elements of the Celestial grade

A body strong enough to withstand ascension, following the Ten Realms' path of ascension.

Fuse them.

Ascendant

Erik felt the power rushing through his veins. His body thirsted for it; it craved it. He *craved* it. He hadn't realized how much it was a part of him.

Seeing Rekha broken had broken his heart. He'd fused her body together as best as possible so she wouldn't die.

He conjured mana blades, bleeding into his gloves. Turning from grey to red, an iron tang filling the air.

Rugrat was surrounded by a squall of destruction; spells, elements, mana, created and destroyed in seconds, pressing Akran back as he tried to defend.

They clashed in a wave of power, splitting the water between as they flew backward. An island was swept away as the water crested over it.

"These blood drinkers have been upgraded a few times, but I wonder what the blood of someone just before ascension would do if directed into a punch." Erik's voice carried through the floor as he charged Akran.

Akran turned and fled, shooting toward the orange formation as it turned yellow, expanding.

"Yes!" Akran disappeared in a flash of light.

Erik glanced back at Rekha.

"Go."

He couldn't hear her with his ears, but his domain sensed it. Sensed her broken body, her weak breath, the elements and mana threatening to kill her, overloading her body. Once they were an aid, now a poison.

Erik roared, blasting through the sky to the formation, gathering elements into a sphere around him. Rugrat was ahead of him.

"Yes!"

He disappeared ahead of Erik.

Do you wish to ascend?
YES/NO?

"Yes!"

Erik careened out of the formation from a tropical wasteland into a wooded utopia. He tore through the forest, clearing a path through the thick trees. Creatures, like tumbleweeds with green glowing eyes, threw spears imbued with the wood element.

He countered with metal shards, breaking the spiraled spears of wood. Releasing the wood energy added to the sphere of rampaging energies around him.

There you are. Erik sensed Rugrat and Akran fighting across the floor as more attacks shot out at him. He remembered the attack that had nearly killed him.

Water turned into an explosion of fog that covered the area under Erik as he charged toward the fight, leaving a trail behind him. The ground cooled as he drew in the heat of the surrounding area, drying out the trees, cracking the ground like a twenty-year drought as he released lightning. It spread through the fog, through the dried-out forest, sparking a flame with the ready fuel, countering the earth element, setting fire to the floor.

Erik thought back to how they had cleared the wood floor in Alva. *Some things don't change.*

With his control over the wind, he fanned the flames of the forest, bringing it to an inferno. He tore across the forest, ripping trees free, the vacuum of his passing drawing the flames along with him. His organic scan reached out through all things living, finding the tumbleweeds, some grabbing onto trees, transforming them into bodies.

Erik ducked into the trees, spinning the wood element into a drill, crashing through the tumbleweeds, shattering their elemental corner stones.

Ascension Trial
You have reached the Ascension platform, laid down by the ascendants that created the Ten Realms. This trial is not for the faint of heart. Complete the trial to control the forces of the Ten Realms. Fail and you may lose your life.
Requirements:
Pass through the ten trials (9/10)
Rewards:
Ascend

Erik shot out of the forest and into the area flattened by Akran and Rugrat's fight. Trees were shredded, turned into weapons. Frost and flame covered the area as metal shone in the sky. Mana condensed into purples and met elements compressed into gem-like weapons.

Erik burned through his stamina, his mana surging as his attacks crashed into Akran's.

He punched with his blood drinkers. It carved out a dome of Akran's power, creating a dent in his domain as the glove cracked.

Erik kept punching, breaking through Akran's attacks. His tails snapped in his direction as Akran roared from Rugrat's hit, cutting through his eyes and snout.

Erik cut off Akran's Water tail.

Rugrat drew out a dual mounted warship flak cannon, pouring power into it, compensating for the dead formations, recreating the weapon as he fired.

The rounds pierced Akran's domain, exploding and tearing chunks of power from him.

Erik tore off Akran's Fire tail. He could feel him weakening. Rekha's attacks and the wounds upon his body were taking their toll.

Akran's power surged, twisting elements into a chaotic beam.

Rugrat's rounds hit Akran. He tossed the gun away, a mass of twisted metal.

Erik charged forward. He had studied Akran's body through the entire fight. Erik's domain condensed, drawn into his body, energy flowing through his body steady and clean. He extended his finger and a chaotic beam shot free, stabbing through the point where Akran formed his own chaotic beam, breaking the ball of destruction just inches from Akran's head.

Erik was blown backward by the explosion. Rugrat helped him slow as they stood next to one another.

Erik shook off the broken gauntlets.

The sky cleared to show Akran missing part of his face, shoulder, and front right paw.

"You just don't fucking die. Power me up." Rugrat threw out spell formations as Erik put his hand on his shoulder, converting his massive pool of stamina into mana. He poured it into Rugrat's mana gate.

Beams of mana *ignited* the ninth floor. As thick as a car, they cut through Akran's defense, piercing him from several directions at once.

A wave of elements and mana washed out from Akran's body as he collapsed.

Erik waved his storage ring, taking his body to make sure he was dead.

They slumped in relief. Erik shuddered, his body in shock from the release and gain of power, thrumming with it now.

"We need to finish this damn thing." Erik flew toward the teleportation formation that was transforming to cyan blue.

They couldn't go back down a floor to Rekha. She was alone in the water floor, wounded. But if they could ascend and become ascendants, they would control the Ten Realms. *There has to be a way to get her out of there.* They landed on the formation.

Do you wish to ascend?
YES/NO?

"Yes."

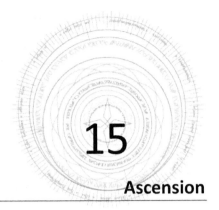

15

Ascension

K ay'Renna threw a spear, throwing a Ravager back over the wall, her sword gutting another, as she grabbed an axe and took off the head of the next.

Her armor was bloodstained from the days of fighting. Shattered had not stopped throwing themselves against Kircross.

"Watch out!" someone yelled as a frigate sunk and spun. Signs of Devourers and the warship's fighting tore out of the hull as it smashed through a tower and crashed into the ground.

The air was as chaotic as the ground. Warships held their line as Devourers in the thousands launched their attacks.

A dungeon core detonated, flattening the area around it, leaving an open crater in the Shattered advance.

Kay'Renna fought to reach the cannons on the third floor. The Shattered had climbed through the cannon ports, engaging the defenders. She hit the formation on the wall, turning the cannons over to the city dungeon. They activated, spewing destruction. She came back out to her party, four less than what she'd started with.

"They are asking us to push to the south. There's a group of fighters encircled," one of the fighters said.

In the fighting, they'd stopped thinking of anything but the next fight, their orders. It was easier. Thinking about one's mortality had no place here.

Kay Renna nodded, rubbing her forehead. "Let's go."

They took off at a jog. Kircross was just one big slaughter. The Ten Realms were burning, and the Shattered had invaded the Sixth, tearing through academic cities with impunity. *Come on Rugrat. We're counting on you.*

Shards of ice peppered the bunker that was really no more than hardened stone and dirt with a slit in it. A team member shuddered and fell next to Storbon, the unarmored regions of their upper body a mess of blood.

"Shit, medic!" Storbon grabbed the man's carrier and pulled him back from the line.

They had been pushed back down the corridor, the wreckage of their retreat filling the space back to the trial's platform.

"I've got him." Yang Zan grabbed the man and pulled him over to the other casualties, checking him. Storbon's eyes tracked to the dead piled to the side of the platform. Han Wu was among them. He hissed and ran back to the fight.

Stack formations created the defenses, reforming them with every attack and enhancing the defenders.

Eli'keen cradled his arm, a savage wound on his side as he used a staff to blast down the corridor. Weebla was using an Alvan machine gun, laying waste to the hallway.

Walking wounded held their position. There was no going back. Cayleigh was propped up against the bunker wall, using an Alvan rifle next to Sam, who was on top of a formation. He was drawn and pale from the casting and the wound on his neck.

Storbon ducked and ran between secondary walls up to the bunker line, and fell against the wall, checking his machinegun.

"They're falling back!" Gong Jin yelled.

Storbon turned and then stood, raising his machine gun. The Shattered were pulling back, or at least not advancing as daylight streamed in from the end of the hallway again.

"Check your ammo. Get stamina water into you," Storbon yelled, turning against the wall and dropping into a seat. He pulled off his helmet, a hand held out jerky for him.

"Thanks, Roska," he said as she ate another strip.

She grunted. They just sat there, everyone slumping in their positions, exhausted.

"Never did I think when we were in Alva that we'd make it to the Second Realm, or even level ten," she said.

"*Huh.*" Storbon slumped back, words too exhausting as he robotically ate the jerky.

She snorted. "We were pretty fucked up."

"You more than me," Storbon muttered, grinning at her.

"Asshole." She bumped him with her shoulder and leaned her head back against the bunker wall. "Been a damn good run."

They had been outcasts, broken children that were useless. People were scared of them, like being around them would make others afflicted. They'd known one another, taking on the worst jobs to earn enough to continue surviving.

"Captains." Storbon snorted, looking at the rank insignia on her shoulder.

She followed his gaze and rolled her head back on the wall and chuckled.

"Devourers!" Yao Meng said, without dread, just monotony, and opened fire.

Everyone shifted, pulling on helmets, and stood on the firing line. Tracers cut down the hallway as it darkened with running Devourers. Rounds sparked off the walls, destroyed by the elemental barriers created by the beasts.

The first fell, and another took their place.

"Level two!" Storbon yelled.

"They've upped their game," Roska yelled as they kept coming.

"Get ready for hand to hand!" Storbon used his sound transmission device.

More Devourers fell. A group of three broke free, stronger than the others. They rammed the defenses, breaking through and sending stone and metal into the platform.

"Regroup!" Weebla ordered, in charge of them all.

George and Davin expanded and attacked one of the trio. Formations blazed in front of Egbert's hands as he stood from the stack formation he was working on. Beams of mana stabbed into the beast as Eli'keen and part of special team seven drew their melee weapons and crashed into the third Devourer.

Spell scrolls activated. Beams of chaotic power burned through Devourer barriers in the tunnel, pushing into the rank behind and the one behind that before they ran out of power. The Shattered rushing forward paused.

The beasts turned and started running back in the direction they had come from.

"What are they—" Storbon stopped thinking and continued stabbing, his spear cutting through Devourers trying to get clear of the room.

They threw elemental attacks to cover their retreat as Storbon stored his spear and grabbed his rifle, firing back down the hall.

"The hell?" He searched for Roska but saw someone else.

He glanced around and saw her on the ground, coughing. She'd been hit in the shoulder, nearly losing the arm. Wounds peppered around the area.

"Medic!" He stored his rifle, pressing his hand to the wound under her shoulder, pulling off her helmet, as she wheezed.

"Fucking hurts." She tried to grin even as she sputtered. The elemental effect of the wound fought his healing spells.

Erik and Rugrat arrived on the ninth level of the trial, a swamp covered in low-lying fog. Buzzing filled the air as Erik reached out to sense the enemies of the floor. Bugs rose from the trees, flying toward them.

Erik reached out, releasing a poison laced with the wood element from his hand. Water and flame created wind. The bugs twitched as they entered the brown cloud, then their bodies exploded from rapid mutating growth, dropping from the skies.

Rugrat controlled the trees. They snapped around the bugs that had not launched, branches spinning together and piercing the beasts faster than a speeding bullet, killing tens in a second.

Ascension Trial
You have reached the Ascension platform, laid down by the ascendants that created the Ten Realms. This trial is not for the faint of heart. Complete the trial to control the forces of the Ten Realms. Fail and you may lose your life.
Requirements:
Pass through the ten trials (10/10)
Rewards:
Ascend

Erik watched the formation change from blue, almost cyan, to blinding white.

Three sections glowed like burning stars, the formations weaving and tying together to create something beautiful, yet filled with a terrible power.

They walked onto the pad as they had done for what seemed like a lifetime, back-to-back.

Do you wish to ascend?
YES/NO?

"Ready?" Erik asked. They looked like fresh hell.

"As I'll ever be." Rugrat circulated power and faced the other direction.

"Three, two, one. Yes!"

Erik staggered under the weight of mana and elements pressing down upon him, threading through his skin, stabbing into his muscles. He grunted, studying the room. They stood in a massive cavern, the kind that made one feel inconsequential.

It was carved out of white crystal stalactites, shaped in hexagons hung from the ceiling hundreds of meters long and tens wide. Runes of every color, like a glowing rainbow, weaved through the opaque crystal stalactites, weaved across the floor in a massive formation. Erik squinted at the light as he followed the center of the runes.

"Is that...?" Rugrat pointed.

In the middle of the cavern lay a semi-sphere of pure light, like a rising sun. It was smooth, without blemish. Erik used his dungeon sense skill and his stomach dropped.

[Dungeon Core- High Divine Grade]

A red outline covered the semi-sphere, getting wider as it spread underneath.

"Holy shit. It's a dungeon core." Erik looked under his feet, unable to take in the size of the core.

"It's as big as the sun."

Rugrat was looking at the surface beneath his feet, too.

"Pretty sure the sun is bigger. Hotter, too." Erik snorted, the banter easing some of the tension in his gut. "The tower didn't send us into the sky. It sent us down, and who knows how far down we are?"

"Leave that to the thinkers. Come on. Things to do, realms to save, dungeon cores to plunder." Rugrat took a step forward, swearing in grunts.

Erik gritted his teeth and took a step. *Motherfucker.*

Mana and elements scoured Erik's body. He felt raw from all the power that had been stuffed into his body. His second step got easier, then the third. *Objects in motion tend to stay in motion.*

Their steps got faster, and Erik pushed up to a jog, drawing upon his elements and circulating his mana, reinforcing his body.

If they didn't get back to Rekha, and soon, she would die.

He picked up his pace. Rugrat matched his speed. Erik sweated tiny threads of black along with sweat. He had to fight to circulate his power. The closer they got, the greater the pressure.

By his grunts, Rugrat was suffering too.

I won't stop. He won't stop for me. Out of sheer determination, he pressed on, pushing through the pain, reveling in it.

Erik groaned as something cracked deep inside him. He kept walking, looking inwards, recoiling in horror. Cracks appeared in his elemental core. As he pushed on, the cracks grew. The pressure of the gathered elements was too much.

The mana he'd been circulating at an ever-slowing pace stopped and collapsed.

Mana flowed through his acupoints inwardly, the pressure mounting around his mana heart. Fissures bled light and mana into his body.

He cried out as the elements and mana started to leak into his body. He had no elements, no mana to draw on, just the power of his body being torn apart by the elements, and mana from within and outside.

Just a bit further, come on.

The mana and elements that had escaped were forced together, compressing together.

He didn't have to draw in the mana. It was like being in a mana cultivation pod where the mana density outside was greater than the mana he held within.

Rugrat was breathing heavily beside him. The two of them broke into a jog and then a run. Erik could sense Rugrat's mana and elemental core cracking as well. They were still so far away. Erik focused on the ground, pushing out errant thoughts, focusing on circulating, on the next step and the one after.

They crossed the open cavern. Erik yelled as impurities from the deepest parts of their mana channels through the depths of their body were *squeezed* from them, it pressed out of their acupoints and pores like clotted blood.

Erik retched, and spat out globs of oil-like impurities.

They must have reached halfway; time was a procession of pain. Erik cried out, collapsing to his knee as elements threaded through his body, stabbing into his elemental core.

His elemental core glowed within his chest, getting brighter and brighter. The core's outer layers collapsed as the swirling energies of the elements combined, growing brighter, shifting, and merging into a flickering light. Erik could see all five elements and their interactions with one another, a rotating pentagon, interconnected, exchanging power. Creation and destruction, life and death.

He cried out as his elemental core detonated. Elements raced through his body, scouring him clean of impurities on the deepest level.

His entire body was drawing in the elements now, not just his elemental core. He resonated with the elements around him, as if he was an extension of the world.

Erik panted, grabbing a stamina potion and drinking.

Rugrat shifted beside him. He'd collapsed into the dirt, but now he rose, taking off his helmet, fire in his eyes.

Erik passed him a potion and he drank.

"Come on, you slow bastard." Erik patted him on the back. His body transformed with the elements without conscious thought. They were a part of him now and he a part of them.

Erik gritted his teeth. If they were to leave now, their bodies would collapse. They were being sustained by the high elements in the cavern.

"Come on! That the best you can do?" Erik growled and stepped forward.

Rugrat stepped with him, half-hearted jogging, their legs like noodles. It felt like they were wading through treacle. As fast as their elemental enhanced bodies could go, this place reminded them of their limits.

With each step, Erik felt pain. He no longer cared for it. He reveled in it, determined to keep pace with Rugrat. His mana system felt like a balloon ready to pop. The pressure mounted within, through his acupoints, his mana gates, right down through his mana veins and into his mana heart.

It rubbed up against the elemental tempering that had left his body raw.

Erik closed in on the dungeon core.

His mana heart gave in first. It shattered, mana leaking throughout his body. He burned from within, his body breaking apart like the bodies he'd taken everything from when their tombstones appeared.

He cried out as he hit the ground and rolled. His body fought on, rebuilding what was destroyed, empowered by the mana. The two fundamentally changed as they combined, the two energies smashing up against one another with nowhere to go except to be compressed within Erik.

Erik reached out to the world and *pulled*. Elements and mana responded, hurling him forward, past Rugrat, who glowed with inner light as his mana core exploded.

The mana and elements *slammed* into one another, swirling and shifting.

Erik pulled himself forward a few more times, but he was coming apart at the seams. He turned his vision inward. His body was ravaged by element and mana, swirling, dancing, as beautiful as it was destructive.

I need to direct it, focus it, or I'll be torn apart.

Erik tried to guide the elements and the mana, but even as he guided it, he didn't know what to do with it. His body was being tempered, combining, and then falling apart. *Like alchemy.*

He stopped and felt the elements around him. The mana was pressing down on him like the elemental beasts he used in his alchemy to refine his concoctions.

I need to shape it—guide it.

The elements within Erik's body condensed, turning into beasts of water, of fire, metal, wood, and earth. He reached out to the mana, and it transformed into a beast as well, six energies all rushing through his body.

The body is a concoction. We shape it with our actions and thoughts, through exercise and eating, through the concoctions we drink. The mind becomes tougher and stronger through experiences.

The air around Erik warped like a wave of heat coming off a summer road.

He guided the beasts of change through his body. They passed, altering and enhancing, combining together.

Fire cleansed him, tempering and preparing his foundation. Mana threaded in with the Fire element beasts, spreading and integrating with him. The Fire element flowed through him instead of pressing down upon him. "The foundation tempered!" Erik found the elements were weakening to what he needed.

"Rugrat, use your crafting on your body. Refine it like you would metal!" Erik hissed through his teeth as he got to his knees and pushed to his feet.

"The soul grounded!" While the Fire element had drained him, the Earth element was like rainfall after a drought. Energy spread through his body.

The Earth beasts faded, their yellow light being drawn into his body. Erik pressed on, staggering forward, standing straighter.

He heard hammering, and he looked back to see Rugrat contained in flames, the Earth element being drawn forth. The element hummed as Rugrat melded it into his body as he had melded ingredients into metal.

Erik turned to face the dungeon core, its power, and the energy of the realms, a fierce gale pushing him back.

"The mind tempered." The Metal element roared, beasts appearing as large as dogs around him. They leapt for him, surrounding him in silver and gray, appearing within and outside.

The elements resonated. Where they had laid in one part of his body, they now spread throughout. Erik opened and closed his hands, stretching and flexing as he stood upright, facing the dungeon core, a smile of grim, dogged determination on his face.

"Not today! Not today! Bones Reformed!" Fire, Earth, Metal, and mana shifted, fighting and warring with one another. Erik held the course, pushing forward, the cavern his cauldron, the elements and mana his ingredients, his body the formed pill.

They fought one another, separate, different. Erik pressed on as they swirled together, combining, fusing, becoming something different, something new. That new energy gathered in his chest, making it whole.

"Muscles that flow!" The Water element rushed through Erik's body, through every opening. Beasts formed, a horde of them galloping alongside one another. They struck the elements and mana at his core, dispersing them, circulating it all. The combined elements flowed back out through his body.

It was as if he was stretching from a decade long slumber. His bones popped and released. He was filled with power. It coursed through every part of his body.

He was now just a few hundred meters from the dungeon core.

"And blood with the power of the realms."

The Wood element seemed to rush toward him from across the world. It flooded through the cavern, surging toward Erik, wrapping around him in a cocoon. Emerald green roots and vines extended through his acupoints, through his mana gates.

Erik reached out, pulled into the air as he crossed his legs and pressed his hands together at the heart, his body radiating, shifting power as the earth element spread within him. It reached into his body like roots. It sunk into the combined elements, into the combined mana, and it *grew*.

His old body was being stripped away and rebuilt anew, regrown. A body not of Earth, not of a human, but formed by the elements and mana of the Ten Realms, shaped by his will, purified by his alchemy.

Pain poured through him, like he was coming apart at his core, burned from the inside. He yelled and screamed, but he remained seated in mid-air, dragging in elements and mana. He increased the rate of absorption, pushing forward, always forward. It was chaotic, without form.

Erik could feel himself coming apart again. *The hell do I do now?*

There had to be a way to guide the power, to reform himself. Shattered had to guide their power. *But we have the ascension formations between realms!*

He pictured the first green formation in his mind's eye and pressed it upon the elements and mana. He felt them calm down and he shifted to the purple formation as his elements responded with his body.

The elements and mana changed, compressed and focused. They were forged anew as he tempered himself, refined himself, as he passed through formations, reaching the final blinding white formation.

His mind felt like it was breaking, holding such a formation in focus. His roar shook the cavern as his body shuddered, the elements and mana rubbing against one another, trying to stop themselves from this one last step.

Erik drew on his last reserves of strength, pulling from a place unknown.

"Come on!" he yelled. The elements and mana snapped into one, and the formation stayed steady within his mind.

They combined at his center like dominoes, spreading through his body. Erik released his hands and legs, the cocoon burning away from him as he rose, glowing with power, elements and mana being drawn into his body and flowing through it.

Erik opened his eyes, feeling resonance with the dungeon core, and control over the power of the Ten Realms. He looked inward, finding his body had changed in alarming but familiar ways.

"I'm a dungeon core?" His mana system network spread throughout his body. His mana heart and elemental core were gone. Instead, translucent energy flowed through. He breathed in elements, fueling his body as he exhaled mana.

He reached out. Elements and mana gathered around his hands. A thick mist gathered from his surroundings. He turned his hand, separating them, then threading them together without any of the instability or chaos.

Quest: Ascend
You have gained the foundations needed to ascend.
Requirements:
Mana of the Celestial grade
Elements of the Celestial grade
A body strong enough to withstand ascension, following the Ten Realms' path of ascension.
Fused them.
Ascendant

Title: Ascendant

> Through trial and tribulation, you have passed through the Ten Realms. You have found the reason you fight. You have tempered your body and your mind. You have cultivated your mana and your soul. You took the harder path and through mounting pressure, you persevered, being born anew, becoming an ascendant of the Ten Realms.
>
> You have gained control over the Ten Realms elements and mana.

Title: From the Grave V

> You've died and come back to the land of the living not just once, but five times. The reaper himself is going to need to rise to kill you.

Rewards:

> +4.0 modifier to Stamina and Mana Regeneration
> +4.0 modifier to Mana and Stamina Regeneration

Erik felt a sense of peace with the world, with everything around him. It was comforting now, the pressure like a warm embrace. His senses spread outward as the power sucked inward like a vacuum, rushing toward Rugrat.

He yelled, the final formation appearing behind him as he shook with power. The entire cavern trembled with him. Erik hadn't noticed it when he'd ascended, too wrapped up in surviving.

Erik realized he was floating. The power of the realms responded to his thoughts, his imagination and feelings.

Rugrat opened his eyes.

"How's it feel to be second?"

"Fucking jackass," Rugrat muttered.

Erik laughed, checking Rugrat. He stepped forward, crossing a dozen meters with the lightest press. A few steps and he appeared next to the dungeon core.

"So, this is a person. Or was," Rugrat said, staring at the core.

"Maybe." Erik reached out and held his hand above the core. "Come on. I don't want to be a dungeon lord all by myself."

"Thanks for the invite."

"Hey, least I can do. Us older ascendants have to look out for the youngsters."

"You're not letting that go, are you?"

"Three, two, one." They touched their hands to the dungeon core.

Do you wish to:

Take command of the Ten Realms

Remodel the Ten Realms

Integrate with the Ten realms

"Command."

Title: Ten Realms Lord

You gain new options with Ten Realm cores. Touch the realm cores to bring them under your control.

Majority of ascendants must agree to alterations to the realms.

You control the Ten Realms experience conversion system.

Name: Erik West

Level: 110

Race: Ascendant-Human

Titles:	
From the Grave V	
Ten Realms Lord	
Reverse Alchemist	
Wandering Hero	
Ascendant	
Strength: ???	???
Agility: ???	???
Stamina: ???	???
Mana: ???	???
Mana Regeneration ???	???
Stamina Regeneration: ???	???

His cultivation, bloodline and dungeon master stats had been compiled into his new titles.

Erik and Rugrat linked directly to the Ten Realms core, which enhanced and merged with their own domains and allowed them to see through the planet and to the fighting above.

Rekha was still on the water floor. Concoctions and needles lay around her as ships from the fleet fell from the sky.

"Get Rekha," Rugrat said. "Heal her. Get her to ascend. I'll go to the fleet,"

"But—"

"Do it, Erik." Rugrat threw out a teleportation formation.

Erik gave him a terse nod and flew, the wind cracking as he tore across the open cavern. He felt Rugrat teleport as he reached the formation they'd arrived on.

The formation shifted to its orange formation and activated.

Erik tore through the air across the ruins of the floor. He slowed, using elements to remove the blast wave of his arrival, and knelt next to Rekha.

She was unconscious, pale. Her body was a mess from having Erik and Rugrat's cultivation shoved into her and then tearing it out to shove back into them. She was barely holding on.

Elements from the surroundings weaved around her, creating a cocoon of light.

Elements and mana flowed into Erik. He transformed them into what he needed and guided it. Rekha sighed as he healed her wounds and worked on her cultivation. He fused power into her, synthesizing it through his own core.

He picked her up, creating a barrier as he tore across the floor, the formation changing as he teleported to the ascendant floor. He pushed back the elements and mana, gathering it within.

Rekha gasped, opening her eyes as Erik held out a hand, stopping her from getting up. She stared at his hand, then at him. "You, you're—"

"A human glow-light, yes," Erik muttered as he released more mana and elements into her body.

"What are you?" She stared at his hand, her eyes going faraway. "How are you?"

"I'm ascendant, baby. Got some cool new tricks."

"Baby?" she muttered.

Erik coughed, feeling awkward. "Uhh, sorry. I, umm, distracted."

She raised an eyebrow. "I bet you are."

"Umm, well, healing?"

"Uh-huh." She bit her lip, seeing something past him. Her eyes rounded. "Is that...?"

"A dungeon core, yeah. Biggest friggin' one I've ever seen. You're on the ascendant floor. Your cultivation was forcefully raised all the way. I'm healing you up and topping you off." He explained how the floor worked.

"So destroy my cultivation and fuse it into my body and then recreate my body. Sounds really simple."

"Hey, come on, it's nothing worse than one of Xun Liang's training episodes." Erik removed his hand from her chest.

She gave him a sad smile.

Erik sighed and gritted himself. "Are you ready?"

"No," Rekha said and reached out.

Erik helped her to her feet a little too hard. She braced herself on his vest and met his gaze, holding them there.

Erik's hands moved around her back, pulling her to him as he kissed her. He released her a moment later. His stomach turned as she smiled and pulled him back for a longer drawn-out kiss.

They pulled back, breathless.

"Ascending," Erik said.

"Yeah, ascending." Rekha bit her lower lip and shivered, shaking her head with a smile.

"Well, I hope that was a good shiver."

"You'll have to find out later." Rekha winked and stepped away from him, facing the dungeon core. Her expression changed, firming as she circulated her power.

"Alright, I'm letting everything back in. Remember, use your crafting techniques and then the formations."

"I've got it." Rekha grunted as the power fell on her. She called on her elements, transforming her body.

"I'm not holding anything back now," Erik said.

"See you in the Tenth." Rekha took off at a jog, running for the dungeon core.

This was her trial—her ascension.

Erik wanted to help her badly.

He felt the teleportation formation activate as Egbert appeared next to the High Divine core.

Erik flew over to him as Egbert accessed it.

Rugrat stepped off the teleportation formation at the camp. A frigate fell toward the camp, the crew doing their best to shift their course away.

"Take cover! It's coming down!" a man yelled.

Ships across the fleet shuddered with attacks, giving as good as they got, an iron curtain across the sky.

Rugrat reached out. Elements and mana surged in titanic quantities, compressing around the frigate. He grunted under the strain as the frigate's descent slowed and then halted, shifting away from the camp as Rugrat manipulated the metal elements, pouring them into the ship. Panels smoothed out and formations ignited, holding the ship aloft.

Rugrat released the ship as it limped backward.

People stared at Rugrat as he stretched his domain over the camp, through the fleet above, across the battlefield and into the ascension platform.

"Egbert, set up your teleportation formation and go down to mine. Erik and I claimed a dungeon core. Take over administration as our interface. Clear out the ley lines to pull back everyone else to the fleet."

"The elements are too heavy here. It's interfering with the teleportation pad."

"Get it setup and ready to move the minute you can." Rugrat stepped forward and appeared on the main wall.

Shattered were still pouring into the Tenth Realm from tears, a seemingly endless horde that battered against the camp walls and rushed to meet the aerial mounts and ships.

Rugrat gathered the elements, the mana, and *pulled.*

His body shook with the effort as he forced energy together, compressed to become visible threads of colors, swirling, twisting. They spun together, the elements transforming, altering, destroying, and creating one another. A wind picked up as elements from across the plains were pulled together into an elemental storm towering a kilometer high and half as wide.

Shattered were torn from the ground as other elemental storms touched down with the delicacy of a sledgehammer.

The fleet pulled back, their formations shimmering as their ships shook in the turbulence.

Tears were washed away, losing stability. Devourers were pulled into the funnels and dragged from the skies, torn apart by the energy of the clouds.

"Get down!" Rugrat's voice boomed. He lowered his hand. The storms compressed and shifted, chaotically interacting with one another before they crashed into the ground.

Rugrat was the only one standing on the wall as he created a barrier, diverting the blast that rolled through the plains, tearing through the ranks of Shattered. It was chaos; it was destruction; it was creation. To Rugrat, it held a perverse beauty.

He called upon the heat and water, creating wind and rain, washing over the battlefield, settling the dust.

The ground shook much harder than the bombardment. Something deeper, something within the planet.

Rugrat frowned and stumbled, looking to his right.

The ground cracked, and a mountain crumbled as the plains shifted, pressing against one another to create a new mountain range. An elemental storm of magma exploded out in the distance. Elements surged as the whole world seemed to breathe in. Tears shuddered, weakening.

The ground rumbled as mana surged outwards. Several volcanoes blew their tops.

Shattered, unprepared for the mana increase, were crushed by the pressure while Devourers panicked, trying to flee as tears collapsed like sandcastles against the sea.

What did Egbert do?

"Fire!" Glosil ordered as the ships attacked, surging with new power.

Those in the camp stood and opened with their guns and spell scrolls. The Shattered fell apart, attacks seemed to fill every open section of ground.

Devourers were hunted down with impunity as Shattered ran in any direction that they thought offered safety.

He felt Erik appear on the teleportation pad, and flash forward to stand next to him. "That's a little fucking terrifying."

"Yeah." Rugrat looked at his hands. "I've never felt mana so dense; the elements are balancing out.

"The ley lines were blocked. We blasted a few of them open. Got it from what Weebla said about the Kanesh mana drill."

"Rekha?"

"Attempting her ascension." Erik turned from the carnage. He cast a hallowed ground, layering it over the camp. "We need to regroup and head to the Seventh Realm."

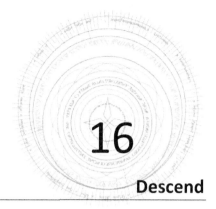

16

Descend

Kay'Renna drew a barrier of stone around herself as the wall to her side collapsed as a Devourer fought another party.

They swarmed the creature in its beast form. Their enchanted blades bled its energy, putting it on the back foot as its sworn Shattered lay dead or dying around it.

The battlefield had moved to the streets of Kircross, the walls breached.

"The city guards are trying to link up with us. They have level three Devourers in the way!" one of her aides said as he tore through a Shattered, panting as he flicked his halberd clean.

They won't be able to get through something like that.

"All right, we'll continue to withdraw toward the command tower!" Kay'Renna said, forcing away the fatigue. A Shattered jumped from a roof and she threw a spear before it could hit the ground. The force nailed it to the wall, away from her party member, who beat back another Shattered.

A tear opened in the street leading toward the command center.

Spell scrolls activated, hitting the tear, killing Shattered. A Devourer rushed out, flame spewing from his hands, coloring her party member's barriers.

Another tear appeared in a side street. "Smoke it and go west!"

She threw out a formation that spread smoke and illusions, messing with one's senses.

More formations covered the street as the other party defeated their Devourer and followed them. Fire blasts blindly hit two of their members as she ran.

They sprinted down the street. They ran for several minutes, finding a manor that had been turned into a base. Defenders waved them into the manor.

"Who's the leader here?"

"One of the city guard. Highest floor. Stairs are inside to the right," a man at the gate said, his features covered in the smoke and smudge of fighting.

"Get some food and water into you," Kay'Renna said to her party and jogged into the manor.

She ran up the stairs three at a time and was waved through doors into a large room with windows looking out over the city, the walls visible in the distance.

"Liaison Kay'Renna," the city guard leader said as she arrived, relief in his voice. "We thought that was you. Your command tower took a direct hit."

"Yeah, those level three Devourers are no joke. I made it out with some of my people. We've been trying to contact the other units, but all of the sound transmission channels are being used."

"People were panicking." The man took out a list and passed it to her. "These are the new sound transmission codes."

"Thanks. How are things?" She started adding them, nodding at the map.

"We lost the outer wall, so we're moving back to the old city. The wall there has been raised. We have pockets of defenders all over the city."

The new wall and the old city wall were nearly five kilometers from one another. *A lot of room for us to have people go missing.*

"The attack fleet is back!" The excited voice came through the general channel.

Kay'Renna moved to a window, looking through the cracked glass as ships appeared over the totems. Sections of armor were torn and melted.

While bloodied and damaged, they were poised-ready for another fight.

Just how hard had the crews been fighting to keep their ship in the air? As they closed, tears as large as skyscrapers revealed the ship's innards. Crews raced back and forth to repair what they could as the dungeon cores at the hearts of these beasts melded the materials back together.

These ships were supposed to be the strongest warships in the realms. Just what the hell have they gone through?

Fear and hope warred with one another.

The air seemed to crack as two streaks ran across the sky.

Kay'Renna stilled. Chaotic spells lanced down from the sky, crashing into the ground beyond the walls. Elemental beasts grew out from the broken city and charged underneath the duo.

The Seventh Realm seemed to react to them, to greet them eagerly, following their instructions.

A third glowing figure appeared above.

Armor of forged mana and elements weaved around them as George tore across the sky. Rugrat landed on his back as Erik formed a dragon of elements, each head another element, its wings creating a gale that washed through the city.

Elemental beasts formed around her, forming legions to greet their master, surging through the city under his command. Golems with formation-engraved armor moved with them, weapons in their arms, giving them long range attacks.

Wizard incarnations spun from every element, swirling together around a core of mana.

The Ascendants' legions were a flood crashing into the ocean of Shattered invading Kircross.

Rekha sat upon a steed of mana. The trio were the harbingers of death upon the Shattered as they spread out and led the attack into the enemy.

The fleets rallied, beaten and wounded. The Alvan engine roared to life. Corvettes raced ahead, their bombs leaving a line of craters upon the ground below.

Led by their dreadnoughts, the four attack fleets had honed their cooperation through life and death, and they surged. Kircross fleets powered their engines, following the charge.

The very planet seemed to shake as mana and elements shifted.

Kay'Renna shivered as she heard something new in the voices of the Shattered: fear.

"All Kircross forces that are able to move to counterattack. Help is on its way!" Korani's voice was hoarse, filled with tears unshed.

Power filled Kay'Renna from deep within as she laughed.

The other commanders looked at her.

"Mount up! We ride!"

Erik's body was surrounded by power. His eyes were black as night, stark against his blue pupils and the elements that danced within.

The world seemed to bend to his command as he raised his hand like some war-god.

His elemental dragon roared, ice and lightning tearing through the Shattered below. Flames carved through the heavens as the corvettes rushed past on his flanks. Their cannons blazed, their PDCs filling the air with black puffs of shrapnel as their bomb bays opened.

A carpet of destruction followed them as Erik drew the power to himself and looked over Kircross's walls; few of the dungeons remained. The ley lines were clearing, but slowly. Too fast and they would alter the planet like in the Tenth Realm.

The chaotic blasts thinned the Shattered, and the corvettes blazed trails through their ranks, but there were still so many of them pouring in.

Erik's dragon roared, as if disagreeing with his master's decision. He patted the beast. *I wish you were here, Gilly, to see all this.*

He jumped from the dragon as it breathed, its breath crossing overhead as he ducked lower, Devourer hunting. Erik called elements to him as he dropped, gaining speed. He crashed into the ground, channeling the elements through him. The ground cracked, releasing the chaotic elements, killing Shattered and Devourers as it rippled outwards.

He leaped forward, denting the ground beneath his feet. Attacks rained upon him as he shifted through them, reading them and their targets as they left the Shattered.

Erik's beasts tore free from the ground, twisted chaos as they spread through the broken ranks of Shattered and exploded. The wave buffeted the Shattered, but Erik weaved through them. He grabbed a spear from the ground and hurled it through a level two Devourer. Finding a group of them, he accelerated, moving through their attacks.

They could only catch the air around him as he lashed out, every attack deadly and focused, reaping their lives.

George laid down a wall of fire as Rugrat's enhanced beast cut down Devourers in the distance.

"We've got tears to close!"

Rekha rode her steed through a breach, crashing through Shattered ranks leading their raised forces.

The fleets crested the walls of the city, cannons ablaze.

Erik conjured a beast of elements, jumping on its back to follow Rugrat as Rekha moved alongside. They cut a path through the Shattered, following them backward.

They rode through the forests, across the valleys, their attack catching the Shattered off guard as they closed tears in their passing.

"I created new ley lines and cleared out the ones that were blocked, allowing the dungeon cores to draw in the elements, and release mana. It should cut off the Shattered and buff our people! I'm heading to the sixth now!" Egbert's voice came through the air.

"Then the Ninth!" Erik said.

"On it."

Erik could feel the elements decreasing, drawn down as the mana started to replace it. "Regroup on Kircross," Erik called to the other two.

"We can clear out more tears." Rekha said.

"We've only just ascended. We don't know our limits yet. We need to secure the city. There are others that need us," Erik said. He released his construct. Its elements returned to Erik as he drew upon the elements of the air, creating a bird.

George wheeled around. Rekha sighed and her steed grew wings as she followed them back.

17

Across the Realms

ekha walked through the halls of the same command center where they had made their plan to attack the ascension platform.

"Cayleigh!" Rekha flashed forward, knocking Cayleigh over, but holding her in an iron grip so she didn't fall, hugging her.

"Woah! Shiny," Cayleigh said.

"Oh, yeah," Rekha toned down the power she was leaking out, releasing Cayleigh.

"What's the glow? It's like the elements and mana are shifting around you," Sam said.

"Elements, mana blended together. Moving dungeon core. The Ten Realms resonates with what I do." Rekha waved it off, examining Cayleigh and looking at Sam. "What happened?"

"When you went through the platform, we linked up with the special teams. We held the entrance for some time, but Akran's sworn kept attacking us like crazy. What happened with him?"

"He's dead," Rekha said, trying to hide the shiver that ran through her.

"You okay?"

"I'm fine now," Rekha smiled. "So, you held the entrance?"

"Couldn't hold it forever. We had a series of fallback positions. Kept retreating toward the platform. Wounded and dead piled up. The platform was going haywire so we couldn't teleport anyone in or out. We held, then the sworn stopped their suicide charge," Sam said. They'd both turned quiet.

"Next, we know Egbert says the formation works. We evacuated through it before the Shattered could get smart. By that time, Rugrat had showed up and was giving them hell. Closed down the tears and took the fight to them," Cayleigh said. "What happened with you?"

"I finished ascending, came out, asked what had happened. Got the totem down just in time for the fighting."

"How is it?"

"Ascending? It sucks, honestly sucks, just—" Rekha caught Eli'keen waving her into the meeting room. "I wouldn't tell you to try it unless you like pain and your cultivation is at the limit otherwise it's painful and not very fun at all." Rekha sped up what she was saying.

"Go, go. We'll catch up later." Cayleigh waved her off.

"I'm so happy to see that you're well." Rekha hugged her and Sam and flew into the meeting room.

Eli'keen nearly got whiplash from her speed and closed the door behind her.

Rekha looked around the room. She moved to where Rugrat and Erik were standing, talking to one another with mana.

"I don't feel tired, do you?" Erik asked.

"I'm not hungry either. You think we don't need to eat?" Rugrat said.

"Great big glowing plants," Erik muttered.

"Wow, didn't know that we would get such a bonus," Rekha said as she walked up beside them. "Why are you using mana to talk to one another?"

"Cause people are looking at us like we're the holy sunflower gods of the Ten Realms," Erik said.

"The what of the what?" She looked around the room, catching the furtive glances as people looked at them, then turned away.

"Oh, I see."

"Yeah," Erik sighed.

Rugrat grinned and turned his head. Rekha raised her eyebrows, sweeping through the building. She smiled as she realized what he was looking at. Kay'Renna appeared at the doorway a few minutes later.

Kay'Renna scanned the room, staring at the trio and Rugrat. Her eyes shifted to Rekha in question.

Rekha moved closer to Erik as Kay'Renna nodded and smiled.

"We're all here," Glosil said as the door ground to a close and the light formations dialed up. "We have secured most of Kircross with the guards pushing to clear out the remaining areas. Now we need to look to the rest of the Seventh Realm. Most of the tears have closed, but there are still powerful Devourers that can break through between realms. Many are able to get into the Sixth Realm still and we don't know how many there are in the Ninth."

A map of the Seventh Realm appeared, floating in the middle of the room. Cities in grey had been abandoned or lost and those in red were under attack.

"We contacted the Imperium and they're focusing on defending Cronen. If we can free it from the grip of the Shattered, we can use their reinforcements with our own forces to sweep through the realm. At the same time, we need to send people to the Sixth Realm to assist there."

"We have fighting all across the Seventh Realm," Korani said.

"Yes, and we have fighters here in the Seventh Realm that can fight them. Those in the Sixth Realm are much weaker. They have academies instead of mega cities and their dungeons are a spread-out warren. The dungeons here are spread out, but they're controlled," Glosil said.

"We need to secure the Sixth Realm because the Devourers can increase their mana cultivation there. If we allow them to continue without pause, they will get stronger and become a larger threat than they are right now in a short period," Weebla said.

"Are we sure the Imperium head is going to support this?" Kay'Renna asked.

"He is the Imperium head. Even if he is against it, this is the purpose of the Imperium," Eli'keen said.

"And how many lives would have been saved if the Imperium had listened to you in the first place?" Her voice was soft, but Eli'keen winced from the truth.

"Two of the fleets will go to the Sixth Realm with Erik and Rugrat. The other two will proceed to Cronen with Rekha," Glosil said.

"We have only just retaken the walls," Korani growled.

"The Ten Realms are burning, and we have to go where we can do the most good. Kircross is safe for now," Weebla said.

"We need to bring the Seventh Realm together. For that, we need the Imperium," Weebla sighed.

"And how are we going to do that with that idiot in charge?" Rekha asked.

"We will do what we have to do. We need the Imperium on our side and to fulfil their task. They swore to protect and defend the realms," Eli'keen said.

"Once we have the Sixth under control, then what?" Korani asked.

"Then we can cleanse the Seventh and head forces into the Ninth to clear it," Glosil said

"Well, this is just great," Rekha uttered under her breath.

"Good luck." Erik smiled.

"What are you smiling about?" she grumbled.

"Look at this way. If Clive is being an asshole, you have all the power you need to tell him to screw off and do your own thing."

"Yeah, like a big get out of jail or fuck off card." Rugrat nodded.

Some ships would need to be left behind. They had been too badly damaged and supplies needed to be moved to ships.

They organized the logistics between the groups, bringing the meeting to a close after another ten minutes.

"Good luck in the Sixth," Rekha said to Erik and Rugrat as the doors opened and people headed off to their tasks.

"You too, and if you can excuse me, I need to see a woman about a date." Rugrat headed off to Kay'Renna, leaving the two of them alone.

Erik stepped toward Rekha. "If he tries to get you into shit or does anything, just say something. Egbert is connected to all the dungeons now.

He'll let us know."

"I'm a big girl. I was the one beating Akran's ass, if I remember correctly."

Erik grinned. "So, how about it?"

"About what?"

"A date after this all?"

Rekha blushed, remembering what she had said on the ascension floor. "Umm, yeah, that would be nice."

"All right then. I know a few really nice food places in Alva you have to try out. Give you a tour of the place."

"Wait, does that mean I have to meet Momma Rodriguez?"

"Well, yeah, probably. Don't worry, we don't have to do that on the first date."

"Oh, God. Momma Rodriguez." Rekha was starting to get flustered.

"You're about to go piss off the guy in charge of the Imperium. You were the first student of the Imperium head, and you're worried about Momma Rodriguez?"

"You just don't get it." Rekha punched him in the shoulder, making him laugh at her expression.

"Look after yourself and don't take any risks you don't have to. We don't know our limits yet, so be careful," Erik said.

"I will. You don't need to worry."

Erik raised an eyebrow and smirked. "Yeah, says the person that charged a level five Devourer by herself."

"It was necessary!"

Erik's mouth lifted into a full-blown smile, pulling her in and kissing her.

She was surprised as he let her go, her cheeks blazing red as people in the room looked away from the two of them. She could see Weebla's grin clear across the room.

She hit Erik's chest and left the room, forcing herself to stay under subsonic speeds, finding Sam and Cayleigh waiting for her.

Cayleigh rested on her axes with a massive grin. "I knew you had it in you."

Rekha groaned as Sam smiled at her and nodded to Erik, who left the conference room.

"Come on, let's get to the ship. We need to get going." Rekha hurried them out of the building and to the dreadnaught.

"Egbert?" Rekha asked the air.

"Ah, right, the fleet. One second. Just need to move that mana from there to there and then… Teleport in five seconds!" A massive fiery number five appeared in front of the fleet.

"Thank you," Rekha said.

"No worries. It is all rather easy. These damn ley lines are rather difficult. Might need a few attack formations hooked up to the dungeon-ascendant core."

"Is there another core in the Seventh Realm?"

"Seems like there is a dungeon core in each of the realm planets, seeded into the actual core of the planet. The dungeon cores that come to the surface are shavings of the main core that have come up through the ley lines. Have fun on your trip!"

The fiery numbers hit zero, and they appeared above the forest.

"Targets sighted!" an officer called out.

"Take them out," the captain ordered.

Rekha checked the map, a few tear markers on the map updated. *The increased mana density is working.*

She headed out of the command center with Sam and Cayleigh. Elevators and lifts took her through the dreadnought behemoth into the lowest deck. Mages stood at casting balconies, raining spells on the tears and Shattered remaining below.

Rekha studied the other ships in the fleet. She should see the peak of Cronen in the distance. She stepped onto one of the formations at the front of the warship and called the elements together.

Chaotic pillars crashed into tears, destroying them as she widened their beam and sent it across the Shattered.

It was a calculated slaughter as they advanced, tearing through the Shattered rear. They took out the tears connecting them to the other realms or across the Seventh and whittled down their forces.

Devourers made to attack the fleet, but their power had been greatly restrained and Rekha targeted them mercilessly.

It was slow and laborious as they advanced, sweeping fire and carnage through the landscape, driving the Shattered ahead of them.

Rekha dropped chaotic spells ahead of the fleet. They detonated, leaving plumes in the sky, thinning and scattering the Shattered.

The early morning turned through midday as Rekha's sound communication device rang.

She activated it.

"The Imperium head is requesting your presence," the captain of the dreadnaught said.

"Right now?" She frowned, looking at the city in the distance. They were nearly there, but Shattered were still filling the ground.

"He is rather insistent. He threatened to take my ship from me." The man snorted. Clearly unafraid. *How would he be able to take a ship from the Gnome faction?*

"Understood. I will go," Rekha said and put down the sound transmission device.

"What was that?" Cayleigh asked.

"Imperium head wants to see us."

"Well, at least we can give him the message sooner rather than later," Sam said.

"You think he's going to be happy either way?" Cayleigh said as they headed back into the dreadnaught.

"No, who does like getting told to do their damn job?"

Rekha walked into the association buildings that had been taken over by the Imperium command.

"They've turned it into the headquarters of the entire Imperium," Cayleigh said as they passed guards, being led into the heart of the building.

"There are no buildings that the Imperium own in the lower realms. It was done that way to show that they would not mess with the lower realms and that if we lost the higher realms in our duty, then we would be losing our homes," Sam said.

"Seems like they're pretty comfortable," Rekha said as they arrived at the command room.

"Rekha Bhettan!" Clive snapped, drawing himself up to his full height.

Rekha raised an eyebrow at him.

"Do you not know how to greet the head of the Imperium after you went against my orders in a reckless and fruitless attack on the Tenth Realm?"

"Who said it was—"

"Silence!"

A wave of mana spread through the room, probably meant to pressure her into silence. It felt like a light breeze as it curled around her, coming under her power.

"You went against my orders, took ships without permission and now you return to the Seventh Realm to beg forgiveness! You should be executed for going against the rules of the Imperium."

She spread out her domain to release the pressure on Sam and Cayleigh.

"You worked with the rebel Gnome and Elven groups to bring about a power change in the Imperium for your own needs."

"This is—"

"You went against me—the *head* of this Imperium!"

"You—"

"*I* am the head now, not your teacher, and you have forgotten to show the respect due to this position."

She crossed her arms, tapping her foot on the floor. "You think that the strongest among us should be the head of the Imperium?"

"Of course, and I have trained for a hundred and seventy—"

Rekha drew all the mana and elements in the room to her. It was as if she had sucked the very air out of the room into her hand, creating a ball of focused elements. "Then shouldn't I be the head of the Imperium? I became an ascendant while you—" She raised an eyebrow. "—are playing stupid fucking children's games to assert your power like a greedy little child."

"Arrest her. She attacked me!"

Several guards advanced, drawing their weapons as Clive drew his own, a smirk on his face as they rushed her.

They have no intention of taking me alive.

People in the room cried out as she blasted them backward, increasing the Earth element, pinning them to the floors or walls and fusing them there. They screamed as she drew power directly from their elemental and mana cores, pulling their power from them.

"There we go. That should be a level of your elemental and mana cultivation. Should take you half as long as the first time to cultivate it."

Clive was fused into the map table, spluttering.

"Your duty as the head of the Imperium is to defend the Ten Realms, to protect the people in it. You thought that you were the only hope in the Ten Realms, you small-minded fool. Nothing but a fighter. I'll give you a tip for free. If you want to be an ascendant, you need to learn how to be a crafter." She created a barrier around him. He yelled, but not a sound came out.

"I invoke the oath that you have all sworn to. The Imperium's forces are to prepare to fight the enemy that has invaded the Ten Realms. Imperium members will report to the frontlines to fend off the attacks on Cronen and then move to the rest of the realm, clearing it of Devourers and packs of Shattered." Her voice boomed, spreading throughout the city.

Many in the room stood up, their chests glowing with their oath being enacted.

Her barrier came down.

"You can't do this! You're not the Head!"

"So what? We are under attack and anyone in the Imperium can announce that we are under attack. Doesn't take a Head to do so. Didn't you say that the strongest should be the Head? Or is that only when you're the strongest?" She glared at him and shook her head. "You are called upon to honor your oaths. Will you serve?"

"Yes!" the room declared, including Clive.

Two of his guards didn't, and the oath returned on them, killing them.

People stepped away as the two dead shuddered and shifted, rising.

"Service in life and in death." Rekha looked at the two undead. "Go kill Shattered."

The two undead lumbered off at a run.

"You!" A general punched Clive, knocking him out. "Sorry, just got annoyed with hearing him talk all the time." He looked at Rekha. "What are your orders, miss?"

18

The Ninth

Glosil stood at the command center of *Crusher,* one of the Gnome dreadnoughts. Weebla, Eli'keen, Kay'Renna, and a dozen leaders and generals from across the higher realms were in attendance.

"The Sixth is mostly secure. Mission Hall parties are moving through the realm as tears and Devourers appear. The locals are able to deal with the roaming Shattered," Kay'Renna said.

"Can we leave them unchecked?" Glosil asked.

"The Mission Hall is spreading to the lower realms to create a network to deal with any large threats. The Shattered, given a generation, will just be like any other Ten Realms creature. Dangerous and new, but manageable," Eli'keen said.

"Many of the demi-human races were once Shattered," Korani said. "With time, this will become their home. It is not an easy life here, but it is a life compared to the Shattered."

Glosil nodded.

"What is the status of the Seventh Realm?" Weebla asked.

"The Seventh Realm forces are sweeping through the realm. Rugrat and Rekha are leading things on that front with the Imperium." Glosil looked at

Eli'keen and indicated for him to continue. He had been given his position as advisor once again, while Weebla had taken command of the Imperium's fighting forces.

"Survivors of the lost cities are mounting excursions to recover their homes. Several cities have been recovered already. All of the major cities have been reclaimed and are rebuilding their defenses currently. There are still Devourers at large, but many of them are surrendering now. Our biggest issue is with the forces of the Ninth Realm pushing down. The ascendants have opened the ley lines of the Tenth, Seventh, Sixth and lower realms, making them much harder to enter and move through with tears."

"But we still have problems there, which is why we must head to the Ninth Realm in order to secure it," Weebla said.

"Once we get to the Ninth Realm and restrict the tears, the Imperium can clear through it."

"What of the Eighth Realm?" Glosil asked.

"The Eighth Realm is a training realm, a sub-planet, with the Seventh and Ninth controlled, the Eighth will become its own prison. The ascendants have changed the rules of the realms. No longer will only fighters be allowed into the Ninth Realm. Everyone will still need to find their why, but that may be crafters and fighters. The Eighth Realm one will come face to face with death and loss."

"So, the Ninth it is," Glosil said.

"Thankfully, we have a point of entry secured already."

Erik looked up from his patients. He'd seen the special team teleport to the camp. He had split his attention among the wounded, able to heal several at once now that he had the sheer power to not worry about expenditure.

Storbon trudged up to him. Erik felt his heart sink. He had seen that dull look in his eyes, the hardness to his features. The weight of loss hung heavy on him.

Erik steadied himself as Storbon brought himself up and looked him in the eye.

"We lost eight. Roska, she—" Storbon looked away, composing himself, then looked back. "She was holding the line. The Devourers charged, got in through the barriers. She got hit in the neck."

Storbon shook his head and shrugged. "The medics worked on her, tried to bring her back, but she—" He took a breath. "There was nothing that could be done, boss."

It was like a punch to Erik's gut. There had been a chance with every mission that one of their people would die. Roska had been like a niece, rambunctious, always there to keep him humble, but they cared for one another.

Erik nodded, not trusting his voice or his words.

He cleared his throat and swallowed. "We're heading back up to the Ninth to clear the realm and secure the academy. Gather your team. You'll be riding with me."

"Yes, sir, I'll get them ready. Meet here?"

"No, meet over by the CP."

"Got it."

Erik used a clean spell, removing the blood from his clothes, then checked on Jen, who was running the tent.

"You need me for anything?"

"No, Erik, thank you. Without you, we would've lost a lot more."

"Just doing my job. Heading off now." He patted her on the shoulder. She covered it with her hand and squeezed it.

He gave her a tight smile and left. A section of the city had been turned into an aid station, filled with wounded from across the realms.

Erik caught up with the special team.

"Egbert!"

"Yeah, yeah."

The group appeared at Cronen city.

"Welcome to the party," Rugrat said, waiting at the entrance to the teleportation pads. Rekha was standing with him, both with their own guards.

"Things all set?" Erik asked, pulling his helmet on and checking his gear as he walked out with his team.

They turned with him, Rugrat guiding them toward the totem. "You bet. Just hurry up and wait. Recon is going through now."

People grew quiet with their passing and moved out of their way to the totem.

Rekha checked her sound transmission device as Erik shifted around. "Get ready!" she said. Everyone stepped onto the totem pad, facing outward. "Teleport!"

They appeared on the teleportation hub that Admiral Peli had hidden in the mountains. They rushed out of the totem, finding Special teams Six and Three already there, as well as Imperium fighters.

Erik's domain stretched through everything around him.

"Area is clear," Erik said.

"You two get going," Rekha said.

"Have fun." Erik nodded to the teams as he and Rugrat flew off the floating island and dove below.

Rugrat led, punching through the ground. Erik followed in his wake, circulating the elements and mana as they crashed through into the ley-line. It was too bright for normal eyes to register. Mana had grown stagnant here, creating mana stones blocked by the elements.

Erik and Rugrat broke through the blocked passages, slamming through ice, roots and dirt, rock and metal and magma. The blockages crumbled in their passing, the mana shifting eagerly. They opened up the blockages as they went deeper and deeper. Erik could feel the planet's core resonating with him.

"Did you find out where the dungeon cores came from?" Rugrat asked, having to use mana at high speeds.

"Started with the Elves. They had a dungeon core on their planet, what's the Tenth Realm now. They tried to recreate it with mana, creating their mana cores. Was only when they came into contact with the Shattered and Gnomes, they figured out they needed the elements and mana to create another core. There are legends saying how the ascendants descended in order to give life to the realms. They could have used themselves to turn the planet's cores into dungeons."

"I heard that they went into the Shattered Realms and spread across the stars to find allies to help against the Shattered."

"Who knows? That's the thing with legends."

They crashed through the last of the blockages, seeing the core below. They were two meteors shooting across the open space around the rotating core. Power entered and left the core, shifting, altering and changing, balancing.

Elements poured through the ley line, purified by the core, and released as mana, creating a mist around it.

Erik and Rugrat approached it, closing their eyes.

The mana mist shaped into dozens of drills, like the mana drills they had used to open their mana gates and form their acupoints.

They solidified as they bored into the blocked ley lines.

Mana and elements surged in chaos, the core shaking in seeming excitement as the mana mist became denser, funneling through the ley lines.

Rugrat created formations in the ley lines to keep up the work as Erik cleared the ley-lines that ran around the teleportation island and along the path to the academy.

Warships appeared, forming into a grand fleet ahead of the teleportation island.

"That should do it!" Rugrat said.

"Back up we go." They took two different ley lines, crashing through the blockages, many breaking ahead of them with the wave of pressure.

Edmond stood at his command table as the fleet pushed out from the teleportation hub, advancing toward the academy. The elements and mana changed, causing him to breathe deeply. The formations were brighter than ever as they surged with the rich fuel to drink on.

"Academy in sight!" a seer said, pointing at the screens.

Edmond looked at the broken wall of the academy grounds, the picturesque rolling hills torn apart by the fighting.

He could see the broken buildings from the fighting as the inner regions of the academy were revealed. So much history just turned into rubble in a few destructive minutes.

Esther let out a breath through her teeth.

"Do we have a visual on the admission hall?" Edmond asked.

"Should be coming up in a second, sir."

Edmond checked the map and then the screens.

"There it is." The seer officer's voice was tight as Edmond looked at the hall. Broken golems lay scattered across the ground. The building had been torn apart, scattered over the grounds.

The warship shook. Edmond swayed with it as officers checked their information.

"Elements are spiking. Nearby ley lines are being cleared. Wait, Lords West and Rodriguez have surfaced."

The duo tore out of the ground, a pillar of mana trailing behind them and spreading out. The holes they had made spewed mana for several seconds before aggressively drawing elements back down.

An unlucky flock of Shattered charged them. Fire and water appeared in Rugrat's hands; dozens of air arrows tore through the flock before they made it within a hundred meters.

The duo stood upon the air as if it was solid ground. The realm seemed to shift and contort around them.

Good thing they're on our side.

Edmond didn't want to think what the Ten Realms would be like if Akran had been able to ascend.

Their protection details rode out, gathering around them on their mounted beasts.

Shattered seemed to have sensed the vast fleet. Ships blotted out the sky as they brought the teleportation island with them.

They rose from underground and flew from where they had been hunting.

The fleet met up with Erik and Rugrat, who moved along with them.

"All ships, fire upon targets of opportunity," Weebla said.

The Imperium announced their return home with spell and mana cannons.

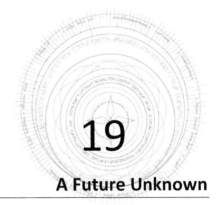

19

A Future Unknown

elilah walked alongside Old Hei. Both of their guards looked upset as they passed through the construction all around them. The Beast Mountain Range had grown ever larger. Delilah could see the roots of the large super-cities in the Ninth Realm spreading out.

It had been a month since the Imperium moved in to the Ninth Realm to reclaim their home.

"I hear that the Imperium has secured most of the academy and is pushing to clear the rest in sections," Old Hei said, his arms clasped behind his back.

"It shouldn't be long till they are able to claim their home again. I've heard rumors that they want to create academies in the lower realms like Avegaaren."

Old Hei chuckled.

"Is that one of the reasons you came to see me?" Delilah smiled.

"Ah, any reason to get away from that stuffy old alchemy workshop."

Delilah laughed. "Is that why it's so hard to get you out of the library these days?"

"Your alchemy workshops are much brighter and airy. Good for the circulation!" He pepped up, making Delilah roll her eyes as they moved around mages fusing rubble and dirt back into a building.

"The Imperium is thinking of altering their internal structure to become teachers to spread knowledge through the realms and stretch the associations to every corner of the realms."

"I hear they're thinking about exploring the Shattered Realms too?"

"Yes," Old Hei frowned. "Not sure how I feel about it, but there are many that wish to travel into the unknown, and there are many things in the Shattered Realms that one cannot find in the Ten Realms."

"Seems that the new head is eager for change."

"She is. Rekha has both Eli'keen and Weebla as her advisors and a sub council of the associations to bring up issues. With the inclusion of crafters in the higher realms, it means that fighting is not the only focus of the Imperium anymore."

"Hopefully, this leads to a time of peace. There has been enough fighting for all involved." Delilah sighed.

"The realms are changing, rebuilding, and repairing. People have come closer together than ever before."

They reached the end of the walkway, looking upon the construction.

"Vuzgal will rise again," Delilah agreed, seeing buildings grow from the destruction. She looked back at the castle district and the main tower. Half its original height, it continued to grow upward toward the sky.

Erik appeared on a mountain top, looking at elemental storms in the distance. Hearty trees thinned up there, but the summer wind made it crisp without being too cold.

Rugrat was sitting on a boulder shaped into a bench, looking at the world below.

"So," Erik said, sitting down next to Rugrat.

"So," Rugrat said, not looking up as he pulled out an old bottle of scotch a few fingers from full.

"Is that—"

"We opened it before we headed off to Africa. When we came back, well, we were too worried about your missing limbs and the curse. We never got to finish it off." Rugrat pulled the cork out with his teeth and sloshed some of the scotch into some cups from his storage ring.

"Hey, don't spill it. We're not going to be getting any more!" Erik warned.

"Calm down," Rugrat said around the cork and held up a glass to Erik and stoppered the bottle, putting it on the ground between them.

They tapped glasses, touching them to the boulder and took a drink.

"Oorah!" Rugrat said, low and appreciatory.

Erik sat back with a sigh. Looking at the gates below, linking them to the Shattered Realms, each surrounded by heavy defenses that mirrored the ascension platform's fortress.

"Don't think that it will get us drunk anymore, though," Erik said.

"Let a man dream, will you?" Rugrat muttered.

Erik chuckled and drank again, looking out over the realm, spotting an ancient elven city that seemed to grow from a mountain side.

He looked at the grasslands far below, where beasts roamed and demi-humans called home. They fell silent, their eyes drawn to the gates flashing as people arrived and departed.

"Nah, not worth it."

"Not worth what?" Erik looked over.

"Wondering if the high proof hundred percent stuff would work. But hell, would take out all my tastebuds with it too."

Erik snorted and took another sip.

"Never thought that things would turn out this way," Rugrat said and patted Erik on the shoulder. "I'm sorry you had to give up your wish to go home, man."

"Don't be sorry," Erik said, and leaned forward. "Earth, my house there… It was just a place. It's the people that matter." He turned to Rugrat.

"You're my family, more than my blood ever was. Alva's my home." Erik smiled and looked at the gates. "I wouldn't change it for the world, not one decision I made. Two Week Curse, huh? Don't seem as much of a curse now."

"Amen to that, brother." They tapped glasses again. "Amen." They tapped them to the stone, Erik remembering the faces of those they'd lost along the way.

He drained his glass, and reached for the bottle, filling Rugrat's cup and his own.

Erik looked out at the plains again. People continued to arrive and leave again, coming from somewhere, going somewhere else.

They sat there, drinking in silence for some time.

The Tenth Realm was meant as the last stop, the final realm of them all, but it was really the start for so much more.

"A place of endings and beginnings." Erik's words carried on the dry winds as Rugrat tilted the bottle toward Erik, who nodded.

"What was that?"

"Life, journeys... You know. Once you get to what you thought was the end, you find that it's just the start of something new."

Rugrat nodded sagely, stoppering the bottle and putting it down. "Maybe that's it."

"What?" Erik asked.

"Life is a journey. It's all a roll of the dice. You never know what's going to happen or where the dice will land."

"Just got to make your best decision, stick to it, and hope to hell they're the right ones."

"Remember your past, develop your present, and pursue your future. All one can do."

"A redneck poet. I wouldn't have thought."

"Hey, marine redneck poet." Rugrat raised his glass with a grin.

"Oorah!" Erik howled, tapping glasses, then the rock and taking a large mouthful of scotch from a planet they had been born on, in the realms they belonged.

"Stronger together than apart," Rugrat nodded.

Erik checked his watch. "Ah shit, come on. We've got that double date with Rekha and Kay'Renna!"

"Goddamn Ten Realms and time zones!"

"Egbert!" Erik yelled.

"Egbert!" Rugrat yelled. "Kay'Renna is going to kick my ass if I'm late!"

"Rekha has been bugging me about it for a week."

"A week! I promised Kay'Renna *months* ago and her dad keeps giving me that where's my shotgun look whenever he sees me!"

"Momma will kick both our asses if she knew we were late to a date!" The two of them paled and yelled together. "Egbert!!"

Those coming or leaving the Ten Realms looked up at the two idiots on the cliff top yelling into the sky, loud enough to be heard through the valley. The fear of the spoon, or flip flop, was strong in them.